The Pleasure of Eliza Lynch

Anne Enright

The Pleasure of
Eliza Lynch

Atlantic Monthly Press
New York

First published in Great Britain in 2002 by Jonathan Cape
Random House, London, England

Published simultaneously in Canada
Printed in the United States of America

FIRST AMERICAN EDITION

Library of Congress Cataloging-in-Publication Data

Enright, Anne, 1962–
    The pleasure of Eliza Lynch / Anne Enright.
    p.cm.
    ISBN 0-87113-868-9
    1. Lynch, Elisa Alicia, 1835–1886—Fiction. 2. Lôpez, Francisco Solano, 1827–1870—Fiction. 3. Irish—Paraguay—Fiction. 4. Mistresses—Fiction. 5. Paraguay—Fiction. I. Title.

PR6055.N73 P58 2003
823'.914—dc21   2002035606

Atlantic Monthly Press
841 Broadway
New York, NY 10003

03 04 05 06 07   10 9 8 7 6 5 4 3 2 1

for Martin

This is the story of how she buried him with her own hands, on the slopes of the Cerro Corá.

A Fish

FRANCISCO SOLANO LÓPEZ put his penis inside Eliza Lynch on a lovely spring day in Paris, in 1854. They were in a house on the rue St-Sulpice; an ancient street, down which people have always strolled in a state of pleasant imagining. In the spring of 1854, no imagination was needed as Francisco Solano López pushed his penis into Eliza Lynch and pulled it back again, twenty times in all. This was quite a lot of times for Francisco Solano López, but something about Eliza Lynch distracted him from the usual rush of his pleasure. Something about Eliza Lynch gave him pause.

Outside, the birds sang, trees rustled and fancy carriages rattled by. Inside, the four-poster bed was hung with turquoise, its enormous baldaquin billowing above them and gathered into a pucker of silk that mirrored, as she lay under it, the lovely navel of Eliza Lynch.

Apart from the magnificent bed, she had nothing. There was a burled walnut box pushed into a corner, an ormolu clock ticked on a mantel of ordinary stone, a simple table of inlaid tulipwood was burdened by a statue of the flagellated Christ. The room was practically bare, if you did not count the bed. But the bed was overwhelming, it was a room within the room; it was a palace, across whose yielding floor López crawled, laughing, in order to engage more thoroughly with the laughing Eliza Lynch.

Which, without further delay, he did.

Many people would come to regret this moment. You might say that everyone came to regret it – except for the two participants, Francisco López and Eliza Lynch, Il Mariscal and La Lincha, Paco and Liz. Already unreal. They were the kind of people who attracted stories – not to mention bias, rumours, lies, rage: the whole tangle pulled into a knot by time, made Gordian by history. The details cannot be unpicked. But this much we may not doubt: there was a joining of parts, and it happened in spring, on the rue St-Sulpice.

Paco and Liz, laughing on the bed. Mme Lynch silently looking at the silently looking Señor López. The tart from County Cork turning towards the turquoise, as the little mestizo handles it into her. It was a moment that garnered the blame of nations, as if everything started here. Something did start here – there are such things as beginnings – but what? But what?

They became lovers. In jig time, in marching time, in twenty beats, they moved from strangers to the rest of their lives. And they knew it. Such luck!

Outside, the birds chirped themselves to sleep, while his hired horse blew into his oats and the coachman snored. The clock on the mantel said midnight, or five o'clock. The clock on the mantel was stopped. And all you could hear was the suck and pull of his breath.

Who was he? He was heir apparent to Paraguay, a country that no one had ever heard of. Who was Eliza? She was very much herself. He had come to her house in order to improve his French, or so he said. The words he learned that evening were 'King of Diamonds', 'Queen of Spades', 'trick'. He learned the French for *sons of bitches*, then *truffles*, *pig's nose* and *tongue*. Also a phrase: 'If I win, you will not like me.' After which pleasant nonsense, they went to bed.

Oh Eliza. In fact, she did speak many languages: she romped in French, married in English, and she ate in the Irish of her childhood kitchen. She had school Latin and spa German, but her fate, now, was in Spanish, and she would die in Guaraní, which is to say, obscurely. The lover in her head spoke Russian, in whispers. The devil in her head spoke Portuguese.

And so, Francisco put his penis, *son pénis*, *su penis*, into the nameless part of Eliza Lynch. He put that thing, which is the same in English, French or Spanish, into a part of Eliza Lynch that is, in any language, obscene.

One:

He was rich.

Two:

He was immensely rich.

He had ordered, that day, seventy pairs of silver-tipped boots – with presumably elevated insoles; because he was small, there was no gainsaying the fact that he was really quite small, but he was stunningly rich, so she, spilled out beneath him, must be magnificent.

Three:

She was silent.

It would not do to shout. Whatever surprise she felt at this, most surprising, intrusion must register as a mere stretch of her eyebrows, a fullness of her jostled mouth; her forehead suffused with a kind of puzzled tranquillity, as though the question – whatever question it might be – answered itself.

Four:

There was no telling how long he would take.

His hair smelt of lilacs and horses. His breath smelt of decay. His shirt was pulled impatiently open at the neck and a filthy leather pouch dabbed at her chest. Money? No – his money was folded and stuffed down the side of his boots. Vast sums. There was a flurry of paper when he dumped them, all unheeding, on the floor. Then his short military jacket; crusted with gold braid and held to lopsided attention by the remarkable epaulettes. After which his pants. His legs very thick and gnarled. His shirt dangling down.

She was wearing her sapphires. Also a *peignoir* of shrugged-off silk. It flowed down her arms and moved under her, like water.

Five:

Her lips jolted apart.

She must be his first woman in weeks. In Paris the whores would laugh at him, of course – that is why they were paid so much. Cora Pearl with her whip. Or Dolores at the Café Anglais with her diamonds and a bloody cough. Because they were all dying. Death in the bedroom and death again at the card table, where they would take his money, trick after trick. Here is the fool in from the colonies, let me introduce you to . . . M. le Duc de something he would not catch. Some ghoul of a German banker. A tart with diamonds in her hair, sitting in to watch. And if he tried to touch her, she would laugh in his face. The game continuing in silence. The stakes going up and up. The tart not laughing, any more. Up, and up and up.

4

Six:

He reared away from her.

She might bite him. She might tear at his bottom lip, if it were not for the terrible breath. When he walked into her drawing room, you could smell it from the doorway. No idea of where to sit or how to stand, until she took his hat in her own hands and said, quite natural-like, that he must leave it beside him here on the floor. This was what they did in Paris, she said to him, these strange Frenchmen, they left their hats on the floor so everyone could see their names in gilt letters written on the band – she spent her first weeks in town convinced that everyone was called Ruget, which was the name of the hatter. She laughed. Tra la la. Then she paused, rising in a rustle of silk, as though arrested, briefly, by the sight of his lap.

Easy.

She pulled the shirt, with rough fingers, up the length of his back.

Seven:

She arched her own back and said, 'Oh'.

Everyone must take a lover, so they would know how to sigh and when to turn. It was an investment. Everyone should love once; there was no other way to learn. Eliza had wanted to love sweetly, hopelessly, but she loved like bad weather. And she only loved once. There was no use closing your eyes and thinking it was him. There was no use closing your eyes and thinking. But she did close her eyes, and saw López's head briefly above her, his eyes red coals, his brain molten, his hair black flames. She opened them again, quickly, and was relieved to see flesh. Only flesh. Francine, outside, forgetting to bank the fire for the morning, as she always did.

Eight:

Who was counting?

She was counting. The first man in Paris, the second man in Paris, two men in Algeria, a man in Folkestone, Kent. Outside, Francine was clearing away the card table as, above her, López held his breath. Silence. The clock on the mantel had stopped. She counted them out to herself. The man who gave her the sapphires, the man who gave her the bed. Two men in Algeria, a man in Folkestone, Kent. Their memories rising now, as a scent might rise when you crush a flower. Each time he drew back, a name provoked – Raspail, Quatrefages, Misha, Bennett – and then hammered home.

Nine:

'If I win,' she said. 'You will not like me.'

He spread his cards down on the table and looked at her. A good hand. A very good hand. He took the ace of hearts and started to cut out the centre of it with his little knife.

'I have kissed the hand of the Empress Eugénie,' he said. He described the ring she wore – a sapphire set with diamonds in a fleur-de-lis, over more diamonds and a pearl.

The Emperor Napoleon had pinned a ribbon on his breast. He put his arm about his shoulders and walked him personally to the door. Along the enfilade, thirty footmen pretended not to notice the fraternal kiss, man to man, soldier to soldier, nation to nation, as he took his leave.

Then he threw the empty-hearted card at her, across the baize.

This was a man who needed nothing.

This was a man who needed it all – but he did not need any *one* thing, except, and absolutely, to be inside her. As he now was.

Ten:

The dressmaker on Rue de Rougemont. Short and quick like a jockey, with burning, slithery eyes. She might like him. In another life, she might quite take to him. He looked her over and the deal, he seemed to be saying, was either her or 20 per cent. So she settled on the spot – lay herself down amid the silks and stuffs; a spool of Bruges lace still grasped in her hand. The lace cost, in labour, a metre a week. She thought about this – about how long it would take some Flemish hag to finish a fancy cuff, an entire dress, and the thought of the hag made her want to cry. She looked at the side of his head and her hand tightened on the wooden spool. She saw his blood on the hammered silk; she saw black blood seeping into the bombazine. When they were done, she asked him about the dresses, and he – as open in his love of warp and weft as he was closed in love (a grunter, a face-puller) – took her round the room, and romanced her with cloth. *Nankin, taffeta, piqué, foulard.* And so she got, on tick, five of everything, morning, afternoon and evening. Her under-linen, she must supply herself. She owned nothing, not even the *peignoir* she lay down in. She was not yet nineteen and she lived like a countess – on credit.

The money! The money! It was running through her hands like water. She tried to catch it, hold it: clutched instead at his neck, or his throat, or his mouth.

Eleven:

His hair smelt of Lilac vegetal by Pinaud. His shirt smelt

clean. She would be rich. She would have a *calèche* like Cora Pearl, the English tart who dyed her dog blue to match her dress. A man said that her pearls were fake – she broke the string and let them scatter. The pearls sloughed from the string with a pull of her hand, spitting out all over the floor. Who picked them up? The pearls bouncing into corners, rolling under tables and little love seats. What fine young man paused at the door and silently stayed behind, then dropped on to his knees and grubbed around on the Turkey carpet, picking them up? Eliza caught her breath. The blue dog, the *calèche* upholstered in sky-blue kid. She would have to change the curtains now, on her fabulous bed, because blue was Cora Pearl. A starving man she saw once, his legs set wide, and his thing hanging down in the gap, lush and fat. Eliza cried out. She had tried to be good, had wanted to be good, but the curtains had cost her a month of fucking and they were far too blue, and the pearls were scattering and rolling all over the floor.

Twelve:

Oh. Her voice in the room. A shudder in the hanging meat of his face, his eyes behind their closed lids like he was trying to squeeze something delicate and large through a very small gap – but only if he could find it. It was in there somewhere, in the centre of his head, and she wanted to kiss him; help him gather it up. A man he saw once, dragged by a horse; the bones sticking out of his ruined back. The man looking at him as though bored by it all, he said. Then slightly distracted. Then dead.

She was writhing away from him now, her eyes fixed.

Thirteen:

They were still there. They had left their traces inside her.

The man who failed, and failed again, and slapped her to keep himself going, and wore her out with trying. The man who wiped his mouth afterwards – picked up a corner of her dress and wiped his mouth – and chucked her on each breast before he put the sapphires down. The dressmaker, with his clever eyes shut, straining against her, his head full of something that kept slipping out of his grasp. And Misha who left – the bills not paid, the sheets still rumpled on the bed. Misha in his Hussar jacket, who loved her better than his horse, he said, who loved her enough to die – who said, open your eyes, open your eyes and kill me, and she opened them to see him staring down at her, with a look so ordinary and hard his eyes might have been made of wood. Before Misha, Quatrefages, his wet stomach sucking against her back, who said on their wedding night that if she kept her chemise on, she might do; Quatrefages just a cover for Raspail, who twisted her every which way, and all she could remember of Raspail were his hands. Raspail a friend of Bennett who was the first. Bennett the doctor administering a cure; Bennett who said, 'Do not be frightened, my dear, and if you are frightened, shout.' Mr Bennett smiling thinly, until he rolled his eyes back to show the whites. She thought she had killed him. He smiled at her, as though her insides were quite useful and nice, then suddenly he cracked open in front of her and horrors, horrors, came spilling out. She was sure she had killed him, Mr Bennett, her father's friend. She was killing him now. She was killing them all. The bed man, the dress man, the man who wiped his mouth, Misha her lover, Raspail her master, Xavier her husband, Mr Bennett, her father's friend. She was killing them in Paris, Algiers, Kent, and Bennett everywhere. She was killing Bennett in Mallow, where he never had been, and Bennett in that room in Bordeaux, and Bennett who had followed her here because he was inside her still, between her legs, and behind her ribs, knocking,

knocking to get out. Every time he crashed into her. In the pause, she caught and held him. And killed them one by one.

Fourteen:

She would have a carriage that was entirely black: Chinese lacquer, trimmed with ebony, upholstered in seal, the windows thin sheets of obsidian, the cushions black silk, punctured with buttons of jet. High and closed; Eliza's carriage was the most expensive shadow ever thrown. She was making her escape in it. She was riding it over the bodies of her former loves. She bounced it across their chests and legs, bumpitty bumpitty bump. And she was gathering speed.

There was more, of course. There was the feel of cloth running across the skin, of blood running across the skin, and other people's hands. There was the taste; not only of the quails they had eaten that night, but of every meal they had ever forgotten. All this now gathered up, as though in a massive cloth, with Eliza and Francisco lying in the centre of it, their lives tumbling down towards them; the sound of a piano, a song they had each heard, the various smells of home. The past they brought with them to this bed was not – how could it be? – populated by French emperors and English tarts, that was just the skin of it. More like, they carried with them the ghostly circle of rice powder scattered on Eliza's dressing table or the unexpected beauty of his valet's hands. They brought the smell of vegetable peelings, his favourite saddle, a pool he swam in as a child. They brought, finally, themselves: the landscape of his shoulders as he dropped his head above her, the tracery of veins on her white breast. All these things glimpsed, or nearly glimpsed. All these things swelling in their minds, a bubble impossibly big. And when the bubble bursts they are showered, not with pianos, valets, saddles, lovers, meadowsweet, silks; when it burst their minds are (pop!) a blank. Hope. The feel, quite simply, of him-inside-her-around-him, the feel of flesh turning to silk, of silk turning to muscle, and wanting everything! everything! because they are nothing now, and afraid that they will be destroyed by it – by the too-muchness of him and the too-muchness of her. And so:

Fifteen:

Pop! Nothing.

Sixteen:

A blank.

Seventeen:

Nothing. Nothing. Nothing.

Eighteen:

Everything.

Nineteen:

Everything!

Twenty:

And a little bit . . . more.

Usually at this point, the man would roll off and look for his boots, but they stayed and stroked each other. He fingered her necklace – perhaps it was this had made him pause. She ran her hands along the flesh of his back – so neatly packed. She started to laugh. They had surprised themselves. He reached down by the bedside, and hauled up a bottle of slightly flat champagne.

'My father,' he began. He talked about Paraguay, the country that no one had ever heard of, a railway line he would build, tick tack snicketty snack across her stomach and between her breasts, until bumph it hit her nose.

In London, he told her, he had mounted his first train. Thirty-nine advisors, one hundred and three trunks, and return tickets to Brighton. What a young fool he was. Outside the window, the city did not stop. Valera, his equerry, would not take the hat off his lap, his knees prissily together, the words stalled in his mouth. England, that wretched country – they did these things so well. He went back to his London rooms, and every day there was another scroll of paper uncurled and weighted on his desk, another engineer indicating this elevation or that point of strain. A ship – the *Tacuarí* – rising in the dry dock at Limehouse, even as he spoke. Plans for an arsenal, a railway line. Above all, there would be railways. Eliza could not imagine it, but Francisco's father never left Paraguay. Before him, the first Dictator, Francia, never left his own bedroom. And now, here he was in Europe, meeting men by the hour, hiring them with a look, these buzzard British, immensely polite and ignorant, Jesuits all. He said to them, Can you see? Can you see? The silted land of the Paraná basin, the groves of orange trees, the willing men, a country with heart. Can you see? A country that will eat you, and love you and make you her own. We will embroider steel across her breast.

No, he said. She must come and teach them to put their hats on the floor, in the cool tiled drawing rooms of Asunción. But really, he was surrounded by fools; she must come with him as far as Rome.

Eliza lifted her hands and let her fingers trail along the turquoise curtain, showing, as she did so, the skin of her underarms and its astonishing, exotic, red hair.

'Roma!' she said.

And so it began. The state visit to Madrid, where she waited at the hotel while he was presented at the court of Isabella; then soothed him when he came back fuming, in a pair of sheets that had once belonged to Napoleon.

'Where did you get them?' he said, fingering the little embroidered imperial bee. 'Oh, Buonaparte,' he said, and buried his face.

The trip to Rome, where she read the Baedecker to him in bed, bought china, played hostess, chose menus, patted a Dutch broker on his knee, laughed at the puns of a Venetian millionaire, flirted with a bishop who happened to be involved with the Vatican bank (but not, as was claimed in the broadsheets of Buenos Aires, an orgy for the Pope).

The Crimean peninsula, a strategic tour, where Eliza held a picnic on a hill, sitting in their carriage, along with several other carriages, some of whose occupants were brave enough to dismount. She would always remember what she ate that day, the feel of it on her tongue, as through her lorgnette she watched one hundred Mishas in their Hussar jackets risk their body parts and lose them, or simply slide down the flanks of their horses to be lost underfoot. She would recall with perfect simplicity the dryness of the chicken, the honey glaze on its cold, dimpled skin; the crunch where fat met the bone; the fizz of champagne, as the guns crackled below.

Everywhere López went, he kicked the door shut and made love, on beds, floors, *chaises-longues*, patches of grass. Everywhere Eliza went, there were dresses, fittings, patterns, flounces, dismissive waves of the hand. Back in Paris, they went to Les Invalides and Napoleon's tomb, where López cried and said he would build the same, the very same tomb, stone by stone in Asunción. He made it sound like an invitation.

They stayed in Paris, waiting for their ship to be finished (because there was no doubt now, it was her ship too). And when it was loaded with the British railway men and engineers and smelters, they sent their baggage on to meet it at Bordeaux.

With everything nearly bought and packed, the last farewells nearly done, Eliza went to the dressmaker on the Rue de Rougemont, attended by four equerries and her maid, Francine. She wore, for the occasion, a Polish pelisse of merino crêpe, with seven flounces, quite simple, in opaline. It was her parasol that was extraordinary, a cane of clear crystal, her monogram woven into each panel of lace. She looked the dressmaker in the eye; she looked at the contents of his pants. She drank his *café au lait* and took his advice as though quite seriously, made him unroll every bolt of cloth, and then she left. The next day, she sent the equerry, Valera, back, with his bad French, to settle her account.

And every night, silently now, she kissed him in the dark. All the bodies, all the mouths, melting away, as she and López tried to finish what was started that first night. La Irlandesa, Il Mariscal. What was started that first night was a war – they both knew it. What started that night was . . . love, perhaps. A sense of great peace, and strange dreams. A stirring. An intimation of all things askew, or all things dreadful. A sudden hunger. A shiver along her arms, an horripilation. A sense that someone had replaced the world with a different world that looked just the same. And with all this came disgust – for the smell of López, for the sight of him eating, and for the food on her own plate. A reluctance to travel, though she must travel. A change in her eyes. A distant look, as though she were listening to her own blood. You guessed it. What was started that night was a child. Deep inside Eliza, a future had dug itself into her, and was now holding on. A tiny fish, a presence urgent and despotic. By the time she realised, they were in Rome. By the time she was accustomed to procure her *bondon*, she was knee-deep in Vatican bankers and Sèvres china. Besides, Francine had no Italian – she could hardly go into a pharmacist and mime.

And so it grew.

But this was, itself, in the future. As yet, Eliza and Francisco still lie on the bed, wonderfully spent. And for the next few weeks she finds, as recently pregnant women do, that she loves everyone, to the point of tears, and that life is good.

The River

Part I

A Melon

TODAY, I ASKED the name of the bird again, but Miltón shrugged. The *Alma Perdita* I was told by Captain Thompson, one of the over-gallant English who has spent some time in the wilderness here or here about. *Alma Perdita* means a lost soul. There are sudden flurries in the branches, but when I look, nothing is there. In the forest, if you hear something, it is already gone. Still, we are followed everywhere by its liquid, ever-falling cry.

We are two days out of Buenos Aires, and no one knows how many days from Asunción. Such a mongrel ship, half-gunboat, half-packet, and massive – the *Tacuarí*, it tossed us on its shallow draught across the ocean from Bordeaux, and is now too deep to find the river channel. Miltón stands in the bow as though it were a canoe. He slings his line into the water and draws it up again, turning now and then to whistle at the pilot. He knows the river, but who along these banks has ever seen a ship like ours? He must think he is guiding some kind of cathedral home.

Though, when I look into those mineral eyes, I do not know what these people might believe; whether they even have souls like ours – lost or otherwise. Everywhere, there is such growth. I think that if these people believe anything it

19

would be that the Devil is a vegetable, and God a wonderful big tree.

The air is so thick and warm, I do not know if I am breathing or drowning. I lie and drink it in, in wonderful lassitude. The river is as broad as an open-ended lake. When we approach the bank, the trees crane towards us, madly still; all festooned and crawling: the immense, busy, shifting silence of the forest. I take in the smell of it and think I may well sprout, or rot: some plant will root in my brain. It will flower better than a hat.

My own smell too, has indelicately changed. It is light, and difficult to match; the smell of grass in the sun; of something green and growing, as my belly grows. And under my arms – because of the heat I think – a hint of mould.

My belly is huge. They have strung me up in the bow, like a giant tick. I am all caught up in the skeins of muslin they drape around me. The breeze is cooling when we move, which is not often. Miltón stands on one foot, leaning on a pole, his free hand lifted to shield his eyes from the glare. He ignores me well. The light plays with his bones, eats at his silhouette, until he is just some narrow lines, loosely jointed and standing against a sea of glitter.

One of the sailors is like to go blind from the light. The water, so cheap and nothing up close, is, from afar, a tangle of brilliants. A dangerous cloth. I can see it, even with my eyes closed. Miltón sits with the dazed sailor and tears some slits in the length of a broad reed, then he wraps the reed around the man's eyes and ties it at the back of his head. The sailor peers through the slits. He cannot speak with the pain. Something about it pleases me. His homely, lewd face, his waxed tail of hair, and this blindfold of green. It seems he has become something else; a thing of random parts. Human, animal, vegetable.

Miltón smokes. And in the small rafts that float by they

hand up chickens and take tobacco. They stay to smoke; all of them, drifting in the shade of the *Tacuarí* and rolling the leaves palm to palm. The women hand their impromptu cigarros to the children's mouths, while the men stretch back, and leave them to it. All of them healthy and quiet, sometimes laughing in the shade.

This evening I have all the candles straightened in the candelabra. They have softened in the heat and bow slowly towards the floor, until the whole effect is of some kind of splayed flower. When they are lit, I try a little conversation. River manners; easy and unaffected. We sit as travellers anywhere – forgetful of our places in the world. Señor López has cognac. Mr Whytehead, the Scottish engineer, has taken to yerba maté, a foul brew they suck out from a gourd here, but which he says is quite as good as tea. Doctor Stewart, my physician-accoucheur, goes native with some rough alcohol. And because Mr Whytehead, from some religious scruple, will not play cards, the maid Francine makes up the numbers for some harmless rummy. She takes her chance and downs some of my champagne, river-cooled – which is to say, warm.

I ask Señor López about the natives, and what they believe. He says that he himself is a native, and, yes, it is true, he believes in nothing. At which, I feel obliged to laugh. He does not swallow his brandy tonight, but spits it into a bowl, which I have placed for him on a side table. For his teeth, he says. The small room is full of the fumes. 'Nothing?' I say. 'Not even love?' Gallantly, he takes my hand and kisses it. And suddenly Paris is a long, long way away.

Mr Whytehead tells a forest tale of a Frenchwoman who was miraculously found, after she and her companions got lost among the trees. A Mme Godin des Odonez, whose husband was engaged in a great measuring project somewhere to the north or the west of us. His wife set

21

out to join him, along one of the tributaries of the mighty Amazon, in a company of eight, two of them also female. On the third day out, the natives deserted their canoe and left them to make their own way. They chanced upon another guide lying sick in a hovel on the bank, but he fell into the river and drowned while trying to retrieve a hat; after which the canoe quickly capsized, with the loss of all their provisions. Three of the men struck out for some place they thought to be nearby, and never returned. The rest: Mme Godin, her two brothers, and two female companions lashed together a raft, which broke up on the rocks and, when the tangled growth prevented them from walking along the bank, they struck off into the forest. Here they lost their way and became demented and one by one they died. Mme Godin, by some miracle waking out of a swoon, took the shoes off her dead brother's feet and stumbled on, she knew not where. Her clothes in tatters, her body half-naked and lacerated (at this he can not help but glance at me) by creepers and thorns, she chanced upon a river – perhaps the same river – and two Divinely Providential Indians, with a canoe.

The candles droop as he speaks and lean slowly sideways. The flames keep their easy, hopeful stance – and then, the crisis – I watch them shrink to a point and then recover to lick back up the tallow, now upside down. The engineer sucks the dregs of his maté and we listen to the night.

Of course, it all happened years ago – he gives the date, being by temperament exact. I say that it is hard to imagine these great trees having weeks and fortnights, as we do: all they know is another day, and another day, and another day after that. Indeed, he says. For eight of these primeval days and nights, she wandered alone in the howling wilderness; surviving on berries and bird's eggs; shouting and singing to keep the jaguar at bay. She went in a young woman

22

and, when she came out again, her hair was turned quite, quite grey.

He pauses in some satisfaction, and surveys the room. I say that she probably ate the brother. She didn't just take his shoes; she took a bit of leg as well. She lopped off a nice big ham and slung it over her shoulder, to help her along the way. Señor López gives a great shout of laughter, and hits the engineer between the shoulder blades, and we have another round of cards.

I like the way he glanced at me when he said the word 'naked'. He is full of slips and blunders. He leaks. He cannot help it. He seems such an unbending, abstemious little man, but I sense the longing in him to give in and live as other people might. The doctor too, rolls his watery eye, and heaves, and sighs. He is very big, when we are so confined in the cabin. Still, in the middle of so much awkwardness – his mouth; small and nice.

Francine says, apropos of nothing, that a mother has only to look into the eyes of her newborn to believe – believe what she could not say. Only that we are ancient, that we come of an ancient race. Señor López looks down at the table and his eyes film over with tears. She lifts her face to the light and says that we spend our first weeks forgetting who we are, and then the rest of our lives trying to remember it again.

This is very pretty of her. Francine started this journey as a maid and will end it as a lady's companion. And so we go. 'And what would you know of newborn babies?' I say, with a sporting glance at the assembled men. At which, quite wisely, she declares rummy, and we continue with the game.

So, she has had a child. It is surprising what a journey will throw up. Poor Francine.

But now, in the river dark, my mind turns to the luckless Indian dying in his hovel – only to be plucked out by these travellers (these angels of death) with their exotic clothes. And so he does die, but marvellously, for a hat.

Of course the hat was important – a white man would die without one. A white man did die without one.

*

This morning I do not move, and the boat does not move. I wake to a clanging sound, then the abrupt hiss of coals hitting the river as they clear the boilers out. Pht. Phht. Pht. I lie in the oven of the stateroom all morning. Through the open door, I see Señor López busy, frantic, intent. He does not notice me. He unrolls plans on the table and calls for his engineer, Mr Whytehead, so I must have the door closed and dress in the airless dark. Outside, the light hits like a brick. My dress instantly wilts. The starch gives way in the wet air and my skirts limp altogether along the floor. So I trail around the deck and look at no one, as no one looks at me; then I lie in my gauzy tent and swing.

At noon they raise sail to catch a whisper, and so we veer from one side of the vast river to the other, at which point, the whisper dies.

Everyone sits about. The English – all sorts of railway-men, fitters, miners – fill the boat with dull delirium. Their voices drift on the hot air, and then stop.

I ask Miltón for the name of a tree on the bank – a handsome tree with red and peeling bark. He laughs and gleefully rubs his forearm, saying, I think, 'White Man's Skin.'

In the afternoon, I have Francine put all my white veils away. They increase the power of the sun's light and the danger of sunburn and freckles. They are also, I think, very injurious to the eyes. Green is the only colour that should be worn as a summer veil.

Freckle wash – take one dram of muriatic acid, half a

pint of rainwater, half a teaspoonful of spirits of lavender: mix, and apply it two or three times a day to the freckles with a camel's-hair pencil.

When Doctor Stewart joins us after dinner, I take him aside to ask for muriatic acid. He says that my complexion is probably subject to my condition, but that lemons may do just as well. He has little French and no Spanish, and so I am forced to speak English to him. Mr Whytehead has everything, of course, up to and including Swedish.

And so we assemble – my little band. It is too hot for cards. It seems that, apart from my freckles, there is nothing to talk about. I try Sebastopol. I recall Buenos Aires. I wonder at the possibility of a garden in Asunción, and what might grow there. But Señor López turns always to the state of the unmoving boat, her inner workings, her boilers, vertical or horizontal, her trunnions, whatever they may be. I have no words for these things, and leave it all to Mr Whytehead.

I long for my piano, but it is deep in the hold. Sometimes, lurching across the Atlantic, I would hear a tinny discord; a distant twang that felt like one of my own heartstrings snapping.

But we must have music, the boat is so still now, and the night gathers about us as though there might never be another day. I have the captain order in a musical seaman, in order to push back the darkness. The man holds his cap in his hands and gives a humble, swelling account of 'Barbara Allen'.

> O mother, mother, make my bed
> To lay me down in sorrow.
> My Love has died for me to-day,
> I'll die for him to-morrow.

Señor López trumps him with something astonishing in

Spanish and Mr Whytehead, prevailed upon by myself, finally opens his mouth – out of which floats, to our amazement, an easy, soaring tenor. The room is all tenderness. He sings a carol, '*Quelle est cette odeur agréable, bergères, qui ravit tous nos sens?*' and all uninvited, *pro patria*, you might say, Francine supplies the descant.

After which, everything is easy. Señor López wants Whytehead to bet with him on our arrival date in Asunción, and he demurs. Everything he does makes us laugh, now. No one can pronounce his name, and this fusses him. Francine enquires, by way of general mirth, what his Christian name might be and, with some hesitation, he brings out the pearl, 'Keld'.

Doctor Stewart clears his throat – to smother a laugh, I think; but then he fills our little cabin with his sudden baritone. Tuneless enough – but large, quite large.

The night has gathered in again.

This afternoon, Francine said that her mother has a friend – whose generous attention she still enjoys, at the age, she must be, of almost forty-five. A pleasant enough man, Francine says. He makes a visit every afternoon at five-thirty by the clock. Her mother calls him always 'my dear friend' – the use of his Christian name being less than respectable, and his patronymic an intimate, formal pleasure that must be reserved only for his wife.

'But Señor López is not married,' I say, quite pointedly, and Francine keeps her head down. Still, I find the conceit quite pretty. I tried it on Señor López, this evening, I said,

'My dear friend.' And he said,

'Yes?'

What was that thing I wanted to say about butterflies? There was a group of them, anchored to the sand, their wings flicking this way and that in the heat and the breeze. One was the most astonishing blue. I have not seen such a blue since leaving Paris. And with it, as though in colloquy, fifty more of every variety. They all sat and stirred like ladies in a garden, their skirts parting to show underskirts of more beautiful hue, a flash of violet, a swish of peony edged with black. They spread them to sit, and played with their fans, and flicked open their parasols in the sun.

I asked Miltón why they gathered together like that, on certain spots on the bank. He shrugged, and looked, I thought, quite comical. He said that they go where an animal has pissed, or a man has pissed. At least I think this is what he said. Then he rolled out his tongue, as though to lick.

And now I do not know what I wanted to say about butterflies. I have been laughing all day, but it makes me sad. I recall the salon of the Princess Mathilde, the richest room I was ever in. And yes, women like myself, newly arrived in town, all clustered and fluttering, when a rich man speaks. And when he leaves the room, a general business with fans, as we settle on his words and eat.

'At least they do not fight,' I say.

'Which?'

'The butterflies. At least they are beautiful, and they do not fight.'

'Enough piss, for everyone,' he says.

The silence, again, is deafening. The baby flutters inside me, and settles. Doctor Stewart's red hair is fading to sand in the sun. He has switched from cane alcohol to a more respectable rum.

*

Today, from the swamp, a new crawling thing. Señor López leapt away from the mattress and swore. *Vinchucas*. Like cockroaches. Evil-smelling. I pull up my nightdress in fright and find more bites. Hundreds of bites. They like white meat, he says, and then he chews on me himself. Also my blood is richer now. Every crawling, flying thing can smell my belly from miles around. They fly in under my skirts and eat. Francine is set to get them out before I put my bloomers on, and gets comically, horribly, buried in the layers of cloth. My dear friend shouts as he watches, and slaps his leg. It is the thing that he enjoys most, in the day.

I have ordered Miltón for my own use, to keep the mosquitoes from inside my shanty pavilion in the bow. Also *jejenes*, which are tiny, infernal things. Their bite does not last unless scratched, but is the most exquisite torture for the first while. Miltón's legs are covered with faded welts, but I have never seen him scratch, except in an idle way. They don't seem to bother him. My very fingernails itch. I want to jump into the river until the water closes over my head. But there are things in the water too (not to mention the English animals on deck) that stop me, the flesh-eating *pirhana* fish, which makes for a great splashing and shouting when the sailors take to the river, and worse – the *rana*, with a barb, Señor López tells me, *so* long, the wound astonishingly painful and slow to heal.

Still becalmed.

I get Miltón to name the birds for me. He does it in his own language first, a guttural mess that makes me think of Gaelic, and then, after some thought, in Spanish. The *Membei*: a tiny blue-winged parrot. The *Mainumby* (in Spanish *El Picaflor*): a tiny whirring gem of a bird, with iridescent feathers. The *Tuca*: a strong, clever bird, the one I saw was carrying a huge banana, lengthways, in its beak. A handsome vulture, or perhaps a falcon, with no Spanish name at all, the *Karakara*. Why? It goes karakarakarakara and then rrrrrrrrrrrp!

We have assembled quite a list, when I spot two birds of my own, of a particular feather: Francine strolling on deck and chatting quite amiably to our own Mr Whytehead. Francine all in green like a little parakeet – the engineer in his frock coat and stovepipe hat; quite the magpie (or gull!).

My hands are swollen. I cannot wear a ring that Señor López bought me in Madrid and all day I am itching with the thought that I have somehow let it slip overboard, or even that I threw it over the side. I almost remember doing it; the tiny splash. I send Francine to check my travelling jewellery case and it is there, safe, as I know it must be, but still I see it dropping through the water to the amazement of the fishes. I see it tilt and sink into the grey sludge of the river bottom. I think I may have done it in my sleep, that I may have wandered at night and, against my own knowing, lost the ring overboard.

This afternoon, I call Francine inside. I have her unpack all my trunks and take pen and paper. There is to be no more rummaging when we get to Asunción. She must know which gloves-boots-parasol, and have them close to hand. I am worn out with describing and so have settled on a method, which is to give each toilette a title, such as:

The Diana: a hunting costume of ribbed velvet in two shades of copper, tablier of dull gold plush, kidskin gilet to match, bonnet of fancy straw with bunch of autumn leaves and berries, though I think all of it too heavy to wear here in this heat, and suspect I have brought all the wrong things. It is sometimes cool, though, in the morning, when there is a mist.

The *Chère Amie*: a visiting toilette, in lilac *barège* with three deep flounces bordered with quilled ribbon in blue, gloves of grey with the same ribbon at the wrist, elastic-sided grey satin boots: society may be limited, but Señor López has two sisters and a mother living, to whom, at least, respects must be paid. He says they look like him. I cannot imagine it.

The *Impératrice*: a ballgown in the style of Eugénie, underskirt of rose-coloured satin, looped overskirt in chameleon silk, being raspberry shot with blue. Gloves, boots, *sortie de bal*, in blue, though I think perhaps white would do. This to be worn with opals, for lesser occasions, or my sapphires, if Señor López allows. He threatened to throw them in the sea and replace them with diamonds, which he can come by more cheaply over here, though looking at the forest, I can not imagine diamonds in there nor gold – only mushrooms.

While I am at tea, Señor López comes in and throws things around the little cabin. He is followed about by his valet de chambre who flaps his hands and then starts to cry. The man actually cries. A thin little fellow with too much oil in his hair, he leaves the cabin and goes to the rail and almost howls. I think the oil attracts the insects, and suggest to Francine she tell him so. She looks at me, quite boldly, as if to say 'Me, talk to a valet?'

But something must be done. Señor López is blithered by waistcoats. He goes out in the morning pleased with his reflection, then thinks the men laugh at him and shrugs the damn things off, to wit: a rust-coloured silk jacquard complete with fob and chain, tangled under some maritime divot or pivot or dah-dee-doo. Then he is angry all over again because of course he is very proud of this rust-coloured silk jacquard and it is spoiled, now, so I have Francine rescue it, and smooth it out myself, I say that there is no point in being rich if you do not know what money is. Which makes him laugh. He says that if you know what money is, then you are not rich.

But it is not so simple, and to make it simple I take the sticky valet aside myself and tell him he is to lay out only caramel and blue and leave the flattery to me. Also wash his hair in vinegar. He quivers a little, as we talk.

It occurs to me that Francine would like to be a *wife*. I

have been puzzling over her since we left France. Sometimes, during the carnage of the Atlantic, she could not cross the cabin to tend to me, except by crawling on the floor and hanging on to the fixed legs of the table and then the bed. I looked at her and wondered what on earth she was doing here. What she might seek across the ocean. What she had left behind.

Perhaps she has dreams. Yes, Francine, I have decided, has *soul*. Of course she is also fond of me, as I am terribly fond of her. And besides, she knows all about me and so I must be kind. The girl learned her tricks at her mother's knee; she kept secrets and carried billets-doux from the age of five: you would think she had fallen off the stage of the Bouffes, if it were not for her face, which is very simple and staid and enjoys an air of genteel sorrow.

So, behind her she has left a baby, alive or dead. And ahead of her she sees . . . a husband – a proper one. Such respectability.

She was sent to me by Dolores the Spanish girl, who found her too pretty, but said she was clean and clever and at home in the world. I decided to call her Francine, for my French adventures. Perhaps I should call her something else now; Speranza or Mercedes.

I have her sit by me. I tell her these are the things she must know to be a wife, as taught to me by Miss Miller, the English teacher at Mme Hubert's school for young girls in Bordeaux; culled from her little book, which she inscribed, as I see on the fly: 'For Eliza – who would do well in the world.' (The pages are rotting a little, in the heat.)

She must not! Look steadily at any one, especially if they are a gentleman; not turn her head from side to side during a more general conversation; nor shift in her chair, nor hold on to any part of herself while conversing, such as an ear or an elbow; nor place her hand on any part of the person she is talking to, such as their collar or one of their buttons;

she is not to cross her legs, nor extend her feet to view her slippers; nor admire herself with complacency in a glass; nor adjust, in any way, her jewels, hair, handkerchief; she must throw her shawl with graceful negligence upon a table and not fret about a hat which she has just left off &c. &c. Neither is she to laugh immoderately or play continually with her fan.

And the reverse, I tell her, if she would be a whore. But the reverse again, which is to say the same, if she would be a *grande horizontale*. We do some preliminary work with a fan, with much hilarity.

I close the book.

The same Miss Miller who, as I left that wretched school, said, 'You will end up with a disease,' and slammed the door. Goodbye, Miss Miller.

Francine says that Mr Whytehead is the son of a ship's chandler, which is to say he is the son of no one at all. And besides, his father is dead. Which fact seems to us to be quite hilarious. I tell her that I do not know what openings there would be in Asunción, but she may do as well to stick by me.

The boat moved. All day it moved! The trees have given way, on our left, to an endless swamp of green and grey. And the thump and slap of the great paddles is thin and distant in its echoless wastes.

Tonight we keep no company. My dear friend tells me ghost stories, where all the ghosts are animals. A thing called the *ow-ow* that looks like a sheep and hunts in a pack. 'Ow! Ow!' he says. A water serpent with the head of a dog – also lascivious – and he yelps and pants like a pup.

Francine has painted my bites with camomile, so I flake and itch. It is very close and still. The boat is full of shiftings, small noises, groans. And in my belly, the child does not so much kick as knock. Does not so much knock as scrabble.

Still, if we attempt, say, three ensembles a day, it will pass the time nicely to Paraguay.

*

In a sort of revenge for the jacquard waistcoat, Señor López complains of my tight lacing and Francine is set to cutting side vents in my corsets. She threads the new eyelets with pink and blue ribbon, to please me. But they are ruined. I should not have to dress. I should be confined, and I would stay so, but that Doctor Stewart orders me out, to perspire.

He has not examined me yet. Not once. He is supposed to kneel at my feet and put his hand up my skirts and do things. But he has not. Every time I look at him I think of it, and he thinks of it, and sometimes, in expiation, he says,

'Still kicking?'

'Yes, Doctor.'

'Very good.'

My dear friend is impatient. He gargles brandy and spits over the side. They are all impatient, and give me a wide berth. I am unlucky and I am slow. I remind them of too much – of women. Of the act that made me swell. I remind them of hopes that do not come to fruit and lowered voices and things that go wrong in the middle of the night.

When I was sixteen, I think I was beautiful. But that was three years ago. Something has happened to my face now. I cannot say exactly what – but colours that should flatter do not flatter, and everything I do to it is wrong. I am waiting for my hair to fall out, but I cannot remember if this happens before or after the baby is born.

Señor López says I must turn into a slack old Doña in black, with a mouth like a chicken's arsehole. I must go bald except for my upper lip, and order people, especially important people, around. And he must grow cheerful, I say, and round, with a baby pulling at his nose and another wetting his knee. But he is already thinking of something else, and leaves the room.

I will have a parrot in Asunción, like the one the Clarke sisters had in Mallow. A green one that said *Erin Abú! Erin Abú!*

But this afternoon: a peculiar advance. Miltón motions to me as I lie in my *hamaca*. He is hunched over a bowl of porridge, and he takes a lump of it and smears it on his britches. I have no idea why he should want me to witness this, but it is certainly done for me. He applies it carefully to the bottom of his drawers; then he approaches, lifts the muslin and tries to assault my person, or, in hindsight, my petticoats, his hands still covered in slop. Señor López comes running at my cry and there is such a ruckus, I am afraid I may lose my new friend to the river. He gabbles ferociously and whines, and suddenly Señor López starts to laugh. He laughs until he has to sit down, which he does, with a thump on the deck, and then he drums his heels on the floor. (I, meanwhile, rearranging my dignity, as best I can.)

Half an hour later, the porridge is dry and his britches stiff as a board. The women of the region use it for starch, and it works wonderfully well. Francine has an order from the cook and by evening my skirts again are five feet wide.

We sit and play cards – for no money still, which is not what I call cards at all. The lugubrious Doctor Stewart and the religious Mr Whytehead, who leans now over the shoulder of the simple maid Francine to point at a three of spades. Señor spits brandy. I sweep and whisper and duck and swish about in my marron *moiré* and make them all sweat beneath their collars, and I do not care. I commission Mr Whytehead (who learns his languages from a book) to settle my Spanish into verbs and participles, and I flirt terribly, and,

'Are you jealous, my Love?' I say, when they are all gone. 'I think you are jealous of me, and where I look.'

'Am I?' He seems quite surprised. The idea of betrayal is strange to him. It is not what a woman is for. (Or perhaps he will have me simply shot!) He approves the Spanish lessons with Whytehead, and so I take courage and tell him of my secret plan – which is nothing less than a match between the engineer and Francine.

'The maid?' he says.

'When we get to Paraguay,' I say. 'She can be whatever she likes.'

But I have miscalculated. There is something uncomfortable between us. He has gone outside to smoke, though I have no objection, I tell him, to his cigar.

Dresses for tomorrow:

The Bluebottle: a pelisse in that colour called fly's wing, a grey so dark it is black. Tablier of dull peacock sheen. To be matched with my black lace parasol and, I think, green gloves.

The Medea: dinner toilette of blood-red velvet, under-skirt pink *moiré* antique. To be worn with diamonds, when I get them.

The Housey Housey: at-home toilette, in otter-coloured taffeta trimmed with black silk moss, with chemisette of organdie in dusty pink. All very dull.

Doctor Stewart, drunk, tells me that he is an orphan. Double consumption. It happened when he was six. He says he remembers nothing of his mother, not even the smell of her skirts as he knelt to say his prayers.

It seems a peculiar way not to remember your mother. I say nothing, except,

'You must check on the baby, Doctor Stewart. When you have time.'

*

I will write English, but I will not speak it any more. If I speak in their own language they will see fit to despise me. Not the doctor or the railwaymen, who know how the world goes, but the men. There are fourteen of them, most out of London – one out of Galway, and he is the worst – all the scrapings of some wharfside inn the captain knows.

The captain allows them rum, and tonight they are dancing. Like wild men. The ship shudders to their thumping feet, things fall into the water, and the words of their songs are unspeakable. I know they are singing about me. I would have my dear friend flog all of them – or at least one of them – in the morning. I would have him sail this ship, magically, alone. And marry me! Marry me, my love. I must say it once. I must say it when no one can hear.

But we took an early stroll in the dawn chill; the mist so thick and white, a solid wall that gave way before us. We might have been alone, on the boat, on the round earth. Sometimes, when we are moving, he leans out beyond the questing prow of the boat, as though to say, 'Tomorrow, Asunción.' And I think that he alone, he alone, could take this ghost ship and fly it home.

Our Spanish lessons commence and Francine is very apt. She sits to one side and sews as Mr Whytehead strolls about the room and occasionally bends to write at my little desk. He will not sit down. I do not think he stands to show his figure. He is neat but he is not vain. He is also quite stern, which looks silly. Truth be told, the lesson isn't much use to her, conducted as it is through English, though we occasionally jump about in French, it being closer as languages go. But she sits and looks pretty enough, and lifts her head from time to time, as though to *behold* him. It is a very sweet, religious look and I am quite proud of her, in a way.

This afternoon there was an incident: Miltón held the swinging *hamaca* while Francine ladled me in to it, and he went to take his place at the bow. Then a sailor (Goggins, I think) came up behind him and kicked the back of his knees, very neatly, so that they gave from under him. He kicked him again on the floor, while Miltón curled up and made a soughing sound, which now I find odd, the silence of it – and all this in front of my very eyes. I shout for help. Whytehead comes running and then stands, inept. Finally, my dear friend, who pulls the men apart and fulminates. He turns to me where I lie, struggling out of my *hamaca*, like an insect flipped over that cannot right herself again. I am obliged to translate – it is all sullen mutterings, something to do with a native woman the sailor wanted for his own use, until Miltón interfered. I do not know how. He is such a slight boy, I guess he cannot be beyond fourteen. But interfere he did, and the woman, who came to look for tobacco, slipped back safe overboard.

After this translation is done, they turn away, as though ashamed. All of them ashamed; because every man on the boat is by now gathered in the bow. The child overwhelms me. It twists with such violence I must lie back down. My friend shouts for the doctor and for Francine, and the sailors disperse while I work my fan of stiffened lace, now turning to cloth again in the sun. Whytehead turns to bow, and thinks better of it, as I lift and let fall a swathe of muslin, and look him in the eye.

Señor López says he is a man of vision and tenacity. And so I must smile.

Tonight we keep our own company. I have Miltón sleep in front of our door. The captain – because they need it, he says – has trebled the sailors' allowance of rum, and they dance off the native woman, and all women, and throw their flagons overboard.

Francine strains the river water through two thicknesses of clean linen, before I will let it touch my skin, and in the middle of the night I have a dreadful urge to drink it from the ewer, there is something necessary about the smell. Also the smell of Macassar. The only wine I can stomach is champagne, and this only because it tastes of biscuits. They haul it up on ropes from the river, so it is fleetingly cool. By the end of the bottle it is hot, practically. Hot biscuity champagne. It tastes wonderful. It tastes like Hell itself.

I do not know if it is the world, or me. I do not know if it is the wilderness or the boat or the baby that keeps me so far from myself. I drink hot champagne and eat with ferocity the dull porridge of the place. I know it is dull, but it is hugely interesting to me. And in the middle of the night I am crazed with hunger. Bewildered by it. I look at Francisco's leg as it dangles out of his *hamaca* (he has abandoned the infested bed) and I think that what I need is meat. Perhaps even this meat, the meat of his thigh. I have a desire to bite into him, as you might into a melon.

And then, perhaps it is melon I need. I think about melon, am smitten by melon. I bite into the golden flesh, and feel the seeds slither in their luscious frill. Is there anywhere in this godforsaken place where a melon might be bought or got? Is there a garden somewhere, at the back of a shack, where a little old man has tied plants on to canes and watered them and shielded them from the sun? And what if he will not give it to me? What if the old man (I can see him in the darkness in front of me shaking his head) says that this particular melon is not ripe, or it is reserved for someone else. This melon is for his daughter, or his sick grandchild, or that this melon is grown in the soil where his wife lies, and that on no account can it be eaten, because the flesh of it is the same as the flesh of his wife. I tell him that I have no problem eating his dead wife. I swing a stone that is suddenly in my hand and hit his round, stupid skull, which splits with a melon-like sound. At first wooden, then thick and wet.

After which hallucination, I groan again with nameless hunger and start to pace the room. I put on a wrap and slip out through the door and into the air, as if there might be something, somewhere, that will assuage me, a piece of rope to suck, skin of tar to pick, frozen in the bottom of a pail. As if there might be a melon, indeed, magically lying there. The moon has risen. The deck is humpy with the bodies of drunken, sleeping sailors seeking refuge from the heat. The scene is catastrophic and still. There is nothing to eat. I lean back against the door, put my hands flat on the wood, and breathe.

The sailors have covered themselves with cloth against the mosquitoes. They look like furniture in a house that has been shut up. Or dead men, pinned by cobwebs to the floor. One of them starts to mutter, I think in his sleep, but when I listen to the words I hear the Lord's Prayer. I can not tell which sailor this is. He says the lines in a gulping whisper. 'And deliver us from evil.' He is near the end of it when I spot him, stretched out on the deck. He arches his back into the night, as though presenting his stomach to the moon.

*

This morning, I tell my dear friend that I am turning cannibal. He looks at me in a considered way, and then decides to laugh. For the rest of the day, he taunts me with food. He talks of meals remembered in Buenos Aires, in London; meals we ate together in Rome. Valera is sent down to the hold and he returns with a menu from that place in Rome.

39

And freely, within earshot of sailors, engineers and natives, the whole busy ignorance of the boat, Francisco reads it out to me. Hors d'oeuvres: delicious prawns, strongly spiced. A Rhine carp *à la Chambord*. Quails stuffed thick with truffles on buttered toast flavoured with basil. Asparagus with *sauce hollandaise*. A pheasant with Russian salad. Pontet-Canet with the first course. Chilled champagne from the second course to the coffee. So cool!

To shame him, I tell him it is the baby who is hungry, not me. He moves to the rail and looks over the side. Then he strides off to talk about boilers.

All afternoon I lie in a torpor. More swamp. In the distance clumps of pampas grass and farther still low, black trees. The channel is ever more difficult to find. The paddles slap the water and the sails snap, and the child moves under my hand. I feel a shoulder surface, or a tiny elbow. My little eel. My only thing.

On our right, forest gives way to savannah and back again. There are hills, far away, green and homely, but with no homes on them. I see cattle, but even they are scrawny and wild and strange. Then a landing stage, where the *campesinos* stand amazed. The reek of hundreds of hides drifts towards us, stretched out on racks and drying in the sun. Tonight, we will have fresh meat.

Doctor Stewart grows eloquent. He says that any country is beautiful when reflected through 'the lovely prism of my laughing Irish eyes'. (God help me.)

Dresses for today:

The *Muchacho*: a riding habit of serge in bergandine red.

The Irish: that green dress, with the puffings of tulle. To be worn with a shawl.

I have not the wit for more. I lie here and think that I am the boat. I am the boat and I am the sky and the baby sails inside me, safe. Despite which romantic notion, I am sad.

They must hear me at night. I am disturbed in my sleep by such dreams that I wake and must have him. Like food. Now. It is my condition. What if I were an innocent? What if I were a girl just married, waking in the night in the aftershadows of such dreams, with half the world waiting their turn, husbands, friends, a stranger with eyes like the lumbering animal I saw on the bank, capybara, a man whose face I cannot see, and Misha who is always there, standing by the bed, whether in delectation or grief he will not say. I wake and know that he is dead. And careless, all aflame, I rouse my dear friend, to straddle him unsuccessfully in his *hamaca*, to end by rearranging ourselves on the floor, as he props himself up on his arms to keep back from my belly, and we make a noise that all the ship must hear.

The child, says my dear friend, is low (he has no shame), the child is filling me up down there. It is a boy! he says. It is a boy. I am glad. I pity poor womankind. I had not thought to pity them, but I do now. I think about my mother – all guts and softness, made stupid by something. Perhaps by this. Perhaps she was made stupid by this.

I am woken this morning by the worst noise I have ever heard. It is the sound of the world ending, the sound of all animals eating all men. I rise in terror and run, and wrench open the door to a wall of white. I cannot tell if the attack comes from the bowels of the boat or the water or the forest – the noise is all around. The air itself is roaring. My only thought is to hide the baby from the danger, which means hiding my own body too. Francisco catches me at the rail, and turns me around in the mist. Monkeys, he says. It is only monkeys.

Mr Whytehead calls them Howlers. They roll their voices

around in a special reverberating gourd in their chests, he says, also, perhaps, the mist amplifies the noise as clouds do thunder. He appears out of the mist, to say all this. He is standing at the rail beside us all of a sudden, talking about thoracic cavities, with me still frantic in my night attire. I don't think the stupid man ever sleeps.

But I think they are an omen, whatever about their cavities. I find myself in tears, and cry all morning. My dear friend is bored with me, lump that I am. I cry so much I am thirsty. Even this liquid I must conserve, in the heat. At eleven o'clock, Francine glues me together for our Spanish lesson, with rice powder and *eau de lavande*, but when Mr Whytehead comes into the room my dear friend says that his time is better spent this morning on matters of state. And so he bows and retreats, and I want to cry some more, even though I do not like the man much. And because I cannot abide the cabin longer, I take a turn on deck.

But they were an omen. I was right – and it is no use keeping an omen to yourself. Because at noon, after a hard morning pushing towards home, one of the boilers bursts, though not badly. There was an unimportant sound, as though of two pieces of wood clacking together. It seemed to come from the shore. Then, after a brief silence, the frightful screams of one of the sailors; scalded in the blast of water and steam. He clambered up to the deck and rolled out of the hatch, tearing at his clothes, which were stuck to his body and burning him still. An attempt to free him of them proved ill-advised (Doctor Stewart came late), and now he lies, half-flayed and moaning, while the ship and all on it are horribly becalmed. I have made a visit. He lies shivering in his cot, loosely bandaged in fat, his lips sweet with morphia. He calls me 'Dora, my Dora' and says yes, he is quite comfortable, thank you. But still the moans seep out of him, until every man on the boat mutters a guilty prayer that he may die between this breath and the next. But the next breath comes, laden with pain.

And so I sit. I wear a dress of extreme simplicity in shades of pink and cream and favour his good side, praying a little that he will not turn to look at me out of his other, boiled eye. I am his Dora still, and hold his hand. I wait for secrets, but there are none. The dying have very little to say, I fear, as we lean over to gather their last whispers in our ear.

He pulls me to him and starts a paternoster for me to finish, and with the sound of the first line, I know who it is – it is the sailor who was praying the night they all got drunk. The sailor who lay pinned to the deck, as though pressed there by the beauty and the weight of the sky. Is it possible that he knew that this journey would be his last? How can we know? But he did know. I am sure, he did.

Now, as the evening wears on, I look for my death. I hunt it out. I prise open the blank future and try to smell it – When and How. When and How. If I were to die by water, surely I would know it, or by fire. If I were to be murdered then I would be afraid of people's hands. But I am not afraid of anything, I think, or was not, until now. Now, I am afraid for the child, the inscrutable span and course of his life, all shut out from me. All the years I face for him; the not-knowing and ever-watching, the fact that there is a part of me now that can be truly hurt, after I had left hurt behind.

The last time I said the Lord's Prayer was on my marriage day. I do not want to sleep. It is a good day, a long one, a clear one. The child is easy, and my mind runs free.

Or perhaps it is the orange blossom that makes me think of weddings; it grows wild on the bank and the scent drifts towards us, across the water. I was married in a dress of ordinary blue, with a posy of violets in my hands – no orange blossom there, though M. Raspail did send a butter-coloured straw bonnet trimmed with some cheap-looking berries. It arrived in our room in Dover and Quatrefages laughed quite unkindly when I tried it on. So I took it off and hit him with it. Despite which it was, you know, quite a tender moment, and makes me think now that we could have been friends.

I think it is liquorice that I crave. I will have a little black child.

I remember playing the piano in Mallow. I must have been very young, the keys looked so huge and Papa stacked books on the seat to help me reach. There was a crowd of people in the room and I wore a sprigged muslin dress. They all clapped and kissed me, and my father was most pleased. Some kind gentleman gave me a bag of liquorice, after. I wonder which gentleman it was.

The sailor talks about pies. It makes me hungry. I should leave him – it is not good for my belly to be where dead things are. The words dribble from his blasted mouth, and now and then, clarity. His shirt is left out in the rain. Dora (myself) did not believe him when he said . . . what? This is important; he really must say this. But the pie is distracting. He sinks back into the pie. I don't know what kind of pie it is, but it is very good. Mmm mnn, he says, like a child. Mmm mmm mnn.

And so he dies. It is four a.m., the hour when the world turns over. It occurs to me that I do not know his name. I place his crocked hands upon his chest – so still – and take my leave of him. Outside, the sailors, when I pass, take off their caps. Who cares whose wife I am, now?

*

This morning they set to repairing the boiler, with a little furnace set up on deck for the soldering pans. We sit on the water, and burn.

I settle myself into my toilette and I want to cry again, not because my face is so lumpy but because of the cheap cake of rouge I am using – a little tin box, with a picture of the tower at Glendalough on the lid. It belonged to my sister once, but did not suit her. I think it is the only thing I have about me from Ireland. There is also a little brush and some *maschara* from Algeria. My bag of paints is a sad museum. The right lip colour, the absolute shade of blush, these are the only things that persist in my life. I think that some potion here will follow me to the grave. And then I think that this is literally true – some stuff here will be applied to my dead face. So I leave the brush down and stare, while Francine bustles behind me. All flesh and blood.

I am the daughter of a doctor. My mother came from a naval family, and her brother fought with Nelson's fleet. There are certificates for all this, and letters, in three or four different countries. I was married in Kent at the age of fifteen to a man called M. Quatrefages who served with the French forces in Algeria. This marriage was illegal under French law, because of my tender age, but legal in England.

I am the daughter of a doctor who specialised in rheumatic disorders at the spa town of Mallow in the Co. Cork. My mother suffered herself from bad health, and took the waters there, and we lived nearby for some years. My sister, Corinne, caught the fancy of that famous Italian musician Tamburini, and lives with him, is married to him now in Paris. Where I joined her, after leaving a cruel husband, a certain M. Quatrefages, who took advantage of my tender years to spirit me away to Kent and marry me there. This marriage is still valid in England, much to my consternation. I have met in my time the musician Berlioz, who much admired my playing, also the Princesse Mathilde, who received me kindly, also several members of the Russian nobility, from whom I became estranged on the occasion of the Eastern War.

45

I was born in Ireland and lived there, near the spa town of Mallow, until the age of ten, when the hunger then raging in the countryside obliged us to leave from the harbour at Queenstown. My father is a doctor and my mother is a Schnock (one of the naval Schnocks). After a brief spell in England, I was educated in Bordeaux at Mme Hubert's school for young girls. I was married in Kent, at a very young age, to the chief veterinarian surgeon of the French forces in Algiers. While there I was much patronised by the Chief of the French Commissariat, M. Raspail, also the Fez of Tunis, who both much admired my playing. My marriage was illegal under the Napoleonic Code, and when this became clear to me I left the deserts of Africa for Paris, where I studied at the conservatoire, and applied for my decree nisi, which was delayed by the complications of English law. When we get to Paraguay I will have Señor López draft a new law. Because I am carrying, or so he tells me, the future of Paraguay.

The baby kicks like a boy. It kicks like it cannot wait to get out of me. Francine cools my temples with *eau de lavande*. She whispers, 'Not long. Not long now.' But I do not know how long it will be. I do not know if we will make it to Asunción. I do not know if it will ever be born, or if I will stay here for ever – for ever on this river, with this water flowing by.

Asparagus

DOCTOR STEWART LIKED Asunción. It was the kind of town where a man could go to pieces in his own good time.

He woke up to it slow. It was some months before he wrote to his aunt to describe this sleepy town of adobe and wood, of red-tiled roofs and secret courtyards. But he could not get it straight in his head. Outside his window, a group of urchins was burying an infant child up to the neck. They were smoking cigars – all of them, including the infant, though his was, of course, handed to his mouth by a factotum. None of them was older than five. They seemed entirely happy.

On the rough desk in front of Stewart was a sheet of paper, stained already with his sweat. It would be handed by a wind-whipped postman into his aunt's Edinburgh fastness, a sort of distant cry. So he filled it full of flowers for her, the smoky blue jacaranda and the bridal orange blossom that would make her mouth purse, as though she were tasting the fruit. What else? In the distance, the cries of salesmen and the complaints of cattle – she had enough of those at home. He might say that the women sometimes wore just the skirts of their dresses, and let the empty bodies flop out behind. Or that they liked to dance with bottles balanced on their heads. Or perhaps not. 'It is all very foreign,' he wrote, then stopped and tried again to think of the distinctive thing to say.

Outside, the urchins sat and watched the infant as the infant watched them, looking from one face to another with an expression that Stewart could not decipher. Perhaps it was quite comfortable, wrapped up like that in the earth. 'The men', he wrote, 'are in the habit of wearing hat brims, without the benefit of a hat, and so our local Indian fellow is jauntily crowned with a halo made of felt.' She would find this image a little Catholic, but it was better than telling her you could tell a prostitute by the gold comb in her hair. Respectable women wore tortoiseshell or wood. A new arrival might get confused (he did not write).

'There is such a lack of iron in the town' (commerce, good), 'that people leave nails to their children and, in their wills, specify how many each should get.' Outside, the chief urchin, in his hat brim and little else, sauntered up to the buried infant and pulled it clear. The child came up like a carrot and, as the red soil fell away, Stewart saw that it was a girl.

'But let us not belittle Asunción,' he concluded, for his aunt was a clever woman, and he liked her. 'It is made, as every other town is made, of casual encounters and minor conspiracies; of friendliness to strangers and small, ancient irritations between friends. It is a frontier place, the gentlemen a little too rough and the ladies a little too "nice". But it is made, as every other town is made, out of talk.'

The little girl had recovered her personal cigar and now squatted with the others, chewing the stub. Her position afforded Stewart a view of her genitals, flatly presented between her sweet little legs and feet. And indeed she was all sweet, from her toes to the same cigar's dangerously glowing tip. Stewart folded the letter and ran his hand heavily along the crease. He had not mentioned that the talk was of one thing only, and that one thing was his former patient, Eliza Lynch.

Stewart listened to it all. He cultivated the trick of disappearing into the company, so as not to inhibit conversation about events he had personally witnessed (though only after a fashion). He wished, sometimes, that he could remember the way it really was, but mostly he gave in to the stories as they became skewed over the months and years into something high and fantastical, and ever more true.

Mme Cochelet, the French envoy's wife, said that the grand entrance of the *Tacuarí* into Asunción went thus (she told it, always, in a sort of mime):

The boat glides up alongside the dock. The crowds that have been running along the bank fill the square. The gangplank is let down. Silence. A cart pulls into the Plaza de Palma with twenty bandsmen hanging off the sides, waving their instruments in the air. They jump off the cart and run to the quay and fall in. More silence. Picture it. The dirt. The sloping, cockeyed customhouse, the smell of the river and, in front of them all, a boat the size of a dream.

Finally, the cavalry; all snorting and stamping. Three old barouches trundle to a halt – and there they all are. Carriage number one: fat old López with his outrageous epaulettes, his sword across his lap. Carriage number two: fat old Doña Juana López all swaddled up in black, with her ghastly daughters, Rafaela and Innocencia, equally fat, equally swaddled; their moustachios bristling, their bosoms heaving, and their armpits stained with sweat. Carriage number three: the younger sons, Benigno or, as we call him, Maligno, and with him the ridiculous Admiral (of what fleet, pray tell?) Venancio, tight and buttoned as the upholstery they sit upon, the springs of the carriage singing and sagging as they shift about.

So, the people cheering now in the heat – thousands of them – the band striking up, there is a movement, a glimpse, a flutter of tulle; and there, at the top of the gangway, is a vision. A Juno. A woman of proportions, in a pale lilac gown and matching bonnet, with a stole of lace to hide – Mme Cochelet would bet good money on it – her shame. She would like to say that the bonnet was *de trop*, or the lilac vulgar, but they were neither, and her first impulse, she could not gainsay it, was to cheer or swoon – this shard of Paris ice that had fallen out of the sky to land on the Plaza de Palma; full now of hushed Paraguayans, who had never seen skin so fair, nor eyes so blue, nor a woman so gloriously large, who had never seen that shade of lilac, except perhaps on a deep forest orchid – the colour of a flower that grows in the dark. Stepping up beside her: the young López in an endless stovepipe hat, too-tight frock coat and excruciating pastel trousers. The apparition takes his proffered arm and floats down to the quay, smiling regally to her right and her left. The crowds part as she drifts through to the first carriage and old López. The son bows and speaks. The vision smiles her visionary smile and lifts a languid hand. It hangs in the air. The old Dictator grunts – at her perhaps, or perhaps at the coachman – and the carriage pulls away at speed, followed at speed by the presidential escort whose polished hooves kick up enough dust to turn the silk lilac ice to soot grey. Eliza Lynch looks down at her dress. So much for Paris.

Up to this moment, Mme Cochelet had hoped against hope that – his satyriasis not withstanding – the young López had somehow married, but it was not to be. When 'La Lincha' was presented to Doña Juana, the old woman (who treated the entire country like it was her own back kitchen) shrieked and struck her breast and ordered her carriage away. This shot off with such force that the now-dusty vision was spattered with excrement. At which,

Maligno smiled his little smile, and followed his mother at a gentle trot, before more harm could be done.

Mme Cochelet was fond of this story, which had grown so much in the telling that none of it (save, of course, the lilac dress) was in any way true. She told it for years, sometimes twice in the same week, but she only told it to those she could trust. Mme Cochelet was, after all, married to the French envoy and had to be careful what she said. She started telling it in 1856 after Eliza had a *quinta* built for her in record time; a simple, easy house of pink marble. She added the dust from the horse's hoofs in 1857, after the young López built a road from Government House straight to its gates in the suburb of La Recoleta. She added the excrement in 1858, after her husband went out there for the first time. They were, you could say, *political* details. And, much as Stewart admired Mme Cochelet, her defiance of the heat in home-knit stockings, her Norman rectitude when it came to things like covering the milk and sacking the servants, still he thought it unwise of her to disdain La Lincha so freely. To say so often, and so openly, that she 'would rather break bread with a *nigger* than eat at the house of the Irish whore.' It was entertaining, but possibly unwise. It was true, but it was not pretty.

Every day, Eliza sallied forth in a carriage so beautifully sprung you could ride it across country without spilling a cup of tea. Every day, Stewart saw them spit as it passed: the old Spanish aristocrats, with more surnames trotting after them than they had horses; they crossed themselves and covered their daughters' virgin eyes. But why should the woman not take the air? Why should she not sometimes walk down the street, with her parasol gently twirling, to dare the men to bid her good day – to dare the men *not* to bid her good day? Because they all went. There was not a man for a hundred miles who had not ventured out to the *quinta* at La Recoleta to see for himself the little oriental carpets, the French tapestries hung in the tasteful rooms, and to drink the political cup of *café au lait* that was handed to them, in person, by the mistress of Francisco Solano López.

The mother, old Doña Juana, spent the day fingering her rosary beads and screeching, 'I will *never* accept that woman. I will *never* accept that woman!' in the tearful company of her daughters; the hirsute Rafaela, the glandular Innocencia. Stewart prescribed laudanum. He did not say that there was no cure for the facts of the case – that the old woman had been outfoxed somehow by her own son; that every time she thought of La Lincha now she saw her own future, and old López dead.

There was nothing like a good root around the López ladies to remind Stewart of Eliza Lynch, who had a different order of flesh from the rest of us, who had the kind of flesh that might redeem a man. William Stewart was the only person in Asunción who was banned from visiting La Lincha – for most people it was the other way around – and it was a sort of private joke with him. Still, he sometimes thought of her with regret. He would never get to palpate, nor suture, nor ease. He would never cool those limbs in the flush of influenza, nor brush from them the bloom of measles. Above all, he would never see them asplay in the blood and terror of childbirth – a scene that he had, in fact, missed, after coming thousands of miles to see it. This might seem a little remiss of him, but Stewart was absent for complicated reasons, in which drink played only a minor role. Quite simply, he could not get off that boat, with its horrors, quick enough. He walked off the gangplank and through the crowd and disappeared into a week he could not himself remember. William Stewart missed Eliza's lying-in because she made him shudder. That was all. He took whatever remnant of him was still decent, and walked it off the *Tacuarí*, and got it drunk as a lord.

He could hardly recall what scruple it was he felt then. He did not name it, because it was impossible to name. Nor did he encourage it – he pickled it. He preserved it in alcohol, like some misshapen curiosity with the label gone. If he held it up to the light now, he would not be able to tell you what it was, or what class of creature it had once been.

As for that other remnant of her river band – when he met Keld Whytehead, they did not speak of it; as if they had both been marked by something, about which there was nothing to say.

And what of Eliza? Alone! said the gallant Captain Thompson. Completely alone. She poured coffee on the balcony, and talked of home. When the day was hot, or the political climate warm, she touched her hand to her breast and said, 'Paris, ah Paris!' in just that tone. Picking out a little melody on the fabulously real piano, taking up a book and putting it down again. There were things in her head, you could see that. Once he had explored one of these volumes and found it contained, not *Geneviève de Brabant* but Voltaire's *Candide*. She laid her hand on his arm, and gently took the book and said, 'Ah. That, it is the story of my life, you know. And you, Captain Thompson, are my own Doctor Pangloss.' No, there was no doubt about it, Eliza Lynch was delectable. To love her was to succeed, the Captain said, to hate her was, quite simply, to fail.

In which case, no one succeeded better than Francisco Solano López. The city was a building site – he had an army of haggard, small boys pushing blocks of stone from the Arsenal to the Post Office; taking the roof off the Library and dumping it on the Shipyard steps. López coming in after a hard day of pointing and striding, the little son crying Papa! Papa! to be nipped on his rosy cheek by his father's dirt-stained, ink-stained, finger and thumb. There was, as yet, just one child. Mme Cochelet said that Eliza had ridden like the furies to purge herself of the second, but Thompson said she had laid the stillborn thing out in a white robe, with little gauze wings on the back, like an angel doll. Thompson had seen it himself, at the most tasteful wake possible, and you could not doubt the mother's grief. Now, there was an ornate little grave inside the gate of the cemetery at La Recoleta that said:

Ere sin could blight or sorrow fade
Death came with friendly care
The lovely bird to Heaven conveyed
And made it beossom there

And so we are finally humiliated, thought Stewart – by spelling. This is what it meant to be far from home. And he would sigh as he passed the bollixed stone on his way back to his house, where he would sit and get his boots pulled off and think about his own, terrible life.

He wondered, from time to time, about the whereabouts of the maid, Francine – no one seemed to mention her, though they talked of everything else.

Doña Cordal and her obscurely ruined daughter Carmencita said that Eliza kept her courtyard full of birds: parakeets, hummingbirds, macaws from Brazil and, tethered to a stick in the corner, a big, fat, Karakara vulture. Mme Cochelet said that Eliza kept a troop of raw Indians dressed to the nines and trained to pour wine like French footmen. She said that, apparently, the food out in La Recoleta was a miracle.

Benigno López mentioned over a bruised billiard table that Eliza Lynch did things in bed that a man could scarcely believe – he had it from his own brother – and he clicked the blue towards the centre pocket, and missed. Captain Thompson said, quite gallantly, that she had a pure soul. But they were all agreed that she was sleeping with someone behind López's back – an Englishman, or that Indian, or a dog. No one said that she was sleeping with the maid, however, which was, in its own way, strange.

Keld Whytehead did not listen to gossip: he built López an arsenal and then he built López some guns. He sent his money home. He went out to La Recoleta as necessary, and sometimes, he said, the beauty of it all made a man's eyes sting. At Christmas he sang carols (perhaps that French carol he sang on the *Tacuarí*), while Eliza accompanied him on the piano. That was all.

On the other side of town, López's abandoned mistress, Juana Pesoa, sifted the truth from the chaff. She said Eliza slept with López and with no one but López, because once a woman surrendered to López there was nowhere else to go. Juana Pesoa had a son by López – his first – and the boy now lived with Eliza. When he came to visit, he brought his mother stories from La Recoleta, as you might bring a caged animal meat.

Stewart sat with her and ate.

Eliza wants to christen her son in the cathedral – she wants to make him the prince, the heir, the most important son. But the boy is a bastard, and will always be a bastard, and the bishop forbids her the use, not just of the cathedral, but of any holy ground. Eliza screams. She raves. She gives López no rest. She calls in a crooked priest who takes one look at the boy – two years old by now, with his mother's blazing green eyes – and declares that he cannot send this small soul to Limbo. If the churches are barred to them, then he will baptise the child there in the *quinta*. For which promise he receives a fat bag of gold.

Juana Pesoa was a handsome, pinched woman. She had an illness which Stewart called 'knowing your place'. She did not rage against Eliza, who was rearing her son with every advantage, nor did she pine for López, who still parked his carriage outside her door from time to time. She went very still and worked on a stomach cancer. Something she could call her own.

Stewart left in a sorrowful frame of mind. He wouldn't mind a go at Juana Pesoa himself, just to cheer her up, just to knock against something that bitter. But as he made his way down the street he found himself wondering, not about the emotional little rictus that was Juana Pesoa's sexual part, but about Eliza Lynch. Were her eyes blue or were they green? he wondered. What was the exact colour of La Lincha's eyes? The colour of absinthe? Or the colour of curaçao? No matter. They were the colour of whatever was at the bottom of his glass, and he was going to look at them, right now.

Mme Cochelet said that Eliza might invite anyone she liked to her unholy christening – no one would go. Old López had put his foot down. And her voice rose with satisfied indignation as Stewart, working blind under her petticoats, tightened the patent truss (after five children, Mme Cochelet suffered from a painful separation of the pubic bone).

'Good,' said Stewart. Ever since Eliza's invitations went out, he had spent his time waving smelling salts under the noses of the López ladies; going from one to the other, from hysteric to phlegmatic, and each of them had a separate and very *mobile* pain. Finally, some respite. On the day of the baptism itself, he decided, he would get nicely soaked.

He did so on his own. The town was so silent and shuttered that Stewart felt like a ghost, roaming the streets. Everyone stayed indoors: the women sewing perhaps, the men mending their boots or reading the broadsheets, the children all subdued. And all of them thinking about the deserted rooms of La Recoleta, the impossible food spoiling on the plates, the splendid wines all untouched; a few household Indians, perhaps, gathered around the specially wrought silver font, while thousands of cut flowers wilted in the heat. They were thinking about Eliza in a dress unthinkably fine, a quiver in her cheek, a tic in her lovely whore's eye, as she looked around the empty rooms and faced, and knew, and ate, and got rightly sodomised by, her shame.

And Stewart hated the lot of them – so smug and delicious with revenge that when the guns opened fire they ran into the streets crying that the demon mistress of Francisco López was coming to kill them all. Of course it was just a gun salute. It was just a reminder that old López may have the country, but young López had the army (as well as something else, a lover sent from Hell and a voice that came from the sky, like Tupa, the thunder god of the Guaraní, rolling out over the town. Boom. Boom. Boom).

A boy pulled Stewart, by now half-cut, through the thunder to fetch up at the house of Doña Cordal. The matron opened the door herself and pushed him upstairs, where her incarcerated daughter, the madwoman Carmencita Cordal, was shouting at her dead lover. Carmencita Cordal told her dead lover that the boy who was christened that day was called Juan Francisco, as their son would have been called, if they'd had a son: that his mother called him Pancho, as she would have called her own, sweet boy. She told him that she had seen the child in the street stumbling after a hoop, and that he was very beautiful. Stewart patted his pockets for laudanum. The guns stopped.

In the shebeen where he found himself, late that night, Miltón (or some Indian) said nothing. They never do. Even so, Stewart's hangover was pounded not only by the memory of the guns, but by some knowledge that he had now, but could not remember: Miltón talking about a land without evil. Stewart agreeing with this place, this idea, quite loudly. They are wonderfully chiming. Miltón says that López is not his father's son. Undoubtedly, says

Stewart, he is more European than his father, fresher, with more *brio*. No, says the Indian, like Jesus – like Jesus is not Joseph's son. It is possible they argued that one, for a while, but there is a kind of drunken sense to it that makes Stewart look more closely now at the squadrons of Guaraní soldiers on the streets. There is a pilgrim light in their eyes. Put whatever name you like on it, they are going somewhere, and you might be obliged to come along. As for Francisco López – that fat baboon – it is a sort of universal joke here: that his father is a cuckold, his mother (in her youth) a pious, trembling whore. The usual stuff – but true all the same. Because the son-and-heir is never the father's son. He could kill his father any time.

High up in the Cordillera, the scrubby hills to the east and north of Asunción, there is a town called Piano. It was named for the fact that Eliza was obliged to abandon her piano there, a hundred miles from nowhere, and another hundred miles from anywhere at all. For all we know, the piano still survives. Perhaps a wooden panel shores up a chicken coop, or the wires are tangled into a fence and sing a little, when the wind is high. The hammers and their moss of green felt must be long decayed, but perhaps a few keys remain scattered in a broken smile, to choke the cattle or confuse the plough. Better still, the piano might grace a parlour, or what passes for a parlour in the Cordillera, with a paper taped to the front, 'El piano del Piano'. Perhaps it still holds the memory of the last fingers to touch it, the doctor's tender hands picking out 'La Palomita', as it stood bravely upright, surrounded by grass and by dead men, a long way from home.

But all this is unseeably distant, as Stewart stumbles around in a haze of scrofulisms and alcohol. He imagines Eliza sitting out in La Recoleta doing bad needlepoint, with the back all knots and the front full of holes. She rearranges the story of her life, 'My mother Adelaide Schnock came from a family that included forty-two magistrates and a captain of the fleet.' She orders patterns from Paris. She keeps house magnificently, and it is said that the servants love her. Servants and men – any number of them – that is all she has. You could say she has everything, except the satisfaction of having it. Also, perhaps, that she cannot relax, because she is not real. It must be hard, to be just a story the matrons of Asunción told each other between the hours of three and four. Everything Eliza does to silence them just makes them talk the more. No, the only way she can become real is by getting married, and she cannot get married until old López dies.

But nothing she did could kill him: no amount of soirées or Italian poets or diamonds or new colours for a shawl. Nothing, that is, until the theatre.

That was the trigger, thought Stewart; though the bullet was slow. He dreamed of the actor Bermejo, with a revolver. Bang! The gun springs a flag from out of its long muzzle. The old Dictator laughs. He clutches his chest. He falls endlessly towards the floor.

And where does the actor come from? The actor slithers, wet and fragrant, out from under the skirts of Eliza Lynch.

A whore needs a theatre and Eliza was a very great whore, so the building was a miniature version of Teatro alla Scala in Milan (no less), though it lacked a roof – also an orchestra, scenery, gas lamps, and women of dubious reputation in very good clothes. Eliza talked to the architect over little glasses of *fino* and sent to Paris upholsterers for the exact shade of red. Who else understood these things so well? It was Eliza who, before the roof slates were sourced or ordered, invited Bermejo in from Madrid.

The news that a real actor was making his way across the Atlantic flung the virgins and matrons into reverie. When he finally arrived, a little redhead with a pretty wife, the blankness of their afternoons was subtly different from the usual blankness of their afternoons. The evenings he spent with Eliza, of course, but during the day they could stroll past the veranda of the Frenchman's hotel where he sat drinking coffee, ignoring them all, and suddenly writing. The excitement of it! He wrote as though pricked all over, as though attacked by bees. Sometimes, he waved his arms to clear the buzz of thought from about his head. He feigned, he ducked, he went very still: then mysteriously the swarm would settle, and he covered page after fluid page, sheathed in a drowsy, dangerous calm.

It was there on the page. It was growing. It was the first ever Paraguayan play.

Dangerous indeed. When a closed carriage stopped beside the veranda one afternoon Bermejo had instinct enough to run out and kiss the hand that appeared on the sill; also the small female fingers that fluttered out of one window or another, obliging him to run around the carriage, and back again. After which kissing, there was a more official *beso mano* at the presidential palace. Then dinner with the López ladies. After which he regretted the fact that he could not attend Eliza's salon again. The first Paraguayan Theatre would belong, not to the whore, but to the nation. The actor had finally come to town.

In the theatre, vast and roofless, dried leaves stirred and eddied as Bermejo's ghosts took to the stage. And as they thickened and moved, old López began to fail. The maiden woke, and his pain turned into a lump: she started to speak, and the lump became a boil. By Act Three the boil had blossomed into an ulcer, livid from ankle to calf and quite likeable in its way. At least, that is what Stewart thought as he dressed it and wrapped it, and bled the old man a little because he asked to be bled. The Dictator made an unexpectedly sweet invalid. He propped his leg up on a chair, and had the shutters closed and let the nonsense that was the theatre, with its actors ordered in from Madrid and its dresses ordered in from Paris, wash turbulently by.

And it was because of the theatre that no one noticed how he failed to appear in the streets any more, or how his personal butcher had stopped bringing shoulders of meat to the back door.

'Chops!' he said. 'It's all chops and broth.' And so the realisation spread. The women, rifling through the bales of georgette and *satin de Chine*, let the cloth settle on their laps and were still. The realisation became a rumour and the rumour a terrible fact – he was dying. He was dying! and they sewed on in a guilty frenzy, as though stitching him a silken shroud. Fear seeped into the town. Carmencita Cordal started to walk at night and was seen abroad, naked, or bloodstained or dressed in white. In the morning, people found flowers jammed between doors and their lintels, and wreaths floating downstream. Cattle died of secret wounds. Eliza sent the measurements of her own body, by personal courier, to the House of Worth.

On the opening night, there is still no roof. The Guaraní stand on the floor of the theatre, ghostlike in their white smocks while around them the walls rise sheer to the stars; a giant dovecote, each nook rustling with velvet and plush. Old López stiffly enters his box and the audience sighs to its feet. He sits. He does not turn or speak. Beside him, the stolidly staring face of his wife and his overexcited daughters in their crinolines; all bands and zigzags, fat and festive as Bavarian eggs.

The box where they sit is strangely off-centre. The middle box – the biggest one – is empty. It is like a tic in the corner of your eye, but no matter. The play begins.

At first, Stewart cannot tell what the audience makes of it, or even if they know what they are watching. The moments trundle by – a maiden lost in the forest. A tender scene with the injured lion (Bermejo, with a tail), a gallant scene with her rescuing Guaraní Prince (the Englishman Captain Thompson, very white).

The Indians are enormously silent. Do they like it? Perhaps they have no opinion, as such, or as yet. Perhaps the play is simply as interesting to them as a new kind of animal, one with three legs, or five. But, no – there is a murmuring in the stalls. The Spanish maiden confronts her Conquistador father. He is too cruel, she says, and someone shouts. A boot, an actual and expensive boot, is thrown on stage. Then a general shushing, then more shouting, women's voices too. The maiden weeps for the plight of the Indian and her father spurns her – the stalls hiss. She defies him – they cheer and hulloo. He strides off to battle – the crowd roars their contempt.

They like it.

After which, the interval. No one in the stalls knows what this is, quite. They look a little foolish while, in the boxes, the better class of people pass their maté and preen. Then a shiver gathers in the crowd. At one distinct moment, everyone turns to the central box, as the most remarkable thing they have ever seen walks in and smiles.

Oh.

In the long silence, M. Cochelet, the French envoy, stands to his feet, and bows. It is not a question of diplomacy, but of the soul. All the foreigners rise, one by one. If Eliza were a horse they would be tempted to salute an animal so fine. But she is not a horse – she has made herself, and it is to the woman who created this, as well as to the woman who *is* this, that they offer their deep and ironical homage, as though, in her beauty, she has transcended herself.

Her dress, it seems, is spun gold. Her underskirts are lapis lazuli, the colour of the night sky when it glows. Five diamond clusters knuckle around her throat, and a deep sapphire pendant hangs over her bodice, so low that, when she sits, it nestles in her lap. So much money.

Stewart finds himself on his feet with the rest, leaning forward to catch her eye. A woman whose hand he has kissed. She belongs to them all. So tender she is, to the poor, the crippled, the ailing, you might think her touch enough to make them whole. But no, that is why the smile is sad, her eyes so wise. Others must suffer, while she can only bless, and offer her beauty for their consolation.

Stewart feels all this as a thrill in his blood, and he knows that he is a fool. But he is not the only one. The crowd watches, rapt, as she picks up the sapphire and opens it. What can be inside? It is the very nexus, as though the entire theatre had been pulled into the world, like the finest shawl, through its pure blue doors. She glances inside – a figuring look. It is a watch, impossibly small. What use is the hour to anyone here, or the minute? Eliza leaves it carelessly open, hinged like an oyster on the blue-gold bed of her skirts, and Time spreads through the theatre, expensive and minutely ticking. Time for the interval to end. Time for the play to recommence. Time for the battle scene.

'A riot,' they said afterwards. 'A complete riot.'

In the stalls the white-clad Indians press forward and lift their faces to the stage, all at the same terrible angle, while men hack at each other with wooden swords and 'Gadzooks!' 'Have at thee!' they cry. At first, it comes from nowhere, a low groan, the rough keening of someone trapped by the action on stage (where they are losing – the Indians of 1750) and then it is all around, it is everywhere – the crowd is growling.

Few people here have seen the sea, the great mournful mass of it, so who could describe the waves of sound that helplessly break against the proscenium's retaining wall? Some of the rich have travelled but as they watch the stage they feel the rough utterance enter through their boots, to lodge in the base of their own throats. As for the foreign diplomats, the engineers and railwaymen, they do not even hear it – transfixed as they are by the thought that the people on stage manifestly cannot act, and so must be killing each other for real.

And when the stage is filled with bodies and pig's blood, the tide ebbs.

Thank God for plot, thinks Stewart, as the maiden walks out into that open, astonishing space to unmask her (very white) lover for the Guaraní Prince he is. And so, the play proceeds, in all its lovely irrelevance. The prison scene, the duet through the bars, the firing squad, the huge roar of the rescuing lion, the cameo appearance of the King of Spain (old López in his box deader than ever), forgiveness, penitence, tears and . . .

Actually, no applause. Silence.

Why do they not clap? The truth is that most of them do not know that they should and the rest check with old López. But old López sits unmoving while, in her central box, the heavenly Eliza Lynch looks merely smug, as though she had created this too.

The Dictator rises to leave. Perhaps he knows that the play has killed him. Or perhaps not – at the time it is neither rebuff nor disdain; it is simply a man turning, painfully, to go. It takes a foreigner, the young poet Hector Varela, who has come all the way from Buenos Aires for this night, to start a snide and rebellious act of applause that crackles briefly through the crowd and then stops.

Just before dawn, the crisis came. It hit him in the chest. And with it, he told Stewart (who was still in his evening clothes), a preternatural flush of horror.

When Stewart looked at the paper that Miltón (or was it another Indian?) handed him the next day, his first thought was that Eliza wanted to know when the old man would die.

'Please come.'

He read the note and stalled. He took a glass of Madeira. Then he shouted for his horse and fumbled his foot into the spinning stirrup (he was a fool, she was dying!). He tried to pace the ride to La Recoleta but it was the only straight road in the country, after all, and the horse galloped the length of it to haul him up, sweating, at her door.

He was shown up to the drawing room – which was, indeed, a glorious sight: it was some moments before his eyes got used to it, and yet another before he saw that Eliza was already there, sumptuously seated among her things. At first he mistook her for another *objet*; her face was made so tiny by the billow of watered grey silk about her on the ottoman. But it was Eliza, and she was very pale.

The doctor thought with a shock that she was lost, or drowning, that perhaps she would sink under the weight of it all. He stepped forward. She offered her hand, as though it were yesterday.

'Whatever I can do,' he said, and kissed it.

'Can you keep a secret?' she said. And then she smiled.

It all happened, he thought later, so quickly. As though they had both foreseen it, this room, his lurch forward, her hand under his lips. There was an understanding, but he could not tell what it was. And so he followed her down the corridor to a distant door with no sense of what might be behind it, except that it would be everything, and his head was almost spinning as they stood outside. She turned to him with a grave look. And then she opened it.

Stewart had no idea when she left. There was a shudder of grey beside him and, when he looked, she was gone. In front of him, sitting on a chair, was a woman in a good dress. Perhaps it was one of Eliza's. A silk dress, in pink, with the skirts arranged somehow to resemble a rose. The pink, he thought, was wrong. It brought out the redness in the woman's face, which was to say the redness of the flesh where her mouth should have been. Also where her nose should have been, but was not.

He thought he knew the eyes. Of course, they were the eyes of every woman who sees death come in the door. Or perhaps it is life they see. The desperate eyes of the dying, that long for something – and it might be you, Doctor Stewart.

'Francine,' he said.

The woman's tears were a torment to the open meat of her face and he told her to stop crying, please, if she could. He tilted her by the chin towards the light and got her to open the remains of her mouth so he could assess the state of her throat. It was a classic presentation, with ulcerations of the nasal and buccal cavity, disfiguration of the vocal chords. He put his fingers to his lips, in case she should try to speak.

'You had a lesion on your skin, some years ago,' he said, and she nodded. And so he proceeded to tell her what she already knew.

Eliza was not outside when he left the room. There was an Indian in the corridor – almost definitely Miltón – who took his script and, rather brazenly, read it aloud. To counter which unlikely erudition, Stewart said,

'Lutzomyia, you know,' and Miltón said,

'Sandfly. They like white meat.'

Stewart wished he would stop being a vulgar, clever man, and start being an Indian again, and this irritation kept him busy all the way back to the bottle of raw cane alcohol at home. He had Scotch, but this was not a Scotch occasion. Scotch would make him weep.

And the next day, from Eliza, a gift – a basket of cherries, red as an old wound, their delicate stalks and their thick, dark skins no more miraculous than the ice in which they came.

When Stewart next called to La Recoleta, he found Eliza playing diabolo in the courtyard with the only son of Juana Pesoa, the abandoned mistress of Francisco López. The doctor looked at the dazed, ardent eyes of the boy (who was far too old for such games), and faltered.

'Go on, now. Run along!' said Eliza, and the young man, in a clumsy imitation of childhood, dashed into the house.

'Poor child,' she said, when he was gone. 'His mother is dying, you know.'

She said it so perfectly – perhaps she meant well. And to fill the doctor's silence she took his arm and said,

'You know, Doctor Stewart, I am the most fortunate woman in Paraguay. So it is a sort of motto with me – one must always *include*.'

Stewart looked at her birds. There was, indeed, a vulture, chained to a stake in the corner, and it was very beautiful. He did not want to touch the woman at his side. He did not want her hand on his arm.

She enquired after his lodgings – did he have a garden? And his aunt, was she well? When all this failed she signed to a servant,

'You must meet Pancho,' she said.

Her son. Whose heart he had heard fluttering through this woman's thick skin. He must be four or five by now. The stories told of a little animal, who bit his nurse and would not learn to read, but when Stewart saw him appear in the doorway he thought him pure beyond the normal purity of children, he thought him pure like a flame. And so his mother played out her scene. She ran forward and embraced him; her lovely knee bent, her lovely silk in the dust. The child fought to be clear, and started to talk, and the angle their faces held was so perfect, the distance between them so radiant and careful, that Stewart forgave her – of what crime he did not yet know. This was the antidote. This was what he wanted. This. He wanted to possess, not the body of a woman, but the still air between her downturned face and the upturned face of her child. Air that is shaped by cheek and eyelash, by smiling lips and hopeful, reassuring eyes. He did not want to have a woman – not even this woman, Eliza Lynch – what he wanted was to give some woman, or to take from some woman, his son.

After which sentimental ambush, Francine seemed to him to be treated well enough; to be properly fed and tended in a room that was small but clean – to be a normally melancholic set of problems, symptoms, assuagements; a tropical illness; a usual, hopeless attempt at dying.

On the other side of town, old López was taking his time. Never a thin man, now he was fat-seeming in peculiar places. The lids of his eyes grew tight and heavy, the lobes of his ears plumped up. Stewart does him with diuretics, with dandelion powder and digitalis, and his piss filled buckets. He swelled, pissed himself smaller, swelled again, and Stewart, no stranger to liquid pleasures and liquid pain, found himself going through a dry time. He was seen, when drunk, to slop his *caña* into the street; the coarse wine gulping and spattering into the dust. Stewart in his cups abhorred drink and when he was sober, he was not so fond of tea.

In fact, rumours of his sobriety had been mistimed. He stopped drinking during the first illness; the ulcer that made the Dictator's flesh become, as it were, runny. He stopped once, and then he stopped again. He stopped six or seven times in all. But he did not actually stop (for the last time, for the first actual time) until that night at the theatre when,

turning to go, he brushed against the virgin, Venancia
Báez.

Or perhaps this was just the story he told himself at
the time – that the two reasons he became sober were
the two brown eyes of Venancia Báez, brown as oblivion,
brown as black is brown (or brown, as he said after they
were married, as a monkey's; playful and wise). Because
the story changed when they were in the middle of the
war and the lovely Venancia became querulous and small,
because the war did not suit her, and she saw no reason why
it should. The war made her hoard things and grow fat, and
she could not make love when the war was on, she could not
be pleasant, even to her own children. When this happened,
Stewart decided it was the Dictator's illness that made him
give up drink after all, because this carnage, the waste of it,
the pile of limbs he harvested from wounded men growing
beside him on the floor, all this made him feel alive and
undiluted. The early days of war made him so simple he
thought he had found his true self; that all wrong turnings
and seemingly blind alleys of his life had led him here, and
so they must have been the right turnings after all.

Another story might simply be that Stewart was more
sick of drinking than he was sick of himself – always
a delicate equation. One night he woke up to his dead
mother's touch and found it was a dog licking at the vomit
in his hair – and what lingered, what won out you might
say, was his mother and not the dog. This was a story for
his old age when his mother – so long forgotten – was back
with him again, all the time.

But no matter how he told it or lied about it as the years
went by, the fact was that Stewart took to English tea and
constant attendance on the bloated form of old López. And
when he was not by the bedside he was under the window
of Venancia Báez, in the Latin style, courting her father
like a woman – getting his love letters written by one of

the elderly spinster Cordals, who poured all her dreams into them, and knew the form.

It was two years from that first sighting in the theatre before he would see the naked breast of Venancia Báez again, two years before he laid eyes upon her bare throat or the skin of her lovely arms. Every Sunday, he looked at her on the way to Mass, hidden under a mantilla of black lace, with her heavy velvet dress creeping over her like moss, and sometimes he wondered if, under it, her body had not changed. He gave her diseases in his head; a goitre pushing at the pearls she wore that night, a spreading psoriasis, a phthisical rattle souring her sweet and easy lungs. Besides, he had fallen in love with a child and she was turning into a woman. There was nothing he could do to hold or stop it – he was caught between his desire for what he had lost already and his desire for what he might gain, and this maddened him, as though he was in love with the future and in love with the past, and his days moved with vegetable slowness, while somewhere inside her deep, cool house, Venancia Báez bloomed.

Meanwhile the theatre was shut. The place was a brothel, after all, and who could think of such pleasures while they waited for the death of old López? He must be dying – the doctor was sober, he grew more sober from day to day, and everywhere there was a frenzy of calm.

Outside his shuttered window the country seemed to stall, but surged ahead at the same time. Railway lines snaked out into the countryside, the rails slapped down one after the other; gathering speed, like a woman who knits faster to finish before she runs out of wool. The orders issued one after the other – or were they imagined? – from the dark room where old López lay dropsical. It was as though his weakness made him omnipotent. His wife Doña Paula took her true place as Cerberus at his iron-studded door, and sometimes forbade admission to

70

her own sons, who sloped about like whipped pups and cut each other in the street.

Everywhere in Asunción, people rode this current wave, not realising that the whole vast tide was about to turn. They said the next president would be a Cordal, they said that Francisco was finished, and they gloated over the humiliation of Eliza Lynch. It was coming any day now. It was here. She was seen leaving at night with a wooden crate full of gold. She was seen with the marks of a beating. She was seen diseased.

When Stewart went out to La Recoleta these days, he found Eliza frozen with panic. Francisco sat in the upstairs drawing room with a distant look, as though listening to his father's breath labouring on the other side of town. One afternoon, she did not serve him herself, but sent their son across the room with the delicate burden of a glass of brandy for his father's teeth. Eliza pushed him in the small of his back, as though sending a toy boat on to the water, and the luminous child wavered and set out on the long journey to his father's chair. He stood in front of the old bull and the brandy flared in the light, and his father looked at him, and the child returned the look with a serious, sweet smile. For a moment, thought the doctor, it all hung in the balance, whether López would take the offered glass, or strike it from the boy's hand. He shifted massively and pushed against the arm of the chair, as though bracing himself to stand. And then he subsided.

'On the table,' he said, meaning the small console at his side. The child set the glass carefully down and López booted him back to his Mama, with a languid kick to the backside.

'Time we cut your hair,' he said. 'Eh, Pancho?'

He showed Stewart a piece of paper – the first ever railway ticket for the first railway in the Southern Americas. He was so proud of it, he did not want to let it out of his hands. He fingered it and flattened it out on the round of his thigh; until he was surprised to see that he had rolled it altogether into a tight little cigarro, which he popped, as the doctor took his leave, into Eliza's *décolletage*.

And: He loves her, thought Stewart. He loves her after all. Because there – beyond the conspiracy of their drawing room and the conspiracy of their bed – was a look passed between them that might well be called 'love', being gentle and fierce and completely empty. Stewart thought of the stories that were current now – that Eliza procured the daughters of distant landowners for him; that she checked with their own fathers whether they were virgins, like buying heifers – and they did not give him the usual satisfaction. In fact they made him sad. Her 'dear friend' loved her. What else was there to say?

The maid, Francine, died gurgling. The cancer that belonged to Francisco's former mistress, Juana Pesoa, broke through the wall of her belly, and she died terribly. And old López revived, to die some more. His daughters cleaned the body of the Dictator down to the waist, his wife tended below. The cloths they used were buried in an unmarked spot, and the priests fought at his door. Then – it might have been the incessant irritation of the cathedral bells, it might have been the first railway train that ran so enthusiastically past the end of the first railway track – but somewhere along the way the people got tired of the Dictator's dying, and with their boredom came hatred and a need to be released from his terrible grasp. It was time to separate the quick from the dead. It was time to sing again, and dance with a bottle balanced on your head. It was time for Eliza's picnic.

She held it onboard the *Tacuarí*.

When Stewart made his afternoon visit to his (now, finally, fiancée) Venancia Báez, he was surprised to see the card that she held out, trembling, for his approval. It was a thick board, gilt-edged, such as Stewart had seen many times – though not, he realised with a pang, since he arrived in Asunción.

'And what is it to do with me?' he said, annoyed by his nostalgia for the life he had left behind – one in which there were many such wonderful, ordinary objects. Venancia's aunt, napping in the corner of the room, opened one cold eye.

'You must go if you like,' he said, and knew, even as he spoke, that liking had nothing to do with it. Venancia pushed the card against her chest and gave him a brown look. The invitation had been issued in the name of Eliza Lynch.

Fifty Basque peasants had lately arrived in Asunción and they sat at the docks, waiting to be shipped upriver to a clearing in the forest. The clearing would be christened Nueva Bordeaux. There would be a fiesta. The men would travel overland, while the ladies made their way to the new town by river, and on the river there would be held a grand picnic.

By now, the laboured breath of old López had turned to a milky pink foam. At the docks, the Basques swiped at the air in front of their faces, their eyes hard with disbelief, as the virgins and matrons picked their way through to the newly arrived bales of cloth. Another dress. Another shroud to be stitched for the corpse of their virtue. A strange, elegiac act of choosing between *crêpe de Chine* and *glacé* silk, spilled out like gorgeous water in front of them. They fingered it and loved it and let it drop, as though they were to be sumptuously married, but all to the wrong man.

Stewart told Venancia to wear blue. He told her to smile. He said that they must think of the future now, they must take their chance. His ambition surprised him. Of course, he was doing it for her – the lovely Venancia who must be fed and housed and dressed in the finest – and so he blamed her too; because the price of Venancia, the price of his future, was to show himself in such a way in front of the clever eyes of Eliza Lynch.

'But it is I who will be shamed,' said Venancia. In which case, Stewart told her, she would not be alone. Venancia cheered up a little. It was true: every woman she knew would be on that boat. They would talk about it for months.

But, in the event, no one talked of Eliza's picnic on the river, once it was done. In 'Nueva Bordeaux' the men speechified and drank and did something Basque with a live duck while they waited for the ladies to arrive. But the ladies did not arrive and, some time before dark, the men left the new colonists in their clearing with a heap of provisions (a few precious iron spades, sacks of seed corn that would turn to mould, sacks of manioc that they would plant at the wrong time), and they rode home. There was talk of a collision on the river, of shifting sandbars, but around a curve of the bank, they spotted the *Tacuarí*, her fires banked and her rigging bare. The captain heard their shouts and answered with a whistle blast, and then slowly the great ship turned with the current, got up a lazy head of steam and followed them back to Asunción.

The men waited on their womenfolk at the dock. They watched them disembark, in single file. They handed the ladies into carriages, or sat them on their horses, or if the horses were worn-out, they took the bridle in one hand and their wife's hand in the other. And if their wife was exhausted they held her about the waist, and in this wanton way the streets filled with couples and their trailing animals and trailing servants; the men silent, the women stumbling and quietly weeping – or laughing, some of them – until the sad bacchanal was fully dispersed and the doors of their houses shut, one by one.

And no one spoke about it, at all.

Of course, the women still gossiped after the picnic, the men still murmured and spat, but a silence crept into the cracks between their words, until the words themselves became inconsequential. Everything sounded like a joke, now, spoken to an empty room.

Stewart, making his move, requested and was granted a meeting with the coming Dictator Francisco Solano López. On the appointed day he was shown into a large white-washed room that contained nothing but a large table. On the table, draped to the floor, was a thick cloth woven with a twining abundance of dull gold. He faced López over this expanse and the same weary joke was in the look they gave each other. 'Who would have thought?'

When López spoke, these days, things happened; when he moved, the world drew out of his way. There was no distance now between seeing, knowing, doing. Francisco Solano López had become simple and Stewart found that he was talking to an animal of sorts, as dangerous and easy. He regretted the two fools of the *Tacuarí*, the little strutting mestizo and himself; the pride of Edinburgh University, stunned and soulful and drunk. Where had he gone? that messy young man who looked out over the swamp and found what he was looking for – a wilderness finally big enough for him to howl into (his aunt's drawing room being, for the purpose, a little small). What had happened to him in the intervening years? He had grown harder and weaker, that was what – and he had called it love.

When Venancia asked him how the meeting had gone, he said that he had secured, as he had wished to do, the post of Surgeon General of the army. He had discussed the export of some yerba maté and had received a licence at exceptionally fine rates. He said that their future was secure. He did not say she had ruined his life. But he knew that, once the thought had entered his head, it would wriggle its own way out, in time.

He asked instead for the true story of Eliza's picnic – this would be the extent of his cruelty to her, for now. They were walking in the walled orange grove behind her house, between trees heady with blossom. Her aunt sat a distance apart and Stewart thought it might be possible to kiss her now, quickly in the dappled shade. It might even be expected, and looking at her lips so intently distracted him from the words that came from between them, for the first while.

Venancia looked at the ground. When she spoke it was in an indifferent, lilting way, and she did not meet his eye.

It was Mme Cochelet who rallied the ladies, she said, frozen as they were in the face of the humiliation that waited for them on board the *Tacuarí*. There were some things, Mme Cochelet declared, that, as wives, they might not avoid; and there were some things that, as ladies, they simply could not do. And so they must suffer, and compromise. They would attend. They would dress. They would walk on to the *Tacuarí* as though going to a *fête-champêtre* and not a funeral. But they would draw the line at Eliza Lynch.

And so on the appointed day, at an early hour, with their gilt-edged cards in their beaded reticules, they walked up the gangway to the *Tacuarí*; in virgin white, in green damask, in candy stripes of grey and rose. They squeezed their skirts between the rails, lifting their front hoops to prevent an indecent tilt at the back, and when they reached the top of the gangway, each and every one of them ignored the woman who stood at the top. La Concubina Irlandesa. Their hostess. She wore a dress entirely of lace. It crawled about her neck and crept down her hands, to be caught in a sort of glittering mitten by the rings she wore. She was *enceinte* – yet again – and this made it easier somehow to suck themselves in as they wove around her, avoiding her bastard stomach and her flagrant emeralds, and the heavenly scent that she wore. Eliza smiled and greeted each of them, sometimes (horribly) by name. Not one woman answered her back. They did not feel capable of it, said Venancia, when Stewart (woken from his kissing reverie), asked her how they could be so sullen. They just *could not*, she said, and the gooseflesh he saw on her lovely forearm did not give her the lie. The disgust was physical. Venancia Báez, he realised, could no more touch Eliza than she could touch a turd.

They filed past, she said, and kept their nerve: blank girls and nervously grinning women; the spinster Cordal with the sudden, hooting giggle, and lesser fools who ducked, or bolted over to the other rail. La Lincha turned to follow each profile as it walked by, now a high Cordal nose, now a pair of bulbous, white-trimmed eyes that announced a daughter of Mme Cochelet. Even her own 'sisters-in-law' Rafaela and Innocencia (well, you could not call them 'sisters-in-sin') she stared at brazenly, as they looked quickly past her to admire, in loud voices, the bunting strung from the masts. She stood her ground, you had to give her that, and, all the time, her face twitched with pride, as if to say '*I know you*. I know your husband, your brother. I even know your father. They tell me things they would not dream of telling you.'

It was horrible, said Venancia, and difficult. It was the most difficult thing she had ever done. Some of the girls had to use smelling salts just to get to the top of the gangplank. But they all did it and, their hearts beating, their eyes glittering, they sat and chitchatted in quite the normal way; enjoying the water and the feel of the breeze as the boat pulled away from the quay.

There was no person on the deck so unwatched as Eliza. Fifty pairs of eyes refused to see her. Fifty smooth brows regarded the place where she stood as containing only air. And so they travelled, admiring the two great paddle wheels, the stateroom with its bolted, slightly mouldy, furniture – that was yet so delicate you might think the boat would bring you all the way to Paris, or discover Paris around the next bend. They sat on the sunny side because La Lincha took the shade, and they waited for the picnic.

Venancia paused to swallow. And as she began to describe the dishes that were set in front of them, Stewart remembered another girl on the *Tacuarí*, dreaming of food. He remembered Eliza at nineteen, whining for melons. He remembered her at table, trying to eat in a casual way; and how she looked at the birds on the water and the animals on the bank. 'Cooked,' said her eyes to a snowy breasted egret. 'Roasted,' to a sleeping tapir. And to a leaping fish, 'Grilled, with a sauce *meunière*.'

'Truffled turkey,' said Venancia. 'Eggs *à la neige*, pepper-cured ham, smoked eels.' As each was set down, a major-domo murmured the name and origin of the dish. The eels were from Russia, the ham from Xeriga, the *foie gras* from Strasbourg. There were also things that pretended to be from Europe but probably weren't – a stuffed and larded 'pike', whose face had a more benign and local cast, partridge wings that looked just like tinamu, though the sauce of chestnut cream smelled real. There were sweetbreads with crayfish sauce, a fresh tunny, plates of roe. There was champagne and claret and, for the fainter-hearted, syllabub, negus and punch. There were leather buckets lined with ice, which held canteens of strawberry juice and pineapple juice, there were bottles of Montbello water for the more dyspeptic. The dishes kept coming, veal cooked with fat bacon in its own gravy, miraculous early peas, all kinds of pastry, *Poulet Marengo*, a suckling pig. One enormous platter contained a heap of asparagus, sown, so the major-domo said, on the deck of a ship in a French port and nurtured on the voyage out (they like salted earth, as Mme Cochelet later explained), through the forced spring of the Atlantic passage, so that when they arrived in the high summer of Asunción the spears showed white at the roots. Ripe. The effect on Mme Cochelet of this green mound was so marked that the ladies on either side of her held her arms. Whether to contain a faint, or contain her greed – either way, it was clear to all of them that Mme Cochelet must hold her resolve, or they would all be exposed – to what they could not say, but Mme Lynch was approaching the table now to preside over what was, after all, her picnic, and those closest to her shrank, quite naturally, away. Fortunately (at least it seemed fortunate at the time), at the head of the table was a mixed contingent of Cochelet-Cordals, and they showed their mettle by closing ranks seconds before La Lincha reached the 'groaning board'.

Mme Lynch made an attempt to get through, but her adversaries shifted quite easily to prevent her. So she stood and watched their backs as the women, flushed with excitement, faced their next big challenge – how would they get the dishes served? Mme Cochelet decided for all of them. She picked up a plate in her own hands and gestured to the 'major-domo' who held a trembling spoon.

'Thank you,' she said.

The asparagus was about to touch her plate, the hollandaise, indeed, was dripping on to the cool Sèvres glaze, when Mme Lynch spoke. She did not raise her voice, but her tone was so clean and clear that everyone heard.

'Miltón,' she said (meaning the man with the spoon), 'throw it overboard.' Quick as a flash, the wild little Indian flipped the implement over his shoulder; the asparagus flew in a wide arc through the air, separating into six slowly turning (or so it seemed) succulent spears, which disappeared one by one over the side. A second later, they heard the splish-splish-splash. The Indian cocked his head in a way that was almost amused and looked to La Lincha, who returned his look with perfect understanding and said,

'All of it.'

And he clapped his hands. Slap-slap.

'All right you sons of bitches,' he said (in Guaraní, of course – which no lady ever affected to understand), 'let's get this stuff into the river.' They elbowed their way through the circle of gasping women, one serving man to each dish – they bore the plates high over the guests' heads, then swung them low as they ran, quite eagerly, to the side. Some threw the porcelain in for good measure and brushed their hands as though after a job well done. And then, to a man, they tumbled down a hatch. It was all gone, even the tablecloth. There was a slight scum on the river, of hollandaise sauce and *sauce à la Soubise*, but even that sank, in time.

It was funny, said Venancia, but on the plates the food looked so delicious – sinking through the water, it looked just like vomit. Not of course that she had run to the rail, to chase after it like a fool – though that was where Mme Cochelet found herself; shouting after a stupid vegetable, bawling at it, in full view. No, Venancia had stayed silent, and simply turned away. And that, she said, was the true story of the picnic. If he must be told.

Stewart knew it was anything but – the week after the women came home was one of the busiest he had known. He badgered her with tales of sunstroke, fits, the two miscarriages he had personally attended, and finally she admitted that the rest of the day had been . . . difficult.

After her grand gesture, Eliza had retired to the shady side of the boat. She stood for a while and looked out over the water. Then she gave the captain orders not to move, and sat down. She stayed sitting for ten hours. On the other side of the *Tacuarí*, women swooned at the excitement and were revived – to swoon again in the afternoon sun. Their dresses were stained, first by sweat, then by the fretful carelessness of heatstroke, and finally, sometimes, deliriously torn.

For a while, said Venancia, she did not know who she was.

If Stewart had looked into her eyes then, he would have seen that this girl knew more about herself now than she had ever wanted to. But the doctor in him needed to examine the scene – the different stages of the ladies' distress: when did they realise this might not end? Did the women sit alone, or did they help each other as needs be? Did they fear for their lives? Did none of them seek to share Eliza's shade? None, said Venancia, very firmly. As for the rest, she did not remember. It was exciting at first, and then boring, and then dreadful. At some stage, Mme Cochelet sang hymns, but they were in French, so no one joined in. It seemed that family members stuck together, though she could not be sure, there were some family fights, too. And what of Eliza, did she eat, in order to taunt them more? No, said Venancia, she sat and did not move. But she was in a certain condition, said Stewart, Venancia must think hard, she must remember.

'I remember she did not eat,' said Venancia. 'I am not a complete fool.' And then she started to weep. When Stewart went to comfort her she hit him away, and a terrible deep wail fetched up out of her as she clutched where (he could not help but note) her womb might one day swell.

'And I will never eat asparagus now. I will never even taste it. Never! Never!'

At which, her ancient aunt appeared all at once and, with a black look, caught her by the waist and wheeled her, like a dancer, away.

After this, of course, the Dictator finally finished with all that dying, and simply died instead. And, of course, young López took one cursory look at the corpse before opening the old man's will and declaring himself the heir.

And, of course, no one else saw the will – there was no need for them to see it, as young López was, of course, not a liar. And so it rolled onwards, the convened congress, the unanimous vote, the inauguration ball. And the invitations to the ball were issued in the name of Eliza Lynch.

Stewart could not interest himself in the general female humiliation – he had a particular, private one of his own to inflict. He was to be wed. One week after young López became the only López, Stewart was made Surgeon General of the army, and the arrangements were made for the transfer, from her father's house to his house, of the lovely Venancia Báez.

Perhaps the engagement had been too long. Stewart did not relish the idea of deflowering his pretty wife, much as he desired to so do. It occurred to him that she annoyed him a little. He thought already that the happiest time in his life was after he saw her for the first time, when he was caught between the child and the woman, neither of whom was in his arms. And indeed he never wavered from this version of the story of his life. The happiest he had ever been was when he was drunk with love, and her name was everything. Venancia Báez. Venancia Báez.

On the morning when she would become Venancia Stewart (a name she could not even pronounce), the doctor took a medicinal shot of fine Speyside Scotch, specially imported for the marriage breakfast. By the time he married her, he was so drunk he looked sober again; and by early afternoon he was roaring.

Venancia did not cry. She smiled. She clapped her hands in childish delight when he fell over his own chair. And so, with all the considerable grace she could muster, she went, one more time, to her doom.

Of all people to accost, Stewart accosted Whytehead. He got him in a corner. He told him he was a machine, an automaton, a thing of levers and pulleys, and where, he asked, was the lever for his heart? Was it here? Or here? And he poked his fellow countryman in the chest and (nearly) in the crotch. He said, What of women, Whytehead? He said he had no appetite for them either, Whytehead was right, the whole business was enough to make you spew. Whytehead had the right idea, work hard and sleep on your front. Send the money home. The money, the money. Stewart had an aunt. Whytehead had three sisters and a mother still living, did he not? Thank God. Thank God they were all alive these women, so a man had something to do with his *money*.

Whytehead sat and did not move. He listened. He seemed to welcome Stewart's words; he almost bathed in them. And the wedding guests, who had seen worse things in their time, slipped some whiskey into Venancia's glass of punch and let the two '*Inglese*' be.

'We have not been friends,' said Stewart, and he took Whytehead's dry hand in his own. 'We have not been friends as we should.'

They sat for a while in silence. 'There will be a war,' said Whytehead.

Stewart slumped. His eyeballs rolled bloodily up to view his new wife mingling bravely with the guests on the other side of the room.

'I like them when they're sick,' he said.

'Doctor Stewart,' Whytehead murmured, to indicate that he need not say what was on his mind; he need not go on. But they both wanted him to continue. They looked away from each other, Stewart with a lurch of the head, Whytehead with a calm so intense it might have been a swoon.

He liked a woman with a good disease, Stewart said. Because they broke a man's heart. And not only that – he liked his women as he liked his men, raw, pushed to their limit. In the body, that was where the truth of it was.

Whytehead did not demur. He was waiting now, his face horribly blank.

'That girl was sick enough. The maid. Did you know?' Stewart finally said, and then he told Whytehead that she had died quietly in the end. But before the end was atrocious, he said, and before that again she had clung to him. For which Whytehead should be grateful, to have another man do his dirty work for him.

And his little surge of rage ebbed into love for the human being on the other side of the table. Tears came to his eyes and he stared fixedly for a while at a posy of flowers abandoned on the cloth.

'Are you asking me to thank you?' said Whytehead. At which he stood, collected his hat and gloves, wished Stewart the best of marriages, and left the room.

The River

Part 2

Veal

December 1854, Río Paraná

OUR DEAD SAILOR has begun to stink sweetly – so soon, in the heat. There are problems about the disposal, and so his remains lie on the doctor's cot, where he died, while the doctor sleeps outside.

The boat was quiet all through his dying as the men were loath to wake him (from what?) with their fixing and banging, so the boiler is not yet mended. Now there is another stillness – the one that opens into the world from the mouth of a dead man. A widening in our hearts. The men are all restless, and large. They lumber about or sit, and every slight noise makes them turn and glare.

We do not move, as though to mark this spot in the midst of the flow. Perhaps his soul is still anchored here. Far beyond us – a mile, maybe more – the green fringe of the bank. Now and then there drifts over the water the vegetable smell of things slick and wet. Sometimes, a distant, settling whisper, as some tree gives way and falls, long dead.

They say the silence of the forest is a waiting silence, but I say these trees wait for nothing, neither do they mourn. They grow, that is all. And I feel myself growing with them. There is a pulse in my fingertips, and when I brush my dress, each line and whorl of them tells the silk and reads the pattern woven into its sheen.

Silence. The air moves and the smell of the sailor drifts until we are maddened by it. Francine soaks a cloth for me to hold over my mouth and nose, and my skin is raw from it. Foolish girl.

Señor López wanted to slide the dead man into the river this morning, naval fashion – but he suggested it in such a doubtful manner that no one felt obliged to obey. He faltered, and the men smiled as they turned away. Another day lost. Now, he is in a studied rage. The captain looks carefully blank. The work on the boiler goes on.

The doctor, slung outside his own cabin, dulls his nose with a medicinal flask and finally sleeps – but the smell must creep into his afternoon dreams, as it wafts into mine. Nothing happens except rot and bloat. I imagine the man's stomach swelling, as mine swells. I imagine it might burst and dreadful things come slithering out.

It cannot be so bad. I should look into the cabin to see his calm, dead face: I would get comfort from the realness of it. I am tempted to sneak there just to see how ordinary he is; this man who enters us all now, we breathe him in, and gag.

He is mottled a little under the skin, purple and black, nothing worse I am sure. Or perhaps there is no colour yet, just a slight puffing; a sponginess where the flesh has started to rise. Of course, the doctor should have embalmed him a little, but the wretched man is too busy embalming himself.

This evening, Señor López wants distraction so I try to make up a table for bezique. Mr Whytehead still refuses to make four. I have seen him watching, and I know he loves the way the cards turn, but he cannot play with money, and the maid has none. Stewart flicks up his skirt tails to split them over a tiny chair, and gravely sits; the cards like little sweetie papers, fanned out in his big hands.

'What is it to be?' he says.

To spite Whytehead I say that instead of money we will bet stories, loser tells all.

'Stories?' he says; like this was a worse thing to lose even, than money. And I tell him to be very quiet and give Francine whatever assistance she might require. So we progress. He leans over the maid's shoulder, very judicious and nice, while Stewart breathes a lot, at my side.

In the event it is the maid who loses. I would spare her the embarrassment of it, but my dear friend is in an expansive mood. So she settles herself quite prettily on the edge of her chair, and half-turns her face away. Her story is kept to a modest length, but it is not a woman's tale, at least not the way I would measure such things. If she wants to be loved, she has misjudged. Or perhaps she has judged too well. In this hot room she talks about the cold and I smell the dead sailor on her breath, though I have drenched all our cushions with *eau de lilas*.

The story is about her grandfather who served with Buonaparte. By the time Francine knew him, she says, he had already lost his fingers' ends and the nose he carried over his dear smiling mouth was lacking by a full centimetre, maybe more. And so on, and in a similar vein, until we reach the Russian Campaign.

'Somewhere in the middle of that vast land,' she says (in a formal singsong tone), 'he sat down on ground that was so cold it seemed warm again. He wanted to lean back and look at the sky, because those winter stars were more beautiful than any he had seen. And then, it seemed that he was lying down, with the shuffling feet of men passing him by. It was so delicious. "Remember this," he used to say. "That death can be delicious too." And the stars came lower until he thought that they were shining only on him.

'He would have died there, quite happy, if a carriage had not stopped beside him. The man who got out was small, and he wore a cockade in his black hat. Can you guess it? He opened my grandfather's coat and worked his hand inside, and "Why are you robbing me?" said my grandfather, "when I have already given you my life?" Le Petit Caporal said nothing, but looked at the papers my grandfather had placed, for warmth, next to his heart. Then he said, "Estella. She has a pretty hand, don't you think? And, see here, the violet she pressed for you, still blue against the page." And the thought of his daughter, who is my mother, brought my grandfather to his feet – numb and blackened as they were, and wrapped in the skins of two Russian chickens. He stumbled on, leaving his trail of feathers on the snow and, when he thought to look for it, the carriage was already disappeared.'

Chickens, no less. I find the shoes as painful and mortifying as the story itself.

'Do you think it is true?' I say. 'Or was it all a trick of the poor man's mind?'

'Well, yes,' says Francine. 'After a fashion.' Certainly, when she was a child, she had looked at her grandfather with awe. The great Napoleon had saved him; what could be more true than that? Though perhaps he was just giving them all courage for the bitter future they faced, once Napoleon was gone.

My dear friend shifts in his chair. He is very moved.

'So . . . Francine,' he says. 'I hope, after this, that you will always lose at cards,' and he toasts her, and her mutilated grandfather, and le Petit Caporal, with his glass of Madeira. After which, none of us has the heart to return to the game.

*

The dead sailor turns over in my dreams and seems to call to me. 'Dora! Dora!' I wake in the middle of the night sick with him.

It is bright. There is a moon, and watery reflections dance

on the walls until it is all about me, a river of broken light, rippling and breaking on the ceiling and on the bed and on my skin. I can not bear it, this flickering tide on my arms, the way my body disappears under it so that I am just another surface in the dark.

Outside, under a blank moon, I am free of it. Here is my belly in front of me again, big and hard and round. I stay close to the shadow of the wall and make my lumbering way to the doctor's cabin. He lies slung outside; the smell of old drink cuts like vinegar the awful honey of the sailor's decay. I pass the length of him, from boots to hair, and he stirs and settles, his mouth seeking the comfort of the cloth.

When all is still, I push in at the door. The smell is stronger now: it is absolute. And, instead of darkness, here is the river light again, mocking me as I strain to tell the sailor from the cot where he lies. We are in a flickering, shifting, underwater grave. And there he is. The light makes him look alive. I step forward and want to say . . . what? That I am here – that I am his Dora, or not his Dora – I have a dreadful urge to whisper it, but I do not know his name.

I let my breath out all at once, and startle myself with the sound. It is a bubble of air soughed from out his dead lungs, I am sure of it. This is how a dead man speaks. They say the last breath rises out of him a day, two days later, and if you listen to it you will hear – a curse sometimes, or a blessing, or a name. What is it, that I want to hear? When I see his face for sure then I will go, and I take a step nearer in the dark.

His eye is open. I closed his dead eye, but now it is open again. It looks, not at me, but at everything – at the light that is all the same and the four shifting walls and at me – it picks nothing out, but lets each fall indifferently into the well of his dead gaze – and we are all the same.

His face, I see as I turn to leave, is not like the face he

had when he was alive. It is more stern. And older too. Ancient, and high in the nose. And the livid flesh and the unburned flesh fall alike, in tranquillity, away from all the sharp bones. He looks quite distinguished.

Back in my room, I see that eye whenever I close my own. Also, the open eye of the doctor fixed on me as I shut the cabin door. There is no doubt this one is alive: his pupil, black and wide with fright.

He is in love with me, I think. You can tell at that moment when someone wakes – the thing that dawns in their eyes. Or perhaps we all love easily in our sleep. Because I think I saw love, or something like it – wonder perhaps – before the fright. So I laid my finger on my lips before he should cry out,

'A little prayer,' I said, and smiled at him, as though I were a dream. I hope that he took me for such.

The ship moves gently on the water, tugging idly, over and over at the anchoring ropes. Holding us all, the coughing, shifting men, the dead man and me, retching into a basin in the watery night.

They say there is a sea in my belly now, and that my child swims inside me. And I think sometimes how dark, how blessed, it must be in there.

*

Today, enough wind to steer for the bank and the sailor's grave. At last. We are almost beached in our eagerness to reach the shore, and the men leap overboard not waiting for the boats.

The sailor's body is lowered on a chain; covered in hemp and criss-crossed with rope, like a doll you might make out of cloth and twine. He is rigid and, I think, quite ceremonial, as he lands feet-first. I would like to put a hat on him such as admirals wear, and send him off in his skiff for an inspection of the fleet. But they angle him down until he is lying the length of the boat on one side. The rower nudges him at every stroke and lifts his oar in fright and so they go in circles for a while.

There is no proper order to all this. Everyone spills overboard. My dear friend climbs down to bury the poor man; Mr Whytehead supervises the digging of the grave (I am surprised he does not draw up plans). Francine, with a soft look, disappears down the net of ropes. Was that a request? Still, I can hardly call her back. She is handed over by the doctor who turns to me to effect a bow, which he then fails to complete. He gives me a fuddled look that has something of last night in it, and then, to my delight, he turns tail and hops over the side.

Only Miltón remains. We look at each other and, for the first time I think, he smiles. It is a very pleasant grin with nothing of the savage in it – but slight and tender; as a man might smile in the theatre, to a woman he once knew and still admires. I smile back – my prettiest – and ask him his age.

'Twenty-two?' he says. 'Maybe twenty-five.' I tell him that he lies. He smiles again at whatever joke is between us now, and moves to the prow, quite naturally, in consideration of my solitude.

Alone. A bare few men remain. The boat is lighter under my feet, and rides high. I have an urge to explore. It is some time before I realise what is the smell that so entrances me – it is the smell of the dead sailor, gone.

I watch the burial party working where the river sand gives way to scrub. The men gesture slowly in the heat and scraps of talk drift towards the boat. After a while they abandon the spot and move farther inland, where the going, too, seems hard. When the two digging men are up to their thighs, there is more talk. They twist themselves out to

sit on the edge, then jump clear when the body is swung –
one, two, three – to disappear into the flat earth. I listen for
a thump, but there is none. I cannot even see the hole. My
dear friend stands in his gleaming black hat and reads from
a book – a Bible, it must be, though I have never seen one
on board. The sailors bow their heads and one, the Galway
man it must be, crosses himself.

And so it seems done.

All this while, I lean over the side – his Dora. I press
a handkerchief to my eye and dream of a cottage in
Portsmouth or Plymouth where I would feed a man mutton
and forget to bring his washing from the line. It is not a bad
dream. If the man had a wife I will write to her myself.

Dear Mrs Titmouse (or some such English name), it is
with the greatest possible regret . . . please believe me when
I say . . . Your husband, though not loquacious, carried
himself at all times with an air of . . . adventures long and
gravely undertaken . . . gifts of simplicity and faith . . . with
you in your grief, Doña Eliza Lynch Schnock y López; as
I would be styled here, as a wife.

I must get a crest for my letter paper. Some sort of
colonial theme – two crossed tobacco leaves under a capybara, rampant regardant – God help us – like some sort of
demented calf.

The crew are in no hurry to return. They should have
brought a picnic. They fill the grave with desultory slowness, one man working while another stands about and
suckles the handle of his spade. Señor López strolls a little
with the doctor and detains him by the river's edge. The
doctor crouches down while my dear friend doffs his hat
and looks towards the sky; then Stewart grapples with his
face. I am so struck by the tableau that I do not notice
the figures of Francine and Mr Whytehead until they have
almost skirted the thin river headland and are sinking into
the distance on the other side.

It seems my friend has something the matter with his eye. What are they all doing? What are they talking about? Men move into groups of two or three, then break into new clusters. When Francine comes round the headland again, she is carrying her shoes in one hand and I cannot see where her stockings might be. She splashes a little in the water's edge. I can see her turning face smiling at Mr Whytehead and, a long moment later, I hear her laughter on the slow air. All the men look at her naked feet. The doctor hurries forward and dips as though to lift them with his hands. I turn around to find Miltón looking, as I am, and shaking his head.

'Very bad,' he says. 'For a white woman. Very bad.'

At least someone has some moral sense, however skewed (he himself being practically without clothes). When I look again, Francine is leaning on Mr Whytehead's shoulder, while the doctor absurdly works about beneath her skirts, fitting her shoes back on. My dear friend stands idly; looking on.

My baby is not blind. I do not know what he may yet have, by way of eyes, but I sense them full and open beneath my skin, watching through the flesh the distant, mellifluous world, as it flows him by.

Poor pregnant Dora stumps from the rail. How can I explain this scene or another to my future child? – it is a question of shoes, little darling, a question of feet. I try to care, but all the world has a sameness to it now, as I rest and he kicks: as I watch and he opens his eyes, and does not see.

I saw something in a jar once, in the private collection of a man on the Rue Vaugirard. And I think, for all my hopes, the thing inside me is still but a thing. I would look closer if I saw the jar now. But all I recall is the crease between shoulder and arm pressed up against the glass. Also, and strangely, the fatness of the gentleman's thighs.

*　　*　　*

There is a grand satisfaction in the men when they return. They have buried their man – because the dead sailor is each one of them, a little further on. So they have saved his body from the river and the idle current, and put him in as good earth as a man could find at home.

Over dinner, the doctor leans towards me and gestures vaguely around his throat. There are flies, he tells me, in the sand, and they bite. I tell him I do not know what he might mean (does he expect me to go about with naked feet?). He inclines the ugly boulder of his head, and for the next while follows me around with eyes that are as large and ready to weep as a four-year-old child's.

I am frozen all evening, as though with grief, and set about, and tired.

Tonight, in the darkness, my friend puts his two hands on my belly; then he places the side of his face there. I think he cries. There is a wetness crawling across my skin, and I am sure that it comes from his eyes. He is so quiet, so secret in his tears, that I cannot ask what grieves him. But it seems general, this sorrow – I am set to bawling myself, though I am not the crying kind, and soon we are both laughing at it, and blubbing and canoodling, and my heart seems to heave in my chest because I do not want to love him, but it seems that I am loving him a little, or at least kissing him, none the less.

I have no secrets my love, except love itself.

He falls asleep beside me. I lie and watch. His sleeping flesh clings close to the bones of his face and to the ball of his eye. I touch his hair and pinch it hard between my fingers. I want to wake him. I feel a terrible foolish, falling urge. It swoops through me – to tell him everything; to have all known, the men who were frantic or fond or kind, and my own cruelty. I would have him know the blackness of my heart.

The first man who cried for me (my dear friend) was

Bennett – the man who liked my father enough to lend him three hundred pounds; who liked me enough to press his lips against my young feet and then rise, weeping, the length of me, as I stood there looking at the wall. This happened, not the first time, but the tenth or eleventh time, in that room in Bordeaux.

I would leave Mme Hubert's school for girls and run down the street, my bonnet swinging in my hand. Some hours later I would return; greet Miss Miller at the door, curtsey to Mme Hubert in the hall, look them (unkindly, perhaps) in the eye. No one said a word.

The room was white and left its dry powder on my clothes or skin. There was a picture of the Magdalen, I remember, painted on tin, hung on one wall. She wore a dress of camel hair and held a skull in her hand. I thought the dress must be made of men's hair – the hair of all the men she had ever known – because this was the greatest surprise to me now, the amount of hair on a man, and the peculiar places it seemed to drift, lodging in the pits and valleys like snow. I was surprised to see that a man's personal hair turned as white as the hair on his head, or as grey, and I thought the Magdalen quite lucky to have a dress that was mostly brown. The skull, too, seemed part of her condition; because during the act, Mr Bennett's skull was always clearer to me than the face he wore over it. When he opened his mouth, I saw the horseshoe of bone where his teeth were set; and suddenly he was all socket and jawbone, and the gaping snub triangle of nose.

And so it seemed to me that the tin Magdalen was not repenting but reliving – the feel of a man's hairy skin and the look of his shapely, dead bones. Because Bennett's touch was sweet as death to me. And oh! Death is sweet when you are fourteen.

I ran to that room. Sometimes I went ahead of the appointed time and the waiting was terrible. It makes me tired to think of it. There was no clock. I could hear the people on the street and, sometimes, the singing class I was missing in Mme Hubert's school for girls. I sat on the bed and faced the door, pressing my feet down hard to stop the trembling. What opened, as the door opened, over and over in my head, was not my legs, or as you might say, my sex. What opened was my stomach and my heart – the flesh you might see on any butcher's block melted into one swooping movement of the soul that yearned over and over again for the opening of that door.

He always looked different and small when the latch clicked up. But that is as you might expect.

This is not yet love, I thought, as Mr Bennett checked about him (though the room was always empty) and then looked over to me, and smiled.

He was kind enough, I have to say, and allowed my curiosity to lead the way. I was very intrigued by the sight of his member, a dull, blushing pink, ticking idly upwards – for the first many times he let me play with it only, to get the cushioned heft of it; its buoyant weight and its ugly, weeping eye. Then, when he entered me and rolled his eyeballs back, I thought I had killed him, which made me frightened and compliant for a week or more. And when I got the trick of it, I did not let it show.

I was waiting for the moment that everything would turn – because somewhere in my fourteen-year-old heart I knew that he was on the brink of it; of some devastation.

And I was right.

I think about it sometimes – the agonies of men in private rooms. I think of the men who would be torn apart by it, the men who would want you to cut their throat, or press into their eye sockets with your thumbs.

There are men who whimper and trick about like babies, as any woman who has worked on her back well knows. I have seen a duke wag his bottom and pant like a dog, and any number of wealthy men giggle and whine. But these things do not interest me. What interests me is that high, lonely moment when you know that you might kill a man and he would only beg to be killed again. And it was the longing for this moment that made me run to that room in Bordeaux.

And so, after a month perhaps, it turned. And here is Mr Bennett weeping on the floor. And here am I, a young girl looking at the far wall, and I am thinking, Now! Now, this is love. And every day I run down the street to sit on the bed and wait to love again. And I take from him, in twenty-one days, the sum of one thousand and seventeen pounds.

One night around that time, I woke to my teacher, Miss Miller, sitting on my bed. At least, I heard the whispering of her dress and felt the dreadful sag of the mattress in the dark. I could make nothing out, and when her hand came forward to touch my hair I ducked and would have cried out but,

'It's only me,' she said.

She sat for a while, then,

'Are you frightened?' she said. I did not reply, and after some moments the mattress lifted and she was gone. I started to laugh. I knew what she was asking – she wanted to know if I was frightened, not of the man, nor of the future (nor even of her own ghostly figure in the dark), but of the act itself. Miss Miller wanted to know what it was *like* to know a man. This was the mystery that had, in its insinuating way, ruined her entire life. She was so reduced by it that she had to creep into a girl's room at night and touch her hair.

The next morning I woke, and put that same hair into forbidden curls with Jeanette Blanchot's tongs. I walked the passageways and went from one room to another, smiling and free. I had already finished. I was already gone.

Still, I have a horror of bed-ghosts, the ones who make

your mattress dip, so all you feel is a weakening – the sense, in your sleep, of something giving way. I am frightened of all things that make you tip in your sleep, so that when you dream it is of falling. These days, I am so big I cannot lie on my own front. If I lie on my back I feel a choking ghost in my sleep. So I stay on my side, crooked around my belly, as my dear friend's child is crooked in me. I would like him to lie crooked around us both, but he cannot stay close. He frets and wakes, then goes over to his *hamaca* to swing and snore.

What was that thing I wanted to say about love? I wanted to say something about the moment when necessity turns to love – because I felt always the tug of my father's three hundred pounds. But still – ask any wife – there is always a moment when necessity turns to love.

He does not know how cruel I am. He weeps against my belly – because we have buried a man today, perhaps, or because he is going home, or because he loves me, I cannot tell. I stroke his hair when he is asleep, and he can not feel it.

Today was Christmas Day. Tomorrow the Feast of St Stephen.

*

This morning, all washed by a night of tears, my dear friend says into the stillness,

'I killed a man, once.'

'Only one?' I say.

He and his brothers, drunk one night, tied the man to their horses' tails and hullooed through Asunción. They left shreds of him on the street. You could see the white of his bones sticking out of his raggedy back.

'But it is not the fact or the flesh of it,' he says. 'It is the why.'

'Then – why?' I say, careful not to look at him.

'Why not?' and he gives a painful laugh. 'I don't know. A woman turned me down for him – a not very attractive woman – and it wasn't that either. It was a thing we had to do. The girl was nothing: Carmencita Cordal. She thought her father owned the town, which he did not.'

Or not any more, I think, and say nothing.

'But the man certainly died. I turned him over and saw his eyes empty. I thought I would be sucked into them.'

'And were you?'

'No. Not in the least.' He sounds disappointed.

'So?' I say, and my breath is so caught in my chest I have to slip the word out by subterfuge.

'"*So?*"' he laughs. 'It was my first truly dead thing. And it changed the whole world.'

We lie there for some time, watching, each of us, the sun-splattered water as it dances on the ceiling, and I want to touch him with the bare tips of my fingers, or with my lips that are all alive, now, with the thought of touching him. I want to touch him where the skin is thinnest so I might drink it out of him, lick it like sweat – a prickling that comes to my mouth from the thought of what lies inside this man.

If I had killed the sailor, say, instead of mopping his brow, would I be so much the stronger? Would I walk upright? Instead of creeping about at midnight to get my *fill* of him? I might, instead, just live. Just breathe. Because my chest is tighter and tighter, now. It is closing up as my belly balloons, and I cannot fill myself any more, not with food nor even with air. These dainty, quick breaths I must take. This prison.

López stands at the end of the bed and, taking my foot, he lifts it high to place it flat against his heart.

'So, ask.'

'Ask what?'

'Carmencita. "Was she pretty?" or "Do you love her still?"'

I turn my face away.

'What way did the world change?' I say. 'Was the sky more blue?'

'Yes.'

'More full of birds?'

'Definitely.'

'Was the grass sweeter?'

'And so on. And so forth.'

I do not know what we are talking about, now. But it is enormous good fun, of a sudden, and not about death at all.

My sister in Mallow would bring me to things that she was too squeamish to kill; childish things; a frog or a daddy-long-legs, and I would dispatch them, and it would make her cry. And then later, of course, some blurted telltale, and the horrified face of my Mama, the two of them clinging to each other as they watch me walk towards Hell-fire. She always was a silly thing, my sister. She ran off with a visiting piano player and decided to call it 'marriage'. Let her call it what she likes.

But I dream, this afternoon, of daddy-long-legs, and I am the beastie with my belly huge and my limbs all feeble and waving, and bits gone, and so on.

It is very hot.

I think of the time I went for a fitting to the dressmaker on the Rue de Rougemont. The dress was so delicate that two women stood on chairs to lift it over my head. They used two long sticks apiece to make a canopy of the skirt, and I walked in under it. Then they settled it down over me, and it was like the sky falling, in a rush of silk.

What is it about soft things that makes us want to weep? I stroked, once, the foot of a statue, its marble underside so cold and tender it made my eyes shut. But my hands were not soft enough to stroke this silk, which was *such* a shade of blue. My hands were too numb and rough: I must feel it with my cheek, with my lips, almost, and be rendered by it disbelieving. I tell you, it was the difference between soft and impossibly so, as if there were a degree of fineness beyond which the world melts.

And I knew, at that moment, what money was for. It was so you could have things that were impossible. And around me there appeared a whole country of things that have crossed this line into the wonderful. Things hard to believe, that are for so long hidden, until that time when you spot the first. After which, they all beckon and clamour and call you by name. The most beautiful cloth for blue; the most beautiful shape to be wrought from a gold stitch on a pink field; the most beautiful black marble to set against the white. All absolute. All at a price.

I stood under that dress and it was like lowering my life down over my head. And the soft blue skin of it was armour to me, and transcendence. I swear I did not so much walk in it as float. I looked in the mirror and knew there is something about beauty that can never be touched, that can never be bad, no matter what the price.

I think he knew when he walked into the room: when he gave his little bow and looked up from under it with glittering eyes, I think he knew he was looking at something quite other. Though the look he allowed me was the look a man might afford not a work of art so much as a good dinner before he eats it – the happy thing being that with Francisco Solano López the eating is never done; there is always another course, and then another, which is why I have so many dresses, is it not? – so that the pleasure of removing them will never be repeated, but always new.

I am so nostalgic for him – even though he is here on the boat; even though he is but sixteen or twenty feet away

– that I call Francine to sit beside me like some sweet and dutiful daughter, while I talk and sigh.

I ask if she had any intimation, when she opened the door to him that evening, of the journey we were about to embark upon – because it is her journey too. And she says that, No. How could she tell him from any of the others?

Which is pure impudence, of course.

Oh, but now she *considers*, yes, there was that look he had about him, of a man who will not be thwarted.

I say that when he walked into my room first, I cannot deny it, I wanted him to be taller and perhaps a little more pale; but she was right about the look he had – it made you feel all squirming, but pleasantly so. And she said,

'Yes.'

I say I enjoyed him at cards, because he played properly, and for high stakes. He looked at me over his hand and tried to seem indifferent, not because he wanted to bed me, but because he had two aces and a king. And I won. I would have carried on winning (it was, after all, my deck) but I stopped and said, 'If I win, you will not like me.' It was important, of course, not to drive him away. But also, you know, I *wanted* him to like me – this man who played a serious game. And I wanted to keep playing, too. And so we were locked into it; whatever amorous battle we are still fighting now.

And he put his cards down.

'Do you remember?' I say, but Francine does not like this break in form. She is a servant. She did not pretend to be in the room at the time, so how can she pretend to remember? To agree would be indiscreet of her, and she wants me to stop talking, now.

And I want to stop talking too, because I realise, as I ramble on, that my dear friend wants to have Francine and that I am bruising her a little, as you might bruise veal, the more tender to have it when the time comes to throw it on the pan.

He bows, and walks on for another round of the deck. Or trots. He is never still. There is always shouting and planning. There is always a huddle in a corner, a call across the room or the deck, a different gathering of men in another cabin for more or different conversation. He gets them one-to-one, and the talk is low and hard, it is all of railway sleepers and branch lines, of wagons and mines and supplies of saltpetre.

I look at him as he recedes. He disappears around the stern and the boat is still. Then he comes back. He is talking to Whytehead, as usual, about the melting temperature of – is it charcoal? – the bulk of it anyway, and wagons. I keep hearing the English word 'wagons'. They are, apparently, the key.

I am swinging in my *hamaca*, talking to Francine about the first time I set eyes on this man. And the fact we all know – except perhaps the wagon-headed Whytehead – the fact that is generally available to everyone who sails on this boat, is that Francisco López, my dear friend, would like to have a certain amount of time, privately, with my maid Francine. And this fix he has makes us back away from them, as though he held a gun and she was a bird. And indeed, her eye is very like a bird's eye, as she does not watch him and yet does watch him, from out of the side of her head.

I want to slap her for a hussy, but I do not.

I say, 'We must bring some needlework out here, and sew where the light is good.' The girl looks at me; knowing I would rather pick hemp than stitch silk; my fingers so swollen now I can not feel the needle. But go she does, which gives me a moment to breathe.

My dear friend closes in, and bows, Whytehead raises his stovepipe, and they turn to walk the starboard side. We understand each other perfectly, it seems.

When Francine arrives back with the basket, her face is flushed, as though the thing were already effected in the brief time it took for her to fetch it and return. There is a giddiness in her that reminds me – like a blow – of the times I came back from that room to the school in Bordeaux. Miss Miller opening the door. Mme Hubert standing in the hall. I look at her with the same level eyes. Half-hate, half-hopelessness. And it amazes me, the power men have. How we make way for their desire.

And now we sit and sew. Or I swing and pretend to sew, while Francine stitches neatly at my side, and the negotiations begin.

But before they do, there are a few things I want, urgently, to say.

I want to say that I love my husband. I want to shout it out as though I were in some courtroom dock. But he is not my husband, and such love is not mine to declare. Such love is not even mine to have. Which is all to the good, because such love holds for me no fascination.

But it is nice, sometimes, to pretend. To heave a sigh and say,

'When did it begin?'

And a knock on the door is as good a place to start as any. My dear friend walked into my drawing room on the rue St-Sulpice and my life changed utterly. It might have been as banal an entrance as any other – there was no way to tell; so many beginnings are false or aborted. A pair of warm eyes is held a moment too long, and in that moment you think, I could fall, I could spend a long time falling, into that man's arms. Or he stays for one night, maybe three. Or he leaves. Or you do not like him, after all.

No, Francisco Solano López played cards with me and I said, 'If I win, you will not like me.' And he put down his cards, because he wanted to like me too, before he had me. And with such an ordinary civility – a sort of weariness you might call it – was my future decided. A tenderness, a consideration, from a man who is neither tender, nor considerate, as a rule. But how was I to know that? I had entered on to my future. It could have been a short future, or a lousy one. But then, also, we were so very happy in bed. And that's not fate: it is a question of the nose. Or so my tutor in these matters, M. Raspail, once said. It is a question of how they smell.

So you were led here by the nose, said Francine, and we both laugh.

I was led here by the nose. To lie, and swing, and dream of dresses on sticks, and of insects with their legs missing. To lie and caress the son of the man who walks the deck in a careful frenzy while I talk to my maid – almost, by now, a ladies companion – who has become the object of that acquisitive lust that men so often enjoy between themselves. Stewart, Whytehead, López. Who is to have her, if not The Buck?

It could be worse.

He knocked, and Francine opened the door. It seems he brought a future for her too. Not a bad one, either. If she has him – who is to say? It might lead to marriage – a settlement of sorts, perhaps even with Whytehead, as I was once settled on Quatrefages. Because dreadful things, I want to whisper (she is so much younger than me), are never the end. They are just the way through.

But tonight, for all my equanimity, I bite his shoulder until it bleeds and beat him about the head. He clouts me, too, across the neck and then, ringingly, an ear, and neither of us makes a sound. There is nothing for anyone to hear except a scrabbling, or the sound of cushions plumped up, or laboured breath, as López keeps my face at arm's length with the flat of his hand: feints, once, twice, then catches one and then the other of my hands. He holds them by the wrist, dragging them strongly down so my face is leaning into his. We are very close. He looks me in the eye, and there is a word he wants to say, or hiss, into my face.

I wait for it to be said. It is in the air, this word. I want it manifest. But he does not utter it. Instead, he squeezes my wrists, and looks at me, while the child in my belly turns and, lazily, turns again.

Truffles

1865, Asunción

STEWART CALLED ON Whytehead to tend to an injury that he did not want to share with whatever doctors – Fox or Skinner – he had to dinner. Or so Stewart assumed as he made his way to Whytehead's *quinta* along the gentle cut in the hillside the locals called *Tapé taú nde yurú*, 'The path where my kisses eat your mouth'. It looked the same as any other path, except perhaps a little more beautiful. He wondered did Whytehead know where he lived.

Apart from Fox and Skinner, Whytehead had Cochelet to dinner. Also Captain Thompson. Sometimes a lady came to dinner at Whytehead's and left thinner than she had arrived, stunned by the mutton and by the dessert of spun sugar in the shape of some recently opened suspension bridge. Whytehead had perfect dinners, where the talk was all of cannon bore and the world stage and whether pelargoniums would mildew in the heat. A six-course, living death. Or would be, thought Stewart, if he were ever invited, as he made his way up Whytehead's driveway. Crunch. Crunch. Crunch. Gravel. Imagine that. A sound to make your very boots weep.

Great Britain inside the door in the shape of Eames, an actual manservant from actual Yorkshire. Great Britain ticking gently in the hall. Great Britain in the drawing room and the way Whytehead sat in the upholstered chair, gazing into the middle distance from behind his florid, solid moustache. The flock, the horsehair, and the incredible curtains of plush: the room was a remarkable achievement. Stewart looked around and saw the Mile End Road, swimming in a mirage of heat.

The injury, said Whytehead, was to his hand – the kind of thing his barber might have attended to, Stewart thought, unless the Chief State Engineer had something more to say to the Surgeon General than 'It hurts'. And indeed, there was enough to talk about. There was the war, after all. There was any number of conspiracies to be entered upon, or unmasked. There was money to be rescued, or even made. What his aunt would call 'tradesman's talk'. What López might call 'treachery'.

Stewart uncurled Whytehead's fingers to find the wound. It was an ugly, complex thing of scars both old and fresh. Not so much a cut as a hole – something, or someone, had been digging into Whytehead's hand, then waiting, then digging again. It had been doing so for some time and Stewart feared a parasite, some strangely fixated fungus whose patience was about to be rewarded – being, after months of hurt and healing, nearly through to the other side.

'I seem to have hit it on a nail,' said Whytehead, when Stewart offered an enquiring look. And in the interests of precision, he picked up the thing from a side table and lifted it for the doctor to see.

'Iron,' he said.

'Ah,' said Stewart.

They both looked at the tip as Whytehead turned the nail between finger and thumb, scoring an imaginary curve on the air of the room.

Well, iron was the man's business after all. Scratching it out of the earth, ounce by painful ounce; smelting, pouring, casting. Sacrificing half a ton of shot because the Minister of War wanted fancy railings around his house, which might have cost the country less if they had been made of solid gold. *You can't sink a Brazilian monitor with golden shot.* As Whytehead might say at one of his dull dinners, where all the dull men sat, pondering the burdensome fact that they were alive.

Stewart eyed the nail. Perhaps he wanted to say that the colour at the tip was rust, and not blood; or that these two things were the same colour, after a time. Stewart knew better than to touch the thing. Let the man have his comfort, his suck, his gouger. His own little crucifixion.

'Precious stuff,' he said.

The Brazilians were on the river. They were far to the south, but they were there – around a bend somewhere, or the bend after that. Nothing came in and nothing went out. No one could leave Asunción.

Whytehead put the nail down. Stewart sat in the matching horsehair wing chair. The clock (another clock!) ticked Britishly on. They were both so terribly tired.

It was a pleasant room. The curtains on the windows were moss-green, with little tassels all down the side. There was a framed engraving on the wall of *The Queen at Balmoral, seated on her horse Fairy*. He would like to marry Whytehead, Stewart thought. There would be enormous comfort in it. No need for speech. Everything ordered and on time. A little woman who works a hole in her hand, when you are away.

And, 'Would you like to see the garden?' said Whytehead.

'That would be lovely,' said Stewart.

They walked out through French windows on to a granite terrace. A row of stone pots held the skeletons of bushes that had been cut into the shape of singing birds. Ordinary birds: sparrows or finches or wrens.

'The ants got to them,' said Whytehead and he stood for a while, looking at the wreck.

Stewart's aunt was of the opinion that all gardeners were insane people masquerading as gardeners. She said the same of men who liked to fish, and she humoured such types in a deliberate, loud voice, so,

'Even in the pot?' Stewart enquired, unflinching.

'Oh they get everywhere,' said Whytehead, and he led the way across the patchy lawn, and on through a gap in the hedge.

The sky was low and kind as they made their way through Whytehead's working garden towards a jumble of sheds. They walked so beautifully together; Stewart could feel the way his own thighs moved as they swung their sticks and paced the land. Beans, manioc, maize: Whytehead pointed them out, with notes of botanical interest, also the decorative rose bushes, carnations and dahlias that were planted between the vegetable rows. They paused at his pigsty. They patted the impossible Jersey cow kept for her milk (made thick as butter, it must be, by this heat).

Stewart was walking the country estate of the Chief State Engineer – Keld Whytehead, thirty-nine years old, half-crucified: whose father was nothing you could mention, whose grandfather had been, at a guess, an Orkney fisherman, which is to say a peasant with three words of English, being 'pence' and 'bailiff' and 'Sir'.

'My goodness,' said Stewart. 'Yours?' A tobacco field stretched ahead of them, all alive with the wind and with the shifting backs of peons labouring among the leaves.

'A good year for it,' said Whytehead. He could not use a word so vulgar as 'mine'. Oh bliss.

They would not talk of the war – like tradesmen, like traitors – they would talk of the weather, like gentlemen, and they would do their jobs, which were to kill and to save on a large scale; to build cannon and hospitals and put their shoulders to the wheel, which was the wheel of History itself.

'And that I grew from a cutting, sent over by Mme Lynch.'

Eliza spent her time these days crusading for the troops. She held grand soirées, at which she stood, taking the ladies' jewellery personally, at the door. 'Gold into guns,' she said, 'gold into guns', and the women went into the ball as though on their way to bed, reaching in a somnolent way to undo the clasps at their wrists and ears and necks.

And still she had time to grow a few lavender bushes, it seemed. Stewart had heard of this slippings and samplers conversation she held with Whytehead across town; a traffic of chutneys and jams, umbrellas for the sun and galoshes for the rain; small comforts such as sisters might send, which were as intimate a sign as might be seen of a nation's grateful solicitation. Eliza Lynch was Paraguay. She had produced, for the honour of the country, three living sons. She was also, since López had deeded his lands to her, one of the richest women alive. And she gave Whytehead dried seedpods she had cut with her own hands and laid in her own wicker basket. Which made it all worthwhile.

'And how is Il Mariscal?'

'In excellent health,' said his doctor. 'Excellent.'

'Good. Good. His catarrh?'

'Greatly improved.'

'Thank God.'

They stared at Eliza's lavender bush with gathering regret. The fact was that it was hard for a gentleman (or what passed for a gentleman in Paraguay) to apply himself to the wheel of History when the driver of the Juggernaut was a tyrant like López. Not to mention the slaves toiling at the ropes. Whytehead's miners worked in chains and it disturbed him just to think about it. To use men so degraded, you needed finer blood – blood that flowed somewhere between blue and pitch-black; blood that was not particularly stirred by the sight of green velvet curtains, or even by a framed portrait of *The Queen at Balmoral, seated on her horse Fairy*.

At the side of the house, they leaned on a very British fence to admire Whytehead's best horse; a big-hearted, gorgeous *colorado* who galloped at the sight of them, then stood, trembling, and would not approach.

'The glory of his nostrils is terrible,' said Whytehead and, when Stewart made no attempt to call the verse, he said, 'The horse. Job: 39.'

'Ah,' said Stewart.

'He saith among the trumpets Ha, ha; and he smelleth the battle afar off, the thunder of the captains, and the shouting.'

Feeling pursued, Stewart pushed back from the fence rail and turned to the house. Whytehead moved with him. He lapsed into an easy tone, as though talking to an intimate; as though talking to someone who quite liked him.

'I had an idling idea of Israel somewhere hereabouts,' he said. 'When I was on that boat. That terrible journey by sea. I was thinking – well I was thinking of how many tons per mile of track, of course, but also, you know, of a lost tribe. Or some *Arcadia*.'

'And all is Arcadian here,' said Stewart, hopelessly charitable, pulled into it by the sudden knowledge that the man he was talking to was going to die. And what of that? he thought. So do we all.

'Yes. It has everything,' said Whytehead. 'Except elephants.'

After Whytehead died the Arsenal would collapse and there would be no more guns. It occurred to Stewart, looking at this man's nervous, disrupted face, that his own death had just moved a notch closer. *How does that feel,*

Doctor? And because he knew they had come to the truth of it now, Whytehead stopped and turned.

'I went to the office of the Minister of War, yesterday,' he said. 'When I got there, I was asked to wait at the gate. In the sun. Of course I did not wait. I have a hundred things to do. I am not a waiting man. But when I wrote to complain of the guard's impudence, he sent me this.'

Stewart took the piece of paper and scanned it from 'Your excessive sensitiveness' to the scratchy signature at the end. *Benigno López.* The wretched brother. The only surprise was that he could write.

'You must rise above it,' he said.

'I cannot rise above it. Any of it. I was not built to rise.'

'Then for God's sake sink. Flatter the man a little.'

'I don't know how.'

This was true. Whytehead could flatter neither rich nor poor. He thought it democratic. Stewart thought it merely *small*. Which is why he would survive this country, Stewart thought, and Whytehead would not. Skinner treated him for a looseness of the bowel, Fox for cervical rheumatism, and now, Stewart for a hole in the hand. No one however could cure him of his dignity.

He suffered, under Fox, a daily morphine injection, in the neck. Perhaps it was this that made him stop, or turn, or sit down without warning. Or, as he did now, lie down entirely on the grass. Stewart sat beside him, close by his head. He found the arrangement uncomfortably erotic.

'But O for the touch of a vanished hand,' said Whytehead. 'And the sound of a voice that is still.'

For a while, one man watched the sky and the other the distant trees.

'I used to hit my sisters,' said Whytehead, dreamily. 'Quite hard. I don't regret it in the least. It is an odd thing for a man to worry about. Isn't it? But I worry about it now, all the time. And who was that boy, anyway? I am not entirely sure if that boy was me.'

He pushed himself up on one arm, and turned to look at Stewart.

'The boy on whose actions I will be judged.'

'And you think we will be judged?' said Stewart.

'I am sure of it.'

'Harshly? I mean.'

'There is only one way.'

'I am very taken, recently,' Stewart ventured, 'by the idea of a compassionate God.'

Whytehead laughed.

Stewart walked back along The Path Where My Kisses Eat Your Mouth. He wished he knew what joined him to this man. Race was the least of it. Every time the threads of their lives crossed, they snarled into a knot. No wonder they avoided each other. Or repelled each other, rather, like magnets – if one or the other turned, even slightly, they swung around and were stuck fast.

They were also rivals in business, of course. López, who liked a foreign bank account, afforded them the same easy deal, though Whytehead was doing rather better out of it than he was. Money, thought Stewart, it was always the money that smothered a man's heart.

It was the money that maddened them now, the better sort of British man trapped in Asunción, or working down the railway line in the huge military camp at Léon. As the war trickled on, somewhere in the Mato Grosso to the north or Corrientes to the south, their pay was changed from gold to silver and then to paper, until it was hard to tell if they were paid at all. Still, they held on. If anyone were to funk, it would be late at night after too much to drink with something blurted and wrong – the chances a chap had of making it overland to Buenos Aires, for example, or whether López was 'sound', or who the war was *against*, anyway. And Stewart, being sober, would sit in a corner, silently answering each in disgust that, No, a chap had no chance of making it to Buenos Aires, since the Brazilians held the river, and, No, López was not 'sound', he went to the wrong sort of *school*, don't you know, and finally that the war was against everyone. Of course it was – it was a war.

He made his way home from such gatherings shouting things out in his head. This is a man, he wanted to say loudly, who has no access to the sea. He is like a rat in a bag.

But more than that, this was a man who never read his Homer; he does not realise that wars are things you wage one at a time, so his war is gradually, inevitably, against everyone – if there is a problem in the Oriental Republic let us annex a bit of Brazil. Let us send our armies across Corrientes, which is now the Argentine. And so on, until the three of them, so recently a bundle of jostling provinces, sign a pact against you; three nations: Uruguay, The Argentine Republic, The Empire of Brazil – all sworn to the destruction of Francisco Solano López.

But more than that again – this is a war that is waged at home, where a man might be shot, for no reason you could tell, right here in Asunción. A man might be shot as you made your way home for afternoon tea. This war was everywhere, like air. It was waged in the silent heart and the silent mouth of the Indian. It was fought for 'Paraguay'. Which was to say, for nothing at all. By British standards, López was quite mad.

But Stewart liked the man; he thought he was quite perfectly himself. He liked his intelligence, which was considerable. And, as he walked home during those early nights of the war, he thought about feeding his animal López with this fact or that. What Cochelet said, for example, what Thompson inferred about the competency of his brother Benigno to construct a defence for the camp at Léon, what Benigno muttered about his friend Eliza Lynch. He might just get tired, some day, of all these drunks, and let slip a word or two in his Master's furry ear.

By the time he reached his own door these thoughts of loyalty and betrayal had fused into the single desire for a drink. There was nothing so tedious as this reduction. Once or twice a month, Stewart suffered a craving. He craved the immoral act. He raged against the unfairness of his life; knew he deserved *something* by way of succour or revenge, something small and poisonous. Something filthy. Or harmless. A nip of brandy, perhaps.

He knew why he hated these men, Benigno López, Thompson and the rest. It was because he wanted to pull the glass they were drinking from away from their lips. But he did not touch the glass and he would not betray the men. He walked. From midnight till, say, three o'clock, he tramped the streets and on to the country roads. He knew that he would always be shut out, now, that this was the nature of it, and so he took pleasure in the darkness and solace from the sleepers he passed; animals or men. He stopped to look at them as they twitched and sighed; reaching, chasing, moving their lips – wanting and having, wanting and not having, wanting and finally getting, all night long.

It was on one of his 'nocturnal peregrinations' that he met, and kissed, Eliza Lynch. Or thought he kissed her. Or no, did actually kiss her. Did something, anyway, for which you might use the word 'kiss'. He also felt – and he was convinced of this – a considerable wetness between her legs. At least, that is what he thought about, afterwards, though he did not, how could he? stoop and lift her skirt, there in the street. He touched her, yes. He touched her, but not so intimately. And it was not the leap his mind took that worried him so much as where it landed – this liquid shock; this symptom of disorder, whether genital or mental, that shamed the doctor in him – mocked as he already was by the desire this too-late encounter provoked, the years it had taken his hand to travel so far into the madness that was Eliza Lynch. He was rendered stupid by it – by a heat that started above his knees and trembled to a fluttering apex under his ribs. The feeling was not simply anatomical – although it was also overwhelmingly so. If it were just a question of the body, he thought later, then at least he would have known where to aim the thing, instead of this opening, heaving urge to be inside, outside, and all the way through: to be over, under and between Eliza Lynch.

But it was also a question of the body. It happened in the dark. But, whatever it was, it did happen. Let us call it a kiss. It was given, or taken, when the war was still just an idea that was being played out to the north and west of them. When Stewart's hospital cots were occupied by broken legs and the occasional fever. It was early June. The brink of things. It was the night before the main army, and half the city with it, decamped down-river to the fort at Humaitá.

Stewart came back to Asunción that night to collect some things; among them, a last sight of his wife. He was not expected, and made his way from the new railway station on foot. After the camp, the walls of the houses were particularly blank, and female and domestic. It was hard to say if anyone slept. There was the sound of scrabbling as treasures were hidden under floorboards, the muffled sound, or so Stewart imagined, of children being conceived and tears shed. Also disappointment, the distant mewling of women who looked at what they were about to lose and cried that it was never that much, anyway. When Stewart faced his own door he knew exactly what lay behind it. He thought, with a shock, that he was in a war now, that he might be killed, and if he were killed it would be for this: his bickering wife, his senile father-in-law, his home, Paraguay.

And so he started to walk. He chose the straight road because the night was dark and he did not pause until he found himself beyond the gates of the cemetery at La Recoleta, where he saw a woman, palely dressed, walking, as he walked, along the side of the road.

They might have been fugitives. She had no horse, no servant that Stewart could see. And he thought that this is what ghosts were – figures who have nothing, who are always walking away. The moon was high and the smooth sheen of her hair awoke in him a kind of dread. He did not want her to turn around. He did not want to see whatever look was on her face, now: some mute and terrible appeal, or an entirely usual expression, made hideous and slow. Was Eliza dead? It was years since he had seen her like this – ever since she became a kind of national Thing, Eliza was never alone.

She was alone now. She walked the road ahead of him on the same side, reaching and passing each in a row of young cypress trees. For a while he did not approach, but matched his pace to her dreamy tread; and although she did not speed or slacken, he knew that she sensed him behind her in the night. She was alive, then. She was more than alive. He could feel her thoughts seeking him out, as his thoughts played at her back. He would have called out to reassure her but there was, he found, a keen, and unexpected, pleasure in keeping silent. And so he matched her, step for step, shortening his stride by so much to keep the gap precise – his pace ever more mincing and predatory, until the moment lapsed and she was no longer afraid.

She turned. Stewart had expected a girl to turn, but it was a woman who faced him, and the greeting she gave might have been offered in any drawing room: it built walls around her and ignored the night.

'Doctor Stewart,' she said.

'My dear Madame Lynch.'

The distance between them made him feel foolish, now that he had to cross it.

'You will see me home?' she said.

'Indeed, it is very late.'

'Thank you.'

She turned and took his elbow – so neatly, they might have been stepping out to dance. But Stewart found that he could not accompany her and there was a little, frightful awkwardness as she pulled at his arm, like a mother might drag at a schoolboy who balks on the road.

He had, he discovered, something to tell her.

'Eliza,' he said.

He wanted to tell her how she was seen, these days. He wanted to warn her of what she might become.

She was, in the first instance, more beautiful. Stewart was at the age when men become addicted to youth, so Eliza's increasing, and increasingly new, beauty was a mystery to him. She was, by general standards, old. She was also fussy. She came into his medical tents with a great show of entourage and ladies, and you might think the men would find it an irritation, but the truth was that her face was a solace to them, her smile a balm, and the few words she uttered (to Stewart's sometime annoyance) a cure in themselves. And it was not just the gullible and the forgotten who felt the force of it. When she entered a room – it might be some bare room in the camp at Léon – when the men scraped their chairs back and stood, it was more than courtesy that moved them, it was the knowledge that, unlike the wives-daughters-sisters-camp girls, she understood the gravity of their great enterprise, and that, in some lovely, easy way, she belonged to them all. The most beautiful woman in the world.

So this was the first thing that Stewart had to tell Eliza, in the incongruous dark, by the side of the road – that she was beautiful. The second thing he had to tell her was that she was evil, too.

It was not a word he might casually use, but the war was exciting as religion to him now, and it was vital to keep López pure. Il Mariscal slapped his crop against his boots, he stalked, he was everywhere; and when the band played 'La Palomita', he looked twice as large and very fine. And in his stalking, slapping way, he might have a man whipped, or a man shot. He might have late dinners, which a woman would be wise not to attend. This is what Stewart wanted to say: that Eliza must strike with her Great Friend an attitude – such a one as you would find, indeed, on an old vase. She might fall on her knees. She might soothe. She might plead. But she must stay away from early whippings and late dinners. And she must never, ever whisper in his ear.

As he had seen her do, quite recently, as they stood on the dais at Cerro Léon. It was during a grand parade. She whispered, he laughed; then they both turned back to watch as men marched past on their way to the grave. Eliza's face, without changing at all, had become implacable, somehow, or greedy. Or hideously serene. She had gone from Angel of Mercy to Angel of Death, without a blink of her lovely eye.

Was it too late to turn back? Was there any other way for her to go? Stewart wished that López would marry her – he almost longed for it. He felt, in the most foolish part of himself, that there might be something this woman could do – a bedroom something that their beautiful Eliza might say to their impetuous Mariscal that would stop it all, the torment and horror that was about to descend on them. Because it was the fate of angels, was it not, to intercede?

And now here she was, her ordinary flesh beside him on

the roadside, and Stewart her protector. She was smiling at him, after pulling at his arm and letting it drop. He had just said her name.

'Eliza.'

'Yes?' she said, and took his elbow again, quite patient and sisterly.

'Be careful,' he said. And this time he walked on with her, because, pathetically, he did not know what else to say.

'I am always careful,' she said (evil, quite evil) and the toes of her satin shoes slipped, one after the other, out from under her dress and on to the grit of the road.

It was not far to her house. She talked, remarkably, of Southern England, the small town in Kent where she had been married. 'For I am married, you know', to a M. Xavier Quatrefages. A beast, but a very minor beast, she said. A horse doctor in the military. But Kent was beautiful, all the same. The Weald – was that Kent? Perhaps it was Surrey. And so they came to the gate of her *quinta*, where she turned and took his hand in hers, and he, like some village Romeo, pushed forward to kiss her on the mouth. Or on the cheek. Or he brushed his mouth against the skin of her face, as she turned away.

He did not even like the woman. It was a part he was obliged to play, and she, to complete the scene, turned and fled prettily into the house. The theatre of it annoyed him, but not as much as the riot in his blood that had been gathering ever since he tracked her in the dark. He felt trifled with. He felt tempted, and scorned. Even if this were true (and it was not true) – no matter. What mattered was the violence with which he had wanted her, a woman talking of Kent or was it Surrey, as though she did not want him too. Was this passion? This *epilepsy*? This urge to destroy, like a child in a fit, the room, the house, the entire world? And that anatomical thing, his member, foolishly forward, seeking a place he could no longer imagine, let alone name, until there, on his hand, an appalling, imagined wetness; poor forked animal that she was. Gone now, through the gates of her house. Gone to bed.

He shook it off like a dog and headed back to town, and like a dog, he felt he had been whipped. But the road was straight and he knew where he was going. He was going to his annoying wife Venancia for some love. Just that. The odorous cushion of her breast beneath his ear.

For a long time, the memory of that night's encounter clung to Stewart like a dream you cannot wash off in the morning. It returned, in one detail or another – the sound of the insects in the dark; the turn in the road; and what might have happened if some different move had been made. If he had spoken more, or better. If he had stopped. If one or other thing had shifted even slightly and he had ravished, or been ravished by, a woman he did not even like, who walked out at night as he did, alone.

Nothing much, of course. The sexual act. A different way of looking at López. His own throat quietly slit perhaps (or perhaps not). A great passion, or no great passion. A mess. Any number of things, none of which would increase the sum of his pleasure in seeing Eliza secretly in the dark, as though she had invited him to this assignation, and him alone.

Of course she was not there for him. What Stewart knew – but did not realise for some time – was that Eliza's stillborn daughter was buried in the graveyard along whose walls she walked that night. It came to him, seven years later, when he buried a child for Venancia, who could not attend, being not yet churched. It was their sixth, a meagre little daughter who died as soon as she was born. They scraped out some earth and put her in. Stewart looked up, and Venancia's absence on the other side of the tiny grave made him think of other ghosts – the lilac paleness of Eliza that night, in the June of 1865, when the war was still something you might win or lose.

The graveyard was beautiful. It was one of those blessed days when you thought there could be no hardship in such a place and with such weather. The jacaranda trees were in smoky bloom, the birds sang into the stillness, and the whole world seemed to whisper 'Afterwards. Afterwards'. It was all finished, now. The war. López. Any number of dead. Stewart found it hard to care, after so much slaughter, for his own tiny child, but of course he did care, and the animal sorrow he felt seemed so unfair – that you should never be free of it, that, like hunger, pain would always be new and hard. And as he turned away he remembered that Eliza's daughter was buried here too. So that was what brought her out along the road that last night in Asunción. She had come to visit the bones of her baby – so light and tentative and barely formed. He thought of them as they lay in the earth now, open and loose; melted back from each other where the cartilage had not had a chance to harden into bone.

Stewart stepped back with a snort that surprised the gravedigger. He had remembered – but last of all – the kiss. And with the memory came the thought that the kiss, despite its opiate clarity, might not have been a kiss, after all. Also, and either way, that it did not matter now. Perhaps it had not mattered then. And Stewart felt a fierce nostalgia for the war. Standing alive, as he stood now, among the great sighing mass of the dead.

It is possible they all saw themselves as standing on a magnificent canvas, one that might run the length of an old hall. It would be filled with smoke. There would be hills with men toiling up the slopes, other men firing down from above. A gorge. A swamp. Far embrasures and redoubts – strategic details compressed into a tea-coloured distance before the Paraguayans run out of wall. In the centre, the river, shallow and lazy, flows or dallies past the story of the war fought along its bank: the battles of Riachuelo, Tuiutí, Curupaití, the trenches at Curuzú and, looming above it all, the besieged fort of Humaitá; its builder, the gallant Captain Thompson, unrolling his plans high up there on the mud wall.

Below him, Brazilian ironclads squat on the river while, from ship and shore, the mouths of cannon spit primitive flame. The river is spattered with shot that falls just shy of the ships: the walls of the fort, though vaguely pocked and dented, are never breached. It seems a pleasant enough stalemate – an expensive way to fish. Along the wicker battlements, men point into the middle distance or click out a telescope to glint in the sun. Their names might be written on ribbon unfurling below them. In the centre, López; with an unlikely white stallion rearing under him on the high wall. Pedro Inácio Meza, the ruined hero of Riachuelo dying of his wound, stiffly, on the church steps. Colonel José Díaz charging, and taking, a battery of La Hitte cannons from the Uruguayans at Estero Bellaco. Huzzah! General Francisco Isidoro Resquin running up the left flank at Tuiutí, General Vicente Barrios on the right, the fierce Guaraní soldiers wading through swamp and thicket under close enemy fire to face the sixty thousand Brazilians, Uruguayans and Argentines, housed in that vast city of cloth. How could one man paint them all? And though we see men throw up their arms and roll their eyes, although we see the bullet even as it enters; the stricken faces of comrades who reach but can not save ('oh, no!' the picture might be called. 'Oh, No!'): although we see plenty of dying, we do not see one corpse – so quickly are bodies emptied and then discarded, even by their own stories – nor do we see the vast heaps of the dead. We might miss the vast heaps of the dead: we have come to relish them; the unexpected anatomy lesson of a man's neck open to the spine; the way a group of bodies tangle and subside; the way we must follow the line of a leg to see whose foot that is, so strong is our impulse to unite the body and give each man his proper parts. Also the horror, of course, when the leg stops short. Ten thousand men died at Tuiutí, and as their skin leathers in the open air, the hill of the dead settles and grows horribly flat (who would have thought there could be so many elbows in the world?). A lone photographer stands on the field of death, and there is no one to paint them: the painters are all fled. What happened at Tuiutí? A battle, that is all. Nothing but swamp was lost and nothing but swamp was gained. But the man who lost the swamp was López.

Still, you must never underestimate the Guaraní soldier. He is there in the picture too, in dull-eyed ranks and rows, ever-advancing. Again and again, facing superior forces and overwhelming odds, the Paraguayan Indian outfoxes, outfights, outdies the combined enemy. His pants are blue and his coat is red. And he takes both off to fight in the swamp, which he knows and calls home.

He is sickened by the meat, though, as Miltón tells it many years later. Not because the meat is rotten, though it is often rotten, but because these men are not used to eating such stuff – they only make it, or become it. In which case, there is plenty meat made in the five and a half years of the war. As the battles slowly creak into place, and one strategy slowly crunches into another, the Guaraní Indian fights on; bilious, gripe-ridden, suffering from meaty breath and meaty wind; and there is no surrender. Ever.

Despite which, the story of the war is a story of retreat. Curupaití held and lost. The cunningly double line of trenches at Curuzú, then back to the fort of Humaitá: three hundred and eighty guns, a mess of defences out front, the ground seething with twenty thousand boys and old men, because only boys and old men are left, now.

The stranglehold tightens around them and the names keep unscrolling in the painterly wind: on the river, the fearless Díaz floats in his fatal canoe; General Barrios makes a sortie, Paulino Alén shoots himself, in the face of defeat; Bernardino Caballero holds Acosta Nu – these are names that must be said out loud. As too must the names of the staunch ships who sailed in this war, the *Tacuarí*, the *Paraguarí*, the captured Brazilian steamship *Marquês de Olinda*, the *Ygureí*, the *Salto Oriental* and the *Pirabebé*. Ships where men fought, and in which they burned; ships from which they drowned.

There is some comfort in listing the brave men of other wars: history is a litany, and all we are doing, here on this earth, is making lists of the dead.

So busy intoning, indeed, that we miss the three Brazilian boats as they cut the chains that have been slung across the river, then run the battery at Humaitá. They are the *Barrosso*, the *Tamandaré* and the *Brasil*: all monitors; blind-looking things of unnatural iron – even the deck is closed over, so that the men inside it are either safe or dead: there is no middle way and no romance to them either. Monstrous modernity, which chugs past the open mouths of two hundred and four guns – from the Curupaití battery to the final array at Humaitá – as though they were going on a picnic. Then moves upriver to pound Asunción.

And so there it is. The city is burning. Somewhere in the background, the ghost of Whytehead lays his hand on the bulge of a cold smelter, looking sad yet proud. So much for the remnants of the maiden Tacuarí – they pale in comparison to the great names of this war, Spanish Creole and Guaraní. At the very end of the canvas it is the gallant Captain Thompson who surrenders, finally, the fort at Angostura, because no Paraguayan knows how.

And where is Stewart? Was he brave? Low down, on a nameless piece of ground, he lifts some dying man by the shoulders, as though to help him face out of the picture. The man rolls his eyes. His last, trembling gesture is back towards Humaitá and the unlikely stallion on the high wall – my captain, López. (Or is that López himself, impossibly dying in Stewart's arms? With more beard, perhaps, and a different look in his eye?)

And where is Eliza in his hour of need? She is out of the picture. Her portrait would be hung on the opposite wall, endlessly looking. Trying to discover where it all went wrong.

She will not find it here. This is a heroic painting – one of the last such – and tenderly naïve. It is full of errors, of course, but that is a different thing. Stewart might have pointed out that the chains slung across the river were, for the duration of the siege, most beautifully clogged with water hyacinth. Every morning he wondered at the line becoming sharper – the water downstream becoming smooth as glass, as the river behind grew solid with vegetation. One morning the whole thing flowered and he had the greatest urge to walk the floating path from the near bank to the freedom of the other side.

He might, either, have complained about the lack of red – that most distracting colour. He might say the painter had failed to capture the various and romantic colours of blood, for example, from the dry rust first pointed out to him by Whytehead, to the liquid red of the river, soaked with light as the sun went down. It might be bougainvillaea shooting, from one day to the next, out of the rich mud beside his hut at Humaitá, or a man's shirt in full bloom just before he died, but Stewart's eye was punctured by red during the war, as his heart was sometimes pierced by the peculiar blue of the sky.

Most important, there would be nothing in such a picture of miasma, or of mud. There would be no mud-covered carrion, or living men covered in mud. Above all, there would be no women slathered with the stuff, or even women who, like Eliza, remained amazingly mud-free.

In fact, the fort at Humaitá was crawling with women. They detached themselves from the mud of the walls to approach in their mud-coloured dresses, and they opened their mud-coloured faces to show the wonderful, clean, inner red of their mouths, livid with teeth of yellow. And whatever they had to say, it was always a bother – a plea of some sort, for news of some man, for intercession over a scrap of cloth, or a scrap of roof to put over their heads, or, later, for food. They offered nothing in return, some of them, except the sight of their winning, female faces, or the prospect of leaving your sleeve alone. They might, either, offer some sexual service of great frankness, but their bargaining powers were in general poor, and they might switch from nothing to everything without seeming to tell between the two.

In the universal muddiness that pertained after that first action at Riachuelo (no one dared to call it a defeat), the merest wipe of a rag was enough to make you advance. The woman who fared best – at least the one whose sleeve Stewart would end up tugging before the war was out – started out with a clean face and a stand of rushes she cut from the swamp to repair your roof. She ended up supplying all kinds of things, from a bottle of French wine to woven baskets for the wall of the fort. She could be seen tramping them like a dumpy skirted engineer in increasingly good boots, with gold chains around her neck and other, dangling things hidden under the cloth of her shirt.

She was never hit. When the water rose, the Brazilian boats drew closer and the thick cushions of earth that were the walls became fatter and dangerously low, like hills. It was hard to tell if they were falling under the pounding or reverting to some more natural state and Stewart could not help feeling that they were quite happy subsiding like that, back into the easeful flat, or slipping off into the river again, as mud. He could not help the feeling that even the earth was betraying them now.

Still, it was fun. Every morning, they cheered a little paddle wheeler that steamed down to lob a few twelve pounders into the Brazilian fleet, making them scurry a bit, whip up a bit of foam. When it was sunk they sent Jaime Corbalan down instead – one man in a canoe full of torpedoes, with a ribbon presented by Eliza fluttering at his throat.

'We'll put a hole in them yet,' said López as they waited for dawn and the sound of the first explosion, the plump ball of water bursting in the air. But there was nothing. There was an uneasy silence, which filled up slowly with the different kinds of misadventure and funk and betrayal, so by the time the first jeering whistle broke, they knew what had happened. The Brazilians had swallowed him up. Corbalan was a rich boy and this was the trouble, said López, who, in his cheerful way, had the man's brother shot.

Then new boats appeared, and the shells flew high over the walls, churning an arc of mud where huts and shanties once stood. Every morning, the women went out to collect the unexploded canisters, then brought them to the gunners to be better primed and shot back. They cheered as they ran towards them, and jostled each other out of the way to keep their courage up, because although the shells looked like nothing at all lying there – just lumps of metal lodged in the muck – sometimes one would, under a woman's gentle touch, revive, and so explode.

Stewart faced the problem of the women whenever their anatomy ambushed him in the operating hut – every time he panicked that a man's member had been blown away and grubbed through blood and hair looking for the non-existent wound. Every time he unbuttoned a shirt and found a breast, or two, beneath, he would sigh at the problem of the women. If Venancia were here, would she scavenge for shot? (Venancia becoming, as the weeks and months went by, as beautiful in his head as a glass of water, a plate of fresh food.)

Why, he asked himself, did the women do such a thing? There was a pot of corn for each shell, but there were other ways and other places where a woman might find food. 'I had a man who died,' said one, 'and then I had another man who died.' When life was so cheap, she seemed to say, love became general. So they might do it for a general love. Or for love of *the* General – López. Or because they were told to – as simple as that; the love of discipline. Or because they loved the risk, as some of them undoubtedly seemed to do. They might do it, finally, because no one likes to lose – which is nothing but the love of victory, with her laurels and her wings.

Stewart was much exercised, philosophically, in his cholera tent and in his typhoid tent, by the problem of love. He thought about it obsessively. Perhaps it had always been thus, he thought, as he lifted a mustard plaster from a cholera victim's chest, or paused to examine the gassy, bulging ground over the pits where they buried the dead. 'My aunt always said I was a worrier.'

'But all love is a worried love,' he said, inadvertently aloud, and more than once. 'All love is fuss.'

He thought that he was beginning to love Eliza Lynch, for example. But properly, this time. This did not bother him much: it was a spiritual, even androgyne love – it was not a yearning thing. He did not wait for her to appear. But when she did walk out – her dress bouncing on its hoops, just clear of the mud, and her parasol glowing like a living membrane in the sun – her eyes were so kind, her whole air so simple and redeeming, that it was impossible to call her a woman at all. She was like a sister when she moved and like a dream when she was still. She was what they were all fighting for.

Of course, he was also *in love* with her in a dashing sort of way – they all were, it was the accepted thing to be. 'We have died and gone to Eliza's', was the joking toast they gave, in the little place she kept beyond the church at Humaitá – meaning no disrespect in this use of her Christian name, but on the contrary, a kind of bantering beatification.

Eliza's house was a haven – partly because it was so well back from the arc of bloody muck that was the ballistic limit of the Brazilian ships. Which is not to say that Eliza was a coward; she walked freely out; a distinctive sight – you might even say a target – a swirl of colour with two boys, fore and aft, to lift and lay boards for her feet. They got so adept, it became a kind of game with them all; Eliza walking faster and faster as they ran around her, forming an impromtu wheel on whose inside rim she walked safe.

Stewart could have used the boys, but he did not grudge her this courtesy. It lifted all their hearts to see her looking so fine. There was not a man among them, would not lay down his life to save her stockings from a splash of whatever liquid might taint her: muck, blood (sperm, he idly thought), pus, noble or otherwise, and, God knows, sweat; the soup of putrefaction; good, old-fashioned shit – there being so many ways in which a lady's stocking might get wet, these days.

Every time Stewart saw Eliza, she had grown. He was not surprised by this; Venancia had, for example, shrunk in his head, until she had become a sort of daughter to him – a body he might take up in his arms, fresh and light and loose as water. And sometimes the body was alive and sometimes the body was dead. Either way, even though Stewart knew she was eating her way through her father's estate upriver, along with his own worthless salary, she still became, as the months and years went by, lighter and lighter in his mournful arms.

He himself, he thought, was pretty much the same size, although he could feel his heart getting bigger. His heart seemed to be, by now, the size of a horse's heart, and as the pile of food shrank and the pile of bodies grew, it felt like his heart would take over the entire cavity of his chest, until he was just a thumping, possibly empty, thing of muscle and bone.

There was nothing wrong with any of this, though he found the massivity of his heart, imagined or real, sometimes affected his lungs. He could not draw breath any more, or at least not a proper, manly breath. It was the grief, he thought. He had heard men complain of it – a tightness in the lungs that eased itself only in tears and that had no pathology that he could see. It was just that, as the number of the dead grew, your lungs shrank. As if to remind a man what it was to inhale and so to live.

His stomach escaped this inventory because he did not think of it as belonging to him anymore, and so it might be any size at all. It might be as big as the wide world, or as small as a bullet lodged in your gut. Mostly, he tried to ignore it, so capricious was it, and independent, and mean. But then the hunger moved to his mouth, and this made him want to wrap his gums around things – all manner of things – in order to assuage it. Or he might, in opening a wounded man, catch a glimpse of his last meal, and find a jealous spittle flood his own maw.

It was not that they were famished. They had food – or some food. It was just not the right food. There was something a man craved to see on his plate, but could not name. And as the months went by the soldiers sat around more, and their eyes became more inward-looking and difficult and complicit with their own pain.

It was around this time that the story went about that

Eliza ate the flesh of the dead. She said it tasted just like pork, but gamier – like the truffle-hunting boars you get in the Auvergne. Some said it was Brazilian flesh she liked – though there was little enough of that about – others said it was their own. The story was universally believed – it was the truffles that did it. You could not *invent* a detail like the truffles: besides, who among them had ever heard of the Auvergne? And the taste of gamey pork circled endlessly in their mouths; the wetness so bad they must spit as they thought of Eliza pulling a long strip of pale ham from an amputated joint. These were men who looked at their own arms now, during a long day in the trenches, and judged the ratio of lean to fat. And though there was a horror to it, they did not exactly blame Eliza her portion, so much as blame this gaping world, into which you threw bodies, perhaps your own body, as though the sky itself were starving.

Then, when she appeared, the cannibal thoughts had nowhere to land. Eliza was, in all the mud-coloured world, the most beautiful thing. And they ate her with their eyes.

But what of love? said Stewart's worried thoughts. What has all this eating to do with love? Of course he found the cycle of life here uncomfortably close. They all did. During the endless afternoons, his medical heap of discarded flesh was often raided by dogs, who might be shot as they worried their human spoils. The shot dogs were then eaten. Of course they were cooked first and this made a difference, but the closer a man got to the line the more important it was to maintain it. And what else would keep the line, but love?

He was not the only one who felt this way. There was a keen trade in priests, these days, or the priest-like – men with a mellow, melancholic wisdom that in peacetime would have tempted you to hit them across the back of the head with a shovel – they drew their pipes on other men's tobacco, and gave, in return, a wise sigh and a story, preferably one of woe. Stewart did not listen unless it was a tale of love, because although love still frantically concerned him (also fate and mischance), death did not trouble him at all. The last death he had cared about was Whytehead's, and Whytehead had died some years ago. It was hard to remember when. Before that first action at Riachuelo, or after? It was certainly before any of the big engagements of the war. Whytehead was missing all the fun. No, the last time Stewart had seen him, the band was playing 'La Palomita', and the crowd were cheering their heads off, and Whytehead was just standing there, looking at them all.

It was the morning after Stewart had, or had not, kissed Eliza Lynch; the morning the fleet was dispatched to break the blockade. The whole town stood in Plaza de Palma cheering, one more time, the *Tacuarí*. With her now were the *Paraguarí*, and five or six more, including the *Ygureí*, the *Jejuí*, and the *Salto Oriental*. The captured Brazilian steamship *Marquês de Olinda* was re-rigged with the national flag and it all looked so fine, and so very much his own, that Stewart forgot about fumblings with this woman or that. No man's heart can resist the tug of ships and, as they pulled slowly away, Stewart flung the stupid kiss, and all kisses, after them, as you might lob a pigeon; a flurry of muscle and emotion, which soared up to drift awhile in their wake.

'Huzzah,' he shouted, and he waved his very British hat. 'Huzzah!'

And Whytehead gave him a narrow look.

So he was almost pleased when, after a few weeks in the field, the news came of the man's death. The ships had engaged in the shallows of Riachuelo and the action had failed. The *Jejuí* and the *Salto Oriental* were lost, the *Paraguarí* laid helpless. The commander of the fleet, Commodore Meza had, wisely, stopped off in Humaitá to die of his wounds. And it was at Humaitá that Stewart heard the news that, upriver, the Arsenal had lost its chief engineer and the army their free supply of *matériel*. And he felt whatever thread tied him to Whytehead snap.

He was curious to find that there actually *was* a thread somewhere, like a tendon in his chest in which the connection he had to this man had been manifest. He was surprised to feel an actual sensation of loosening. The picture of the Fates was, he thought, quite just – their big shears cutting the threads of a man's life – because what the world feels when a man dies, even at a distance, is an unravelling.

The body was found in his tobacco barn and the story circulated that Whytehead had hanged himself from a beam there. His dinner doctors, Fox and Skinner, had diagnosed self-poisoning: he had taken an infusion of nicotine they said; a pesticide he concocted against aphids. Stewart knew he would do no such thing. It would mortify his sisters. And he sat down to write and tell them so. 'Dear Misses Whytehead,' he began. Thinking that the letter would never reach them. Wondering how much of their brother's money would ever make it to the Mile End Road.

In the months that followed, Stewart's thread theory, or tendon theory, was of some comfort to him. It was as though he had a little packet of humanity stored safely in his chest, and he occasionally patted himself there, as a man might check for his pipe, while around him the cholera came and with it all other kinds, shades, varieties and types of shitting – dysentery, typhoid, and the rest. He wondered why God had not designed for mankind a convenient plug. He thought, also, that if he saw another man with his pants stinking, he might kill him, just to save time.

In October the northern army had limped down from the Cordillera and there was little enough for Stewart to do. Only the minor wounded made it back, carried over that great distance by brothers, or friends, or even strangers – who must have been put out when López shot their burdens as soon as they set them down, in order to purge the shame of the surrender at Uruguiana.

The general was shot first – which was the difference between López and other commanders of men. There he goes, thought Stewart. My animal Mariscal with his animal war. He walked up the lines of the wounded and stared each man in the face, checking his eyes as the band played 'La Palomita'.

The great slaughter had begun, and it was years before Stewart cared again.

Then, in June of 1867, a man came up to him and spoke a sentence so clearly that Stewart wondered at the path this news had taken – it had travelled such distances to hit with precision the side of his head, where nature had placed an ear to receive it. The *Doterel* had been let through in June with a new English envoy; perhaps the news had come in a letter that Venancia opened on his behalf. Was it her voice he heard through the man's face, as he came up to him in the middle of a busy afternoon and said, 'I am to tell you that Miss Steerat of Edingbur is dead.' It was news, he said, for 'El Doctor' – who indeed had an aunt called Miss Stewart who was by now long dead in Edinburgh as opposed to any other town. Where the news had come from, or who had paid for it, Stewart did not know. When he lifted his suddenly heavy face to thank the man, he had already turned to go.

'She was a mother to me,' said Stewart, pathetically, to his back, and the man looked over his shoulder at him, very like the statue of Perseus at Albani.

And so the previous, ordinary months of siege became extraordinary months, in which he had been alive, while his dear aunt was dead. If it was possible to experience life in retrospect then that was what he was doing now – a rush of sensibility pouring through the days, a lurch in time, a doubling back – as though he had dropped her death along the path, all unawares, and was returning to collect it, now.

The heavens were open to him. There was no one between him and the wide blue sky any more. Stewart looked up, as though for the first time, and decided that there was none so peculiar a colour as blue. The woman who reared him was dead, and he had felt nothing – no intimation before the news, no emotion on its receipt. And so his thread theory of human connection itself unravelled, many miles from home.

Of course, when he last embraced her, he knew that he would never see the woman again. Which is just as we all do, he thought, because 'Farewell' with a woman is always for all time. Even the small partings. Even if she puts her bonnet on and walks as far as town, which is not very far. Farewell. Because that is what women are for. For leaving, and loving from a distance, very like the way we love the dead. And he thought of the slender angel he would like to set on her grave – he spent his time inscribing the headstone beneath with one phrase or another. Finding the right words and forgetting them, re-making them in his head. Some day the thing would be settled with a pen and paper, but in the meantime he managed and forgot sentence after sentence until the moment when his mind was stilled with some lines that Whytehead had recited to him that day in Asunción.

But O for the touch of a vanished hand,
And the sound of a voice that is still.

And with this, a sadness filled his (already much engorged) heart, and although Stewart still, in general, liked the war, he could not remember how it started, any more.

But now that his aunt was dead, he felt a need to dress in the evenings and to look at the men about him with social eyes. Instead of a jaundice, he might see, for example, a tendency to cut corners. He applied his aunt's horse language to them: that one was a bolter, another a swerver, when faced with the great ditch of life. And, as though Eliza realised this from a distance, one morning, busy (as a man might occasionally be) with his lice, he was interrupted by a small girl with a card.

Mme Eliza Lynch
requests the pleasure of
Dr William Stewart's
company at dinner
on Saturday evening July 7th
at half past seven o'clock.

It was this that brought him, finally, to tug at the sleeve of the woman who walked the walls. He found her ordering the wicker gabions into a high gap and he interrupted her for so long as to request a piece of paper, if it could be found. It arrived that afternoon – quite a good sheet – in return for some future life saved, or lost (she would tell him when the time came), and he rinsed his hands with dry grit before picking it up.

Humaitá, July 4th
Dr William Stewart
accepts with pleasure
the kind invitation of
Mme Eliza Lynch
for dinner
on Saturday evening July 7th
at half past seven o'clock

Spacing one line after the next, so sweetly, filled him with a quiet elation. Just this – the simple cross and return of a pen, made him feel almost noble again.

Her recent confinement, and the birth of a fourth son, meant that it was many months since Mme Lynch had entertained in her little house in the compound behind the church. This was a pity, because Eliza by candlelight was a wonder. She gave her guests the gift of an easy, profound attention, and the liquid approval of her lovely black eyes. Her voice, when she spoke, was both light and proud; her whole conversation so carefully matched to the male mind that one was never obliged to stall or defer. This all he told his aunt as he scraped his face with a bloodied bistoury on the eve of the dinner, and followed the line of cut hair with a blind hand. But because she was dead, his aunt kept asking him questions, as though vetting a woman he might bring through her own door. (Eliza there – good Christ! – in his aunt's parlour. And when her dress falls away there is nothing under the whalebone but more bone, and then more bones. Eliza falling at his dear aunt's feet in a clatter.)

He stepped into what was left of his broadcloth, and attacked a green and spreading stain that fed on its map of sweat. He unfolded the revers across his chest, for lack of linen, and knotted a rag around the collar to keep it all in place; all the time attempting to answer his aunt in his head.

Eliza's Irishness, for example – was she really Irish? And what kind of Irish, while we were at it? The right kind, Stewart answered, in the main – her manners seemed bred, not learned. Though it was possible she was about as Irish as any woman who wanted to do well in Paris where they thought the Irish *sauvage* and the English only spinsters.

But why should she doubt it? (His aunt was being most vexing.) Of course Eliza was Irish. There was the whole business of those 'laughing eyes'. There was the embarrassing tendency towards politics. An insistence, almost.

141

There was the frankness of her habits; a sometimes comic sense of cunning, which seemed to wander wherever, and tease at a man, particularly at his privates.

And what of it? She is more than all that, he told his dead aunt, as he made his way through the muck – she is also Eliza.

Her house was a lantern. A low, ordinary bungalow, quite large; instead of walls there were curtains of canvas hanging from the eaves. The lights glowed through the greased cotton until the whole shallow cube seemed to float in front of a man's eyes: particularly if he was hungry. If he was very hungry, the place seemed to dance and recede, and then it seemed to be in front of his nose and very bright, just a little bit too soon.

A man might push aside the flap of the door as Saladin entering his pavilion, or Genghis Khan his Mongolian yurt. Stewart swept the canvas aside and stepped into the 'hall'. He had brought a copy of Suetonius for Eliza to read, but thought it, of a sudden, all wrong, and slipped it, quietly, on to the card table as he waited to be shown through. The inner walls were also cloth and he followed an embroidered scene down to the dining room; a little miracle fashioned from curtains and tapestry and painted cotton.

'Welcome to my field tent,' said Eliza, with a wave at the vaguely billowing walls, and she walked with a frank affection towards him, raising her hand for the kiss. Then she turned and swept him towards the other men.

'Doctor Stewart,' she said.

It was a small group. Paulino Alén, the Caballeros, Bernardino and Pedro – what might be called the coming men, though the truth was that they were the only men left. Paulino Alén was a boy, and there was something embarrassing about this: his snot-nosed gravitas, his beautiful clear skin. He ran an abrupt hand on the seat of his pants, then held it out. Stewart, quite moved, shook it, then turned to peruse the cloth along the walls. Among the drapes of Pompeian-red and soft olive was the same green as poor, timid, Whytehead's curtains – perhaps Eliza got them from the same warehouse; there were so few in Asunción. Then he saw the tassels, and the thought occurred to Stewart that she might have taken them from Whytehead's own windows, after he died.

A cage of stuffed birds! When there were so many living ones in the swamp beyond the walls. They were not the exotic birds you might trap on your rooftop here, but – even more exotic – birds such as you might find at home. A startled sandpiper chirping its alarm, a pheasant picking up one claw to run. A very Highland theme. The cloth spread beneath was a new tartan, in a wonderful close pattern of turquoise and yellow and grey. Eliza was turning him into a woman, it seemed. Stewart wanted to run the cloth along his cheek; he wanted to stuff it inside his jacket against the skin of his chest. He wanted to *have* this piece of cloth, and love it, and take care that it should not be torn.

'Ah, you have seen my birds,' she said. 'Do they not remind you of home?'

'So much,' he said.

He thought she should have offered the birdcage to him then, so he could refuse it and beg the cloth instead. But she did not.

Why should she? She owned it.

A knocking announced Il Mariscal López – as ever formal when entering the house of Eliza Lynch.

'Let him in,' she said to the servant, who lifted the flap for the Dictator to walk through. After which theatre, he looked a little silly. He was always smaller than you remembered him to be.

López kissed the hand of his consort, then waved for them all to sit down. You could not oblige a soldier to wait, these days, when the smell of cooking was in the air. As the chairs were pushed in under them, a figure slipped into the place beside Stewart.

'Late, Pancho,' said Eliza. 'You must always be late.'

'Sorry, Mama.'

He was sitting beside the Little Colonel, and this made Stewart's pleasure complete. They were all so fond of the boy. His eyes were the lightest green you might see this side of the Atlantic; so green as to look quite blind in strong light. The blankness of them was almost decadent. The lurking passivity of his youth and the slowly blinking lashes made a man think about women's eyes; ask what they were doing – so modest and yet knowing – in the middle of a boy's face.

But he was a boy – there was no doubt about that – as precious and wild. He was also a National Thing, being, one day, the reason why they had all fought this war. And as such he was already glowering at Alén who, quite wisely, examined his cutlery and did not look back.

There was quite a lot to examine. When Stewart caught Alén's eye, he tapped the outermost of five forks, to the boy's hidden relief. If the truth be told, Stewart only knew what three of them were for: meat, fish and pastry – even this act of identification made his mouth indecently water. He reached for a glass and faltered, at which Eliza's manservant leaned out of the darkness and, with a whisper almost sexual in its tact and generosity, called the glasses out to him. 'Water, Chambertin, Latour, champagne.' Then he withdrew.

Stewart sought, and found, the Little Colonel's eyes of mineral green.

'Any good shooting, these days?'

He was about to weep. It was possible he was weeping already. He looked at the boy speaking to him and did not hear a word that came from his young mouth. Perhaps because she understood, Eliza served, almost at once, not a soup, but a camp stew such as they were used to of manioc and meat. A good one. There was a terrible silence as they fell to. After which incontinence, the meal proper was possible, in all its ritual loveliness: soup, salad, fish, game, meat. The salad was a little 'Indian', and the fish was the usual fish bombed out of the river, but it was fresher than Stewart was used to, being snatched from under the snouts of Brazilian guns, and it looked up at him from a *sauce à l'estragon*. All in all the food made him feel quite patriotic. The bird was local game, shot before it reached the enemy guns. The leg of pork was a gift, Eliza said, from someone grateful, and the chocolate mousse was particularly colonial and fine, being made straight from the cocoa bean. But as for the last dish – that last fork sitting so mysteriously on its silver rest – when the last dish came they all cheered. *Sorbet de cassis.* How did she do it?

It was a dream. Sometime during the fish Stewart woke briefly to see, rising above the glittering crowd of cruets and epergnes, a centrepiece of flowers and – could those be grapes? It looked as beautiful and familiar as another life – a life he might have led but had not. And he wondered where it had got to, and who was living it now – Stewart's other life that was intimate with such flowers, strewn with them: purple, orange and blue, they gathered the shadows into their moist hearts, and he found himself sinking his face into the colours and the scent. And then, of course, he was doing no such thing. He was eating a whole fish, and the fish had an amused look in its dead eye and he was talking about Scotland, trying perhaps to claim for himself that piece of new tartan, with its overlapping squares of yellow and turquoise and grey.

Over the pork, he seemed to mention his aunt, but he must have forgotten to say that she was dead, or that she was his aunt, because Eliza was laughing. The pork had very hairy crackling, and it was most distracting – perhaps he had been witty, all unawares.

'Oh, the English,' said Eliza. 'The English have no mothers. They grow like cabbages in a garden: they are entirely self-generated. Or if they have such a thing as a mother, it is always a matter of furniture. "I am expecting my mother's furniture" or "This armoire, do you like it? It belonged to my mother." Behind every Englishman there is a woman in a mob-cap surrounded by lumps of walnut and mahogany, and completely beside the point. Frenchmen – now their mothers write novels, or burn novels in their drawing room grate, their mothers are distinguished lovers, or know how to mend a clock that has not ticked since 1693. A Spanish mother is an object of terror, an Italian's mother an object of piety absolute, but an Englishman's mother ... mob-cap, a little needle-work, and a Queen Anne writing table of oak inlaid with yew.'

Stewart was comfortable with none of this. He was not English. He was about to remonstrate – he was quite strongly moved to it – when he remembered that he was not wearing any linen, so instead of banging the table and shouting, he brought his clenched hand up to his mouth, and cleared his throat,

'You are too harsh, Madame Lynch,' he said.

'I am delighted to hear it,' said Eliza. 'We Celts have enough reason for harshness, we must not renegue.'

It was becoming clear to Stewart that he had missed some essential link in the conversation. Or perhaps it was not just this conversation, but all conversations. Perhaps he would not be fit for society, ever again. Something about this prospect seemed disastrous to him. So,

'And what of the Irish mother?' he bravely said.

'The Irish? Oh we eat them,' said Eliza. 'You should see it. We start at the toes and leave nothing out.'

146

They all looked at the pork, and there was a small silence, into which Pancho, for some reason, cheered.

'Diabolito,' said his mother, while Stewart's mind nibbled along the legs of some poor woman to arrive at a most unthinkable place. The woman was, of course, Eliza, but it was also, a little, his poor rotten aunt, or the clean bones of his long-dead mother, and Stewart felt the violence of it so keenly he wanted to shout 'Whore!' or some other desecration. 'Irish bitch!' was the phrase that sprang to mind. How strange, he thought. And useless. How could he explain to Paulino Alén, or to any of them, that this woman came of an irksome race?

Then the sorbet appeared, and Stewart tried not to groan aloud as he ate. Through all the meal, not one word had been uttered about the war or their current situation, and the dull splashes of shot landing in faraway mud were, when you remembered to listen out for them, almost pleasant to the ear.

Then López pushed back his chair.

'Señor,' he said to the boy Alén, with mock formality, and Eliza stood to allow them retire. They went to a table in the corner, where a map was unrolled while Pancho's eyes grew wide with rage and pleading.

'You must come with me, Doctor,' Eliza said. 'While Pancho has his war. You must keep me company and pretend to listen to my pulse.'

'A pleasure,' he said. He offered his arm, hinging it stiffly from the shoulder like an old man. As they left they paused for López to kiss his mistress's hand. And it really was like being in bed with the two of them, the way they looked each other in the eye. The galvanic charge of madness from López (for he was quite mad) made Stewart feel quite dizzy. But Eliza seemed to like it, or soothe it, or take it in – at any rate she looked straight at it, as though she would quite like to bed it, by and by.

'Coffee!' she said into the air in front of her, and she walked on – dragging Stewart a little, who had some difficulty getting past the pathetic piece of tartan under the bird cage, his desire for it still shamed him so.

For a moment, in the small space that was Eliza's reception room, Stewart felt the burden of future conversation. What could he say to this woman? She was too large and he was too tired.

She walked a little away from him, and begged him to sit. Then she paused. Then she walked back to join him, and turned her head a little away as she sank into the matching chair. There was a silence; it seemed easy enough, but a bubble of misery rose quickly to the surface, and broke with,

'You know, Doctor, I am immensely weary of it all.'

'Of the war?'

'No. Of this, my dear Doctor. Of all this.' She turned and indicated, it seemed, her own skirts – unless it was the floor she was pointing to; the Aubusson blue of the rug that toned so strangely well with the beige of the mud floor. She swept her hands wide and then let them fall into her lap. Then she lifted her face to his with a gaze that might well have been called 'radiant and sad'.

'I am immensely weary, Doctor, of being Eliza Lynch.'

Ambushed again, thought Stewart, as the urge to free her came over him, not from the mud or the bullets – though these played their part, as he threw her over the pommel of an imaginary horse and rode her out of there. No, he would grab her and kiss her and take her most violently, and in so doing release her, not from the war, nor the world, but from the terrible prison of herself. This hair, these clothes, this high and graceful look. Come with me and we will simply live. There will be butterflies in the meadow, and so on. Christ, he was tired.

She picked herself off the chair to trail a little across the room. Her dress was the most beautiful thing he had seen for a long time – if you did not count the sunset that daily broke his half-mended heart. It was green. What kind of green Stewart could not say. Green that bristled with a silvery light, there in the dark room. She picked up a photograph of López, then set it down again and drifted on. She had sunk, Stewart realised, at least three bottles of champagne. Eliza always was a hearty girl.

'I work quite hard you know,' she said.

'I know that,' he said.

'At table for example, I work quite hard to keep it smooth, and I am not looking for admiration, Doctor, not so much – but these bitter little looks and the sentences that creep out of people's faces, these Ungenerosities, when I have waded through hail and fire to put an acceptable something on the table in front of them. The centrepiece – those careless flowers in their urn – I copied from an oil by Jensen, the Dane. The work, Doctor. The work! And why do I do it? I do it for love. And high endeavour. I do it so that we should not always be so *small*, and it is vulgar of me to say so, Doctor, but pearls before swine is one thing, at least the swine don't despise the pearls, the way these men despise me.'

'My dear lady,' said Stewart, surprised by her nonsense. 'You are beginning to sound like . . .' He was going to say 'my wife', but he skipped, quite quickly, to, 'a quite ordinary woman'.

For one gaping moment Stewart thought he was drunk. Then he remembered that it was the war that made him feel like this; the war and this room within the war; this house – a bowl of light like a diamond in mud, or a diamond, even, in some man's turd – and he had some memory of a man with his belly slit – or was it the entire length of his intestine? – he had a memory of a man, at any rate, with a jewel inside him at Curupaití, or Tuiutí, or Curuzú, or in a dream he had right here in Humaitá, a dream of difficulty and kidney stones and something astonishingly beautiful, precious and hard, that was deep inside a man. Which was when he lurched awake to find Eliza still talking; the murmur of her husband's voice in the next room a hushed counterpoint. No time had passed at all.

'Why should I not sound ordinary, Doctor,' Eliza was saying. 'I am ordinary. I am ordinary *as well*.'

'As well as what?' he rudely asked. Well, she had woken him, after all.

'As well as a whore?' he might have said – but who cared these days? They were all meat. (Though could 'meat' be said to sleep, as he now needed to sleep, and was it not the blissful thing about Eliza, after all, that she was absolutely meat, and absolutely not meat at the same time, which is to say, a woman, as opposed to a potential corpse? This whirligig of philosophy taking no time at all in his head, or just exactly the time a man needed to shut his eyes and open them again, which is an eternity, or about as long as a blink.)

'As well as being the First Lady of Paraguay,' said Eliza, her voice a little hurt, and proud.

'Of course,' he said.

'But they would hate me anyway, I think. Honestly. You might as well be in Ireland. You might as well be in Mallow – where I grew up you know – a bitter town, it made my mother weep – but we all come from bitter towns, do we not, Doctor? Every unfortunate on the surface of this earth comes from some or other bitter little town.'

He could not but agree.

And as he slept and woke for the next while (sometimes while looking straight at her) she continued to speak. She was most eloquent, though she had the disconcerting habit of suddenly appearing in a different place in the room.

'My dear friend's greatness is a burden to him,' she might say.

Or,

'All I want is to be with my family at this terrible time.'

The surprising thing was that she meant it. Here in the middle of everything, she was talking about nothing at all.

'You know that I came to Humaitá to escape his brother's contempt, and the contempt of his mother and sisters in Asunción. That is why I came to the field of battle, even though I was with child at the time. Because real bullets are as nothing to me when compared to the slights I suffer at the hands of those women. I came to tell him as much. I found him and flung myself at his feet.'

Stewart woke. He sensed a conclusion in the air.

'For every enemy that he has, I have two, because for every man that hates him there is another who says that whatever he does it is at my urging; because a woman's ambition is a fathomless thing – as though I was some witch who hexed him into my bed, and whispered, "You must, my darling, invade the Mato Grosso before the spring." And so we suffer, Doctor. A woman has no limits, because she may not act. She is all reputation, because she may not act. So, even as we do nothing, our reputations grow more impossible, and fragile, and large.'

This seemed to him partly true, though a little bit dull. To say that women were beside the point always struck him as being – well, beside the point, somehow.

'My dear Eliza,' he said.

She paused. She had let herself down. And feeling it keenly, she tried to make him hers again. Stewart was entirely awake as she turned to him with ardent, very female eyes.

'We have come a long way together, William Stewart – you and I. Sometimes I wonder how we got here, at all.'

There was a lot to disagree with in what she had said. He might start with the word 'we'. He might point out that, though they were together in this room, they had 'arrived', each of them, in very different places. And he had a huge yearning for the life he might have led – a life that was familiar with flowers and unfamiliar with Eliza Lynch. But as he tried to enter it, and imagine it, he found he could not. Whatever life he was living now, it was the only one he had got, and it was bound, however loosely, to this irritating woman. He could not conjure one without her.

'At least I have a friend, in you, Doctor. At least I have that.'

He stood rather smartly, and bowed and sat back down again. Perhaps she meant it. Their silence was so profound it drew López at last – he snatched back the door hanging and put his mad face into the room. For a second, Stewart was afraid, but López was not jealous in the least. Such was Stewart's smallness, in the scheme of things. And indeed, Eliza stood and walked towards him as a Great Woman might walk towards a Great Man. At which, Stewart's stomach notified him, of a sudden, that he had eaten more in the last few hours than in all the previous week.

On the way back to his hut, Stewart tried to remember that he was in love with this woman, in a dashing sort of way. He tried to relive the high, more spiritual love he felt when Eliza walked out on her big wheel, with a boy laying a plank in front of her, and another boy snatching one up from behind.

'All love is fuss,' he said, not for the first time, and perhaps out loud. He sought a sight of the moon. And it was there. The moon was white, and he loved Eliza Lynch. Of course, a spiritual love is a question of faith. You say 'I love' and it is as true as mutton. And so we survive.

At the edge of the compound he passed some of the mud-coloured women scrabbling under the door of a shed. It might have been a privy but, from the human whine that came from it, Stewart realised that it was some sort of lock-up or oubliette. The women – there were two of them – were scraping a hole under the door. It looked as though they were trying to feed the person inside. Such generosity, he thought. Such love.

'Goodnight,' he cheerfully said, to the cheerfully saluting sentry. López had his own private prison; another hole where rumour might breed – that he locked up men for Eliza to eat, or that Eliza locked up women for López to ravish, such was the love they had for each other – and with the genderless whine of the prisoner teasing his back, Stewart made his way back downhill and into his bed. And as he fell asleep in his broadcloth – even as he pulled away the rag at his throat – he thought that if he had his war again he would not tear up his last linen to save a dying man. If he had his war again he would treasure his linen – of which there was so little – and leave the dying, of which there were far too many.

A few weeks later, word came that the *Ygureí* was sunk and the *Tacuarí* scuttled by its own crew. Stewart escaped with López across the river into the swamplands, leaving Paulino Alén with a small force to defend Humaitá. The boy had got his promotion. Eliza must have liked him, at dinner.

The River

Part 3

Champagne

December 1854, Río Paraná

WE HAVE ENTERED Paraguay!

Sometime in the afternoon, after long hours spent slapping about this vast puddle, we found the channel. The tan of the water began to grow thin. I did not notice until Whytehead pointed it out to me, but the general muck that we have lived upon for so many days was splitting, by liquid degrees, into the red of the Río Paraná and the clearer grey of the Río Paraguay.

The meeting of the waters. Over to starboard, the red thickened and settled into a streak of colour that clung to the bank, as though some huge painter had cleaned out his brush, far upstream. We were watching this, myself and Whytehead, and being very geological, when my dear friend gave a shout and all the home contingent ran to the rails. They pointed at the rusty discharge that was not yet a separate river, but still a current within the larger stream. And I thought of all the waters of the world, twining themselves in a watery plait like this, on their way down to the sea.

My friend came over to announce that we were approaching friendly territory.

'My country,' he said, and gravely bowed.

I took the moment to talk a little. I pointed to the wash of red in the clear grey. I said that this was the way that we should be, now that the course of our lives had met. I said we should mingle our two watery souls.

He looked over the rail.

'It might be some battle,' I said. 'Or a wounded god, staining the far waters red,' and he blushed almost, at the insistence of my tone. My wrists are bruised with his finger marks, and we are not easy with each other, all day.

'It comes from the far north,' he said. 'From the Mato Grosso and the mountains of Maracaju.' Then,

'When we are old, we will tend our garden there.'

For which I was grateful indeed.

And so the river forked, and in the widening crotch, or so I was told, is the country that I will learn to call home. I looked at the spit of land where it exactly began. Paraguay. It looked like an island in the middle of the river: but from one side of the island came red, and from the other grey, and we chose the grey. And so our path diverged from itself. We were beyond the confluence of the two rivers, and I bid farewell to the Río Paraná, hidden behind the swell of new land. And I said goodbye, too, to the far country it brings to us, spilling into the stream.

Later in the morning, Miltón sidles by to say that the red earth comes from a place without evil. And yes, he says, I was right about the blood. It is indeed blood that comes downstream. Surely not so much, I say, if the place is innocent. He looks at me, and I see the calculations run across his face of how much to say, and how it will be received.

He has taken, my little savage, to telling me things. It is a flattery of sorts – at least I find it so, as he lets something indifferently drop about this daemon or that tree. Of course he is young. I tell him that he is a very leaky Indian. If he keeps talking he will leak all his soul away.

And now, my dear friend's country is on the right-hand bank, while, to the left, a grey swamp sheers flatly from us, all the way to the horizon's line. Sometimes it lies quite low, this flatness: other times, the whole plane of it seems to rise up and bisect the sky. The effect is quite distracting. I tell Miltón to sling the *hamaca* the other way, so I might look at the other bank, and this he does, quite solemnly, unstringing and gathering it, and turning it and hanging it up again, while I stand there and look at him. Then I see the futility of it, and laugh. It is very dull to be this stupid, it is very wearing, and it puts me to endless trouble. Still, Francine hands me into the about-faced sling while Miltón stands proud enough – as though the pointless west-to-east of it had given him some satisfaction, too.

And so I lie, watching, now, the right-hand bank: which is Paraguay. It is indeed an Arcady, as my friend promised; all wild orange groves, and 'bosky glens'. It looks soft. You can see the mist hang on distant forests and the hills are quite medieval, in their trackless pastoral. Endless and ancient, and waiting for the story to begin.

'Tell me about your daemons,' I say to Miltón. 'Are they very bad?'

'They are big,' he says.

'How big? As big as a jaguar, as big as a tree?'

'Not big like that,' he says, after a while. 'They are big like a song is big.'

They are like a song, which you cannot hear – except that sometimes you *can* hear it. They are in the shape of things, but they have no shape. I tell him that he is a very philosophical Indian. He says that, actually, some of them *are* as big as a jaguar. And they look like a jaguar, and all the rest of it. It seems I have insulted him then, because he wanders off and I must coax him back with a smile.

Later, I tell my dear friend all this, and he gives me a sharp look – not annoyed, just close. And I feel, once again, that he knows me to the bone.

But since we have entered his own country, there is a kind of innocence to him, an ease and an urgency. He wants to be doing things. He wants to get things done.

We come in sight of Humaitá; a busy little place, with a bright Spanish church gleaming on the hill. My dear friend waves like a boy while the captain blows the whistle and a bright flotilla disentangles itself from the general trade. The sharp canoes run across the water; a shoal of fish, or a litter of boatlets, coming to suckle at our big wooden side. The Indians have decked themselves out with ribbons; they flutter from the ends of their spears, and it all looks very gay and savage. In each prow a man stands easy, with his cloak drifting back; revealing, in each case, his 'all'.

I am a little giddy with it, the sun and the ribbons and all the rest. Who would have thought it? Of all places – who would have thought I might end up here, in this distant spot, looking at so much male flesh, and with such equanimity? Because it is very brown flesh, I tell myself, and, as such, no great insult to my virtue – this last *aperçu* I cannot turn to say, half-laughing, to my dear friend, whose nativeness seems less an affectation now that the sun has licked the white off him. It has, I realise, made him quite black or, at the very least, nut-brown – as brown as the men in the boats; as brown as the faces that peer from between the trees on the bank, so utterly still they seem at one with the bark.

In the canoes, the men wear spurs and hat brims with neither hats nor boots. My dear friend tells me that the spurs are just for decoration; these men have, most of them, never ridden a horse. He seems almost proud of this fact, and it is borne in on me that these are his people and that he loves them, and so I must love them too.

'How funny,' I say.

The hat brims, he says, are all that is left of Francia, the first Dictator, who required the entire country to wear hats so they could be doffed when he passed. Over the years, the hats fell apart, but the brims remain. It is a way of telling the people that they are governed, he says. And I say,

'They will be lifted, some day, for you.'

I look at these naked men, their heads and heels circled with silver and felt, and think them already innocent and lovely. And they do doff the brims; they wave the little circlets in the air, and hulloo.

We receive the Governor of the district in his own parlour – a mismatched little man with a frock coat and nankin pants. He will come with us now, as far as Asunción, but first we must dine in his courtyard, and have speeches, and roast a pig, and all the rest. At dinner, I notice he hides his feet beneath the table and takes off his shoes. Despite which, he is altogether very sonorous and grave.

I take my chance to ask him about Francia – whose name, I realise, has been in the air ever since I met my dear friend. So – gravely, sonorously – he describes a man dressed all in black with a tricorn hat; a man who read Rousseau and Voltaire; a man 'who would be his own revolution, his own guillotine'. When Francia walked out, the streets were empty – all the shutters in Asunción were pulled to. Even the dogs were shot, so they would not bark at him while he rode, like Lady Godiva, through the town. *El Supremo*, they called him. And every fifth man was a spy. He closed the borders and started a nation, which was the nation whose soil we stood on, now. The Spanish colonists were his particular enemy. There would be no such thing as 'pure' blood, he said. From now on, all blood was pure, all blood was Paraguay.

My dear friend, always watchful of my conversation, catches this last, and makes a toast to 'Mixing it all up'.

(He has been swallowing his brandy tonight.) 'Here's to my nigger father, *El Excellentissimo* Carlos Antonio López, and my Creole mother, who is bastard Spanish mixed with any bastard you like.' I check around my little band, to see how they are taking this. Whytehead looks like a duchess who reaches for the sugar bowl, only to find it missing from her tray. Stewart lifts his glass high and gives a heaving hurrah! At which, López leans towards the British to say,

'Don't worry. It is the Spanish who are the canker here, not you.'

Oopsa! And in case he should think me one of them, I say, 'Not like poor Ireland,' with a smirk that seems to offend everyone, even my dear friend.

There has been quite a lot of champagne. To get us over the hump I declare that my dear friend should speak to us of this man Francia, as one statesman of another, and so he stands and gathers himself for an address.

'You could not touch him,' he says, with a sudden frankness. Then he looks down at the table, to score it with a thumbnail. 'The man would not suffer himself be touched. You could not look at him. It was the law. So when he died, no one would approach the corpse. Besides, who could believe that he was dead? He lay there for three days.'

He looks up into the night, and when he speaks again his voice is thick with unshed tears. His own father, he says, had Francia's lanky bones dug up and thrown half-rotting into the river at Asunción. His own father. And it broke his heart to do it.

'My father', he says, 'is the loneliest man in the world.'

And so to bed, where I comfort him from fathers and from men in tricorn hats, and I keep the world, with all its necessary exhumations, at bay.

Dresses for today: in the old empire style.

The Josephine: a high-waisted white muslin frock over

scarlet slip, of utter simplicity, for sitting about, when it
is hot, also for my condition, and for pleasing my dear
friend when he will not be distracted from matters military
– such as all this afternoon with Whytehead; a discourse on
lanyard shooting, and the rifling, or otherwise, of the gun
barrels on the *Tacuarí*. This to be worn with a white lace
veil, almost bridal.

The Josephine *à Visite*: a high-waisted ditto in grey glacé
silk, with a waistcoat bosom, quite masculine, in lilac; to be
worn with long kid gloves of dove grey.

The Corsican: a pelisse in army blue, the shoulders
mock-epaulettes, with a tablier of scarlet, and deep cuffs
of same, for levees, or for reviewing troops, as my friend
proposes; his plans being large and very rationalising. I
am to become their mascot, he says, I am to become their
Higher Thing.

The Sot: my drinking dress. Something green to take
down the flush in my cheeks. When I looked in the mirror
tonight, I found myself pure scarlet.

Also there is a banging now on the inside of the ship; a
thin sound made booming by the river. It comes from so far
below the waterline, it makes my very skull feel hollow.

'What is that?' I finally say, and, getting no answer from
my sleeping friend, I open the door of the stateroom, to find
Valera, the equerry, seated outside. I do not know why he is
sitting outside my door. Or why he is awake. Or whether
he is there to guard or protect. I gather my dignity along
with the front of my open *peignoir*, and enquire in a clear
voice what the matter might be.

There is, he tells me, a prisoner in the hold.

'Who?'

Valera does not so much as glance at my dishabille. With
great reluctance he disgorges himself of the name I require.
It is the Governor of Humaitá.

The little man in the nankin pants? But I saw him come

up the gangway myself and it was Valera who guided him by a drunken elbow to his quarters. So they locked him up. It must have been done on a look or a nod – I saw nothing, at any rate. And now the little fellow has found something to bang – it sounds like a tin cup – and the whole ship is uneasy. Also, I think there is a wind coming, because a faint rolling under my feet makes me feel a little sick.

'Why? What did he do?' But the equerry just looks at me, with something like contempt.

Back in bed, the knocking drives me to distraction: it is as hard to ignore as the moans of the dying sailor were, in their time.

Tock.

Tock.

Tock.

Has he stopped?

Tock.

No. Or, perhaps, yes. He stops, not once but a hundred times. He stops, after each and every knock. Then, after each and every knock, he decides not to stop. He decides to knock one last time.

Some time before dawn, I take courage and go over to where my dear friend lies suspended in the wakeful dark. Perhaps the man should be let free now, I gently say, or at least given enough *caña* to tip him into sleep. At which a clear voice comes out of the darkness where his mouth must be. It suggests that I might want to join the man in the hold – we could have a good time down there, we could discuss some more Voltaire.

'Oh Voltaire,' I bravely say. 'That fool. Everyone in Voltaire has a buttock lopped off and it is always the one on the left. At least the women do. Not one of them left double by the end.'

'Good enough for them,' he says. Then he fights free of his *hamaca* to stamp across to the door.

'Tell him to stop that noise, or he will be shot.'

Valera, or some rat of a sailor, scurries off in the dark, and a little while later all is still.

Later again, I wake to find my dear friend disappeared. There is a low, urgent noise from the next room – the one that leads on to the deck. Someone is talking. I realise that I am trapped here. I think that Valera is behind it all – squatting like that outside my door. I think my friend usurped – dead! his body already floating out behind us, a ragged thing on the flat river. The voice goes on, and the tone is so conspiratorial I am afraid to open the door. I press my cheek against the wood and ease the latch and, on a breath, break open a crack to see who the new masters of my fate might be.

The first thing I see, by the flare of an oil lamp, is the face of my dear friend, as the Spaniard Goya might have done it, all brown and livid in the smoking yellow light. There are two crystal schooners of brandy in front of him; pushed away and half-full. López buries his face in his hands. He raises his head again. He is, I see, talking to the little Governor. He turns to him, and then away. He lifts his hand and brushes his fingers together; clicks them, once, twice, in the man's face. He holds, briefly, the bridge of his own nose and says something with quiet emphasis, as though for the hundredth time; his eyes still closed. The Governor says nothing: his face is completely still, and somewhat ecstatic, and wet with tears.

The child has not moved since four in the afternoon. I should not have stayed with the dying sailor. I know it. Or perhaps it is the champagne.

*

I do not think he sleeps. When I wake, he is already gone, but he comes back in with my morning chocolate, to kiss me where I lie. He picks up my forearm, and looks at the marks his fingertips left there. Then he is up and away.

No breakfast. Later I watch him from behind my muslin veils, stalking the deck. There is always something to be pounced upon, worried at, cleaned or polished or heaved overboard. And none of it, it seems, has anything to do with me.

'We are in Paraguay now,' he says, when I ask him to take a little lunch with me – meaning 'I am busy', meaning 'This is who I am. I have come into my own.'

And so I lie weeping and plotting indoors and sleep all afternoon. And yet I am not abandoned. When I wake, heavy with dreams, I see he has come to sit and perhaps to look at me awhile. He is there in the chair, staring at the floor, his eyes agape at some dull horror. But when I stir he looks up and, quite naturally, smiles.

'How is the boy?'

'Good,' I say. 'Your little wrestler.'

And then he heaves himself up, and is gone.

He is so impatient with me, now. I do not know what he wants. Oh I know he wants me to choose, in the morning, what clothes he will wear. He wants me to speak French with him. He wants me to tell him about Voltaire. But more than that. He wants me to twist some knife in him, and I do not know where, or in what wound.

There is something wrong now, over and above what is usually wrong – what will never be right – with him. There is a bargain: there is some bargain I must keep, and when he looks at me I try to remember what it is. I knew it once but have forgotten. He wants something. It may be something small. It may be the pivot. Of course – he wants the maid. Let him have her then. If that is all. What is it to me?

I have Miltón bring me back to my *hamaca*, but she comes running, to help me in – and a large business it is, as we take each other by the shoulders and grapple, until I, safely, fall.

'Stay with me,' I say. And she sits on a little folding stool by my side.

The maid. She has a good enough profile, quite pure, in the way that simple faces sometimes are. A hidden saint. Her father is a dolt and her mother a whore, and there she is – my clever girl Francine. The tricks that she knows. The secrets she has been obliged since youth to keep. Which is why she was for me such a very excellent maid.

Sent by Dolores the Spaniard because she was getting too pretty. And I looked at her, and thought her perfectly fine, and not too pretty at all. 'I will call you Francine,' I said, and she bobbed a little and was pleased to be hired.

I wonder what her given name is.

'What's your name?' I say.

'Why, Francine, ma'am.' She seems perfectly surprised by the question. And so I let it go.

Now that she is beside me, my dear friend comes as far as my pavilion on his endless round, and he bows on the turn. Beside me, I feel her prickle and go still. And by the fourth or fifth turn I am bored by it – but massively so – and I tell her to go inside.

I want to tell the silly girl that she might get a marriage out of it, as M. Raspail married me to Quatrefages. And even though this is not Paris, it still might be done. The equerry Valera might suit, or someone a little lower down. Though any hopes of Whytehead are perhaps now gone.

'Would you like to know how I got married?' I say as she folds up the stool. She looks up from her crouch.

'Why yes, ma'am.'

But I find I cannot do it. 'Another time,' I say.

She leaves, and I lapse into a greedy silence. And so the ship ploughs on, while I rehearse my woes.

He wants the maid.

Dressing for dinner, I am so overcome by the tedium of it all, I must chuck the string of pearls on to the table in front of me. The maid absents herself, as does the valet, and my friend comes over to fasten the string himself. We watch one another in the mirror.

I say I will not have the equerry Valera about me, I do not like the look of him. My friend says he is a very effective young man, and I say that I do not care how effective he is, I do not want him outside my door at night, because I don't like his long nose and the way he looks down it, at me.

He says, in that case, he will have him flogged.

'For what?'

'For impudence, my love.'

But that is not it, either.

I turn from the mirror and stand. I am close to tears now. I want to run away from him, but there is nowhere to go. He takes me by the shoulders, and looks at me, and shakes me a little – tenderly. Then he slips his palm along the length of my arm to find my hand, which he touches, holds, and lifts for a kiss: all the while fixing me with a stare.

And his eyes promise everything.

I want to sneer. But this is not a vulgar bargain. It is an invitation. He is inviting me to join him in his life – his impossible life, where the sky is more blue, and the grass more green, where you can have things just by taking them. He is telling me to hold my nerve. He is saying that if I hold my nerve, like him, then I can have anything I want.

'Francine!' I call her back.

When she comes in, López squeezes past her in the narrow doorway and makes a clicking noise with his tongue. Then he is gone.

The room is so small. The maid looks at me, then she tucks her head down and strikes out for the dressing table, but I halt her where she is. I tell her to stand so I can look at her, and she fumbles one hand in the other, while I take my fill.

She is seventeen. She has already one child, dead or abandoned, and the marks must be under there somewhere, to prove it. I pull the hair behind her ear to check for lice eggs. I want to slap her, but instead I point to the soap and say, as I leave the room,

'Wash.'

It is very nice soap. Attar of roses.

I can not smell it off her, when she comes through after dinner. Perhaps she does not like attar of roses. This annoys me. It puts me in a perfect rage.

And so we sit for cards.

'And what are the stakes, tonight?' asks Stewart. 'Another story? A kiss?'

So he can sense it, too. Francine does not even blush. My friend leans back from the table and casually gropes for the decanter behind him. I bustle around and serve him myself. I say it is too dull – Mr Whytehead is to blame; we must play for money, because what is an evening without the promise of ruin? I turn to my dear friend and I say, 'You must give Mr Whytehead more money, my dear, so that he can overcome his scruples and play. (I think I am a little drunk.) Or give the maid money, at least, so we can have a proper game.'

It seems I have stumbled on a solution. And a charming one at that. My friend looks at me, and lifts his glass. And so he is pleased with me, at last.

'Here's to the generosity of Madame Lynch.'

And he shouts through the open door for, 'Money!'

We play just as we were some nights ago. My friend looks at his hand in easy contemplation. Stewart is massive again, heaving and glowering over two hearts and a spade. Across the table, Whytehead leans stiffly in, over the shoulder of the trembling maid.

From time to time, he whispers. And once, he points.

So at least I have some pleasure. To see the girl hazard more than she could earn in a year. To see her handle it – the heft and clink of it in her palm, the gathering feel of the metal rims as they slither into a column between finger and thumb, which she then sets down on the baize. The hand withdrawn. So careful.

I can see a vein flutter on her neck.

I know money. I know the value of, for example, three hundred pounds – how a maid could live a lifetime on such a sum, how my father could live a month, how my mother might have raised her children on it for more than a year. I burned a note, once, that belonged to Mr Bennett. A fifty. I said to him, as I did it, 'This afternoon, I think I'll love you for free.'

These are the things I could tell the maid as she makes a timorous throw into the centre of the table, and then flinches when one of the coins begins to roll. I could tell her, as she loses, hand after hand, a modest dowry – which is to say, a life; a husband, a child she might keep – that money is the least of it, my dear.

And my goodness, she does lose. It takes a little over an hour. It takes a minute at a time. Whytehead leans over her shoulder, his superior mind in a welter of calculation, and is no use to her. Stewart, who bets promissory notes on his future salary, takes her money too. He reaches over and pulls it across the baize: once, twice. He takes it five times or more. The solid fact of it goes into his pocket when the game is done. Which it is done when the maid has nothing left to lose.

'I have the best of it, tonight, it seems,' says Stewart, all good humour – as though she might get it back from him, another time. Then he makes his way to the decanter, with ponderous regret. But his hand trembles, as he pours.

My dear friend smiles, and excuses himself to smoke outside. No one follows him. Perhaps because they were not asked. But still – Stewart, who eats cigars, who has a passion for them, runs a finger over the cut of the crystal in his glass. Whytehead, who sticks so religiously to my husband's side, has, it seems, finally become unglued. And it amazes me again, how we make way for other people's desire.

Even I am unmanned by it, until I say,

'You may go.'

She picks herself up and she walks, not towards the stateroom where my clothes need laying out for the night, but into the open air.

He is not my husband. Of course he is not. I must train my turn of phrase. The man who is not my husband comes back fifteen minutes later – I have counted it by the clock. His cigar is still lit, though now it is a stub that he chucks, unceremoniously, out the porthole window on the far side of the room.

'And why is it', I ask, 'that a man must come inside to fire the butt of his cigar through a window, when he has the whole vast river to throw it into, over the rail?' I say that he must have the satisfaction of the porthole, because men must always be throwing things; but more than that, they must be aiming them too – and the smaller the target, or in this case the hole, the better.

Everyone laughs. My friend looks at me with a new admiration. And I quite frankly meet his eye. It is as though we have done this thing together. And this makes me feel lonely and quite giddy, both at the same time.

Later, Francine comes to unlace me in the dark. I have fallen asleep in a chair, because to lie down seems to strangle the child, or strangle me, one or the other. So she whispers quite close to me and heaves me a little forward to get at the hooks and then the stays.

I groan a little. And, in my sleep-weakened state, all I can think of is the closeness of her belly to me and the hope that there is not a child in her too. I can smell him off her, and this makes me gag a little. Because in the bargain, whatever it was, there was nothing agreed about smell.

And then she has me undressed and under the bedclothes, free of my corset, and happy as a boiled egg, all peeled.

In the middle of the night, I stir and find he is not yet come to bed. It is some time before I remember why this might be, and when I do I am awake and raging. He must not sleep with her. These hours, I think, are meant to punish. And, if so, he will be punished in return. Because he has started the wrong game here. He has started a small game and I am hugely, wildly bored by the small game. I was not sure I wanted to play, but if needs must, then I will play big.

Such is my ambition, in the middle of the night.

I hear the darkness breathe and stir; an animal close to my ear. I never sleep alone. I had Francine crawl in with me in Paris, when there was no man in the bed (I can hardly call for her, now). Because there was always my sister and, when my sister bolted, there was any number of girls at Mme Hubert's. The first, the only, nights I spent alone were in that inn, when Mr Bennett brought me to Paris.

Or did not bring me to Paris. He was sick with something like grief – stiff with it, in the corner of the post we took. It was as though his back would not bend into the angle of the seat. He looked at me while I gazed out the window or played with the cards I had in a little walnut box; clever things – three children playing with their kites made up the three of hearts, I remember; though all the ones I turned were spades, with women weeping, and skeletons.

'Your fate,' I said, flicking them into Mr Bennett's poor lap – mostly to amuse the man who shared the post with us, a fat fellow with a glazed eye. Mr Bennett was, by that time, so maddened by the presence of men around me that it turned the ends of his fingers blue, and I hoped he would not die before we got to Paris, which is to say, before my fortune was made. I was fourteen. We passed though Orléans and I could smell Paris on the road. I could see the smoke of it ahead of us; there was a smudge of Paris on the clear blue sky.

We stopped a night in Artenay, and Mr Bennett, out of jealousy, I thought, locked me in my room. I do not know when he left. He may have stayed to take some supper. The innkeeper had instructions for me to stay where I was – the bill was already paid.

This I found out in the morning, after a night of horror. Then another. And a third. They left me like that, as you might lock up a dog; the better it will love the man who sets it free. I think about it still. I had money – quite a lot of money – in my trunk and variously hidden in my clothes. I was not, after the first night, locked in. And still I craved the rescuing knock. And then it came.

It was the fat man who took the post with us. His name was M. Raspail.

The baby turns. If it is a girl, I will drown it, that is all.

Not that there is anything so terrible about Raspail. He was protracted, endlessly so, in his pleasures, and very private – he would never, for example, let me witness the spasm, if there was one, which I sometimes doubt. But he was clever, and always turned my strength against me. And I am disgusted still, by the thought of his hands.

So, if it is a girl, I will drown it.

I do not believe in the baby any more. Stuck in me now like a ship in a bottle: it is too big. It will kill me on the way out. Either way, I do not think that I can love it, which is all to the good. My poor mother suffered from excessive love of her babies, so when she lost them her health went too. 'Wait,' she seems to say to me now. 'Do not love it when it is small. Do not love it when it suckles. Do not suckle it. Do not allow it by you until it is weaned, and then not for any length of time. You may start to love it when it toddles over to your skirts. You may love it a little more when it starts to talk. But you must not actually love it, until it walks away from you, into the wide world. Safe. Arrived. Alive.' Poor Mama. Poor Adelaide Schnock. So blonde and Saxon-stupid, offering *tisane* in her little china cups to the unbelieving rakes of Mallow.

In the morning, I hear my dear friend try the door. There is a long silence when he finds that is locked. I wait for the sound of his receding footsteps or a shot fired on the lock; an axe through the walnut or the sound of running men. I wait for his pleading, or the sound of his body abjectly sliding down the wood. I feel his silence. I test it and match it with a silence of my own; longer, more indifferent.

I slide a stiletto blade through the keyhole. All the way through.

I will always sleep alone, now. I will fend off my ghosts how I may. And in this way he will never be able to walk away from me, he will only be able to approach my door.

I pull back the knife. He knocks. I open up the door and smile.

Later, I go out to my *hamaca*, and the maid appears in

order to wrestle me into the net. I do not even bother to check her face.

I heard a woman say once that birth was like falling asleep – being just as simple and mysterious. Who could tell you what it is like to fall asleep? So when my baby draws his first breath I will know what some insomniac angel knows when it wakes for the first time. 'So that is what it is all about. So that is what we crave.'

I lie in my tent and lift the thin curtain and say, 'Miltón,' and he runs to my side.

'Miltón, I hear him shouting. Will you see what your Master wants?' The boy gives me a steady look and spits as he walks away. The whole world insults me, I think, and then I close my eyes and think no more.

Coffee

1869, Paraguay

THE CARRIAGE WAS an old-fashioned Spanish affair, high and closed, and the blackest thing you ever saw. Black as obsidian. It was the black of ten coats of lacquer, maybe more, and though a black coach wasn't in itself remarkable, this one unsettled the eye by being unrelieved by any other glint or colour – leathers, harness, bit, all so deep a black you might fall into it. The wheels, it was said, were made of iron, and you would swear the glass in the windows was black, if such a thing were possible – it looked as though she rode behind a widow's veil, as though coal dust had been mixed in with the glass. Perhaps it was the ordinary difficulty of seeing inside a place so lambently dark: the seats gleaming, the dangling fringes of jet, the cushions of black silk embroidered on black. It was some kind of witticism; one that no one but Eliza could understand. 'I wanted it *black*,' she said, and laughed.

The horses were so black they would run in your dreams. Though there was a flowering of pink where sores had erupted, veined and flyblown from the thickness of their hides. They pulled a heavy load. The trunks were packed with jewels and gold plate – there was no doubt about that. There were diamonds slipped into the stuffing of the seats, the cushions might rattle if you shook them, and under Eliza's own crinoline was a curved, fireproof box filled to the lid with American mining shares. Or so they said.

Sometimes they thought of the heat in there. Eliza rode with her mistress of the robes, the widow of General Díaz. The Little Colonel, Pancho, sat up beside the coachman, and strapped himself upright in case he should fall asleep, or loosed his ties in case of attack.

And, with a guard in front of it and an assorted rabble behind, the carriage proceeded north and east. They were going where the light was thin: soldiers and prisoners, travelling shopkeepers, some mad people, girls with babies in their arms; they followed the high, bow-sprung box, as it lurched and bobbed over tree roots and stones. They carried it over streams, levered it out of swamps, coaxed and rolled and rescued each sharp iron wheel of it, pressing their cheeks, as they did so, into ten coats of lacquer. And not once did she open the door.

Sometimes they forgot there was anyone inside. When night fell and camp was set, she would step out, and she looked just like herself: but during the day the changing landscape played changing tricks on their minds, so as they moved from rock to high grass, as they reached a ridge, or rounded a spur, a man might think that he had been in this place before – perhaps as recently as yesterday – or he might think that his life had slipped forward somehow, that he had moved into another day, or another week, and no one to tell him where the lost time had gone.

One evening she stepped out of the carriage with a newborn baby, and it might have been her child or the child of the widow Díaz for all the sound they had heard. Whatever woman gave birth in there did so in silence, like a Guaraní woman, who knows better than to shout. The father made up for it. When Eliza held it up to him, López took the child and, holding the naked thing over his head, he galloped down the straggling line, hullooing and making the horse veer and swerve. So the child was his, then, they smiled to say – though that still did not answer the question of who the mother might be.

Stewart had not attended this birth either, but he was called upon to pass a nurse for the baby, which obliged him to check the breasts and teeth of three clamouring women – together with their clamouring babies who seemed to know it was their birthright that was being bargained away. As it happened, the teeth were bad and their milk too little and too thin, so he set the lot of them on a cart at the end of the cortège, passing the infant from one dug to the next, until a girl wandered out of the trees with a dead baby in her arms, and dripping. When he saw her standing there in the dappled light, Stewart felt a spreading stain on his own chest, as though he had been shot – but when he looked down, there was nothing there.

He was always being shot, these days. He was following his own hearse through the hills for the longest funeral a man had ever known. It had started indecently early, before his corpse had even a chance to climb into the coffin, and it was getting away from him now, the mourners, the horses, his own death. At other times he was following a London cab, and might hail it, if he had half an English crown. And once, it looked like a hat, Stewart thought, an enormous hat, worn by some tiny man, who sang and waggled his head, as he pranced ahead of them down the endless grass road.

After the coach, came the carts. The first cart was for her clothes: it was stacked with leather boxes, twenty of them or more, and all with some sad blue growth creeping out of the seams. The next cart was for her piano which was roped down in its upright, playing position and covered again with a red toile; a vast sheet of careless shepherds and pretty shepherdesses on their swings – also a small dog, endlessly rampant and yapping, and all of them repeated and folding into themselves from one end of the shroud to the other. After this, a cart for servants and younger sons, then food. Finally, a closed wagon for the mother and two sisters of López – which looked like a cage, since the awning had rotted from its wicker arch. The López women sat on sacks of manioc flour and beans as they lurched along. 'I am pissing in your soup,' Il Mariscal's mad mother was reported to have cried. 'I am pissing in the soup of every man here.'

She might look a while for men – there were few enough of them: there were families, and the scraps of families; widows and orphans. There were the remnants of men, who made up the army now. And every so often, it was true, there were men. They turned up. You saw them, squatting beside the morning fire, in their spurs and hat brims, the male contents of some village who had joined their quest – for it was hard to call it a war any more, or even a fight. And yet it was not nothing. It was the last battle, said Bernardino Caballero, a man who had seen enough last battles, you might think, to give him some inkling of when a war might end.

Or even, thought Stewart, of where the ending might have begun. At Angostura, perhaps, where the gallant Captain Thompson walked over to the enemy and handed up his sword. Or later, on the Azcurra heights, after yet another last battle: twenty thousand Brazilians against a battalion of women and children, with beards on their faces made of grass and wool; the new capital (a poor enough town) Peribibuí lost. After that, Acosta Nu, held to the last minute by Caballero, so that López might escape to San Estanislao – another 'capital city', this one lost without a bullet shot. Curuguatí, then eastwards to the heights of Panadero. All of these places boldly marked on a map that López had – though Stewart could point until his arm was sore at this far place or that, waiting for a Guaraní to lend him its name.

After the carts and wagons came certain prisoners who were never shot. They comprised the life story of Francisco López. Some woman he wanted. Some woman he did not want. A man who scorned him. The son of the sister of the man who betrayed them to the Brazilians at Curupaití, or Curuzú. They were given more food than the common soldiers, so that they should not die when they were flogged. Some of them were quite hale, and Stewart wondered why they did not escape. Though how could they, when everyone here was escaping? They had been escaping so long, it made a man think that this was what life was – a regrouping against forces that are large – yes, admittedly very large – but also clumsy and beneath his contempt.

'Hah!' said Stewart, to illustrate his point, and the small girl who walked now with her hand always on his stirrup looked up at him and smiled.

She was a Guaraní girl, of uncertain age.

They do not listen to words, Stewart noticed. These children only look, and it is always at the wrong place. They do not watch your eyes but your mouth. Or they do not watch your mouth but your hands. They make you feel not so much wrong-footed as wrong-faced. Or they might *watch* your eyes, but that is not the same thing as meeting them: a man might long for another human creature just to return his gaze. Perhaps that was what dogs were for. And he spent a while that day thinking about eyes – whether they were the door to the soul, or the soul's mirror. Do they open, or reflect, and what was the anatomy of it all.

He thought of the blue and stupid eyes of George Thompson at Angostura, looking at him while he fingered the hilt of his soon-to-be-surrendered sword. The table where they sat, with a sheet of ants lapping up and over the edge of it, on their way across the room. The rest of the ants walking happily on the floor.

Thompson's eyes of cerulean blue; a flare of white around the pupil, a matching outer ring of a darker smoky blue – there was a pattern to this dark rim, as it fell towards the pupil, a kind of gothic veining. Which blue came first? Stewart was a doctor. He should know about such things, about the previousness, or lateness, of colour, and how colour grows. He should have paid more attention, at the time, to the bruised, navy colour of his own children's eyes, as they shifted into brown.

A British boat was waiting down river, Thompson said. It would take them to the Argentine, and then home. Stewart did not answer. He looked at the ruin of his hands, his cannibalised nails. He did not want to go.

And so his life was shaped by a kind of stickiness. He did not want to leave his family in Asunción – those little strangers his wife had reared for him. He did not want to leave his wife – herself a stranger to the woman he had once loved. Besides, he could not abide Thompson. And so he drifted along with the war, which was not so much a stream as a sequence of separate moments, each so vivid and different from the last it made him feel quite hilarious, the way that nothing now was connected to anything else.

Thompson gave Stewart his horse that day. How did he surrender? Stewart sometimes idly thought. Did he walk?

The languorous dip and buck of the creature's back beneath him provoked thoughts of a slow, abrupt congress, but it was also conducive of other rhapsodies and regrets – that he had not made a contribution, for example. There were trees around him demanding botany, and birds their taxonomy. There were things his aunt would have admired, if you set them on her mantel in a glass jar. There was the fame of exhibition: 'A series of glass eyes, blown and variously pigmented to the specifications of Dr Stewart, with a brief note of their metamorphosis and pathology. The eye of the diabetic patient, the eye of the bereaved woman, the eye of the blind.'

And there was a gorgeousness too, in not doing these things. In never having done anything, except go with the stream, which, although he cavilled, was not finally the stream of duty or obligation, but the flow of his own desire. The only time he went against his own inclination was when he stopped drinking: the rest – exile, marriage, the army, children – each an annoyance to him, and each the only thing he wanted to do at the time. He regretted the fact that he had lived a life of constant regret, and called an end to choice, with all its teasing grief. He looked instead at the life around him, from fungus to flower, and thought about eyes.

Sometimes he felt, as he rode, as though he were inside something; that he was looking out through the sockets of his eyes, as an antique soldier might look through a slit in his helmet. He felt that, between his skull and his self there was a gap, an area of darkness, across which he must peer.

At other times he felt that his eyes were as big as his face, and as open; his face itself was wide as the sky. But then the helmet was back again, and his eyes were darting through the gaps. Like bullets. He shot his gaze at a tree, at a bird. He never missed.

He wished he had a pen, or even that Venancia were here so he could share his observations with her. He was grown most chatty, and so he told the girl with her hand on his stirrup that the eye was not a door or a mirror, but a weapon, at war with the world. And she looked at him.

Some days later she surrendered. She met his eye, and then she did something with her own eyes. A kind of swoon, but without looking away. She made her eyes flat and unjudging, so they looked, he thought, quite gelid. Then – did they open? They became inviting, somehow, like water. The tiniest shift. A liquefaction. Just enough to say, 'Yes.' Or even, 'Please.'

Stewart's pleasure was not what it had once been. It was thin and weak and he did not know what to do with the body of this girl under him, which was very small. It seemed more like a bundle than a body, though hot inside – which struck him as sad. His desire was a meagre, hard blade with which he stabbed himself, not her, where once desire had been (he could hardly remember what it had been) – oceans, rivers, forests, God help us: everything. The girl was younger than he had thought and he did not take her again.

The last time Stewart slept with Venancia there was nothing to be done. Perhaps there had been some physical exchange, but he could not remember it as a carnal event. If, for example, he were to die, and in his dying try to remember the last time he had been inside his wife and the last time she had been about him, he would not be able to do so. As the journey went on, as the landscape unfolded in front of him and unravelled behind, he wondered if the people he had left in the past still existed. He wondered if there was any way to stitch the path back up, and make his way home to them. And he regretted the night he had lain in the dark at Venancia's side talking about warehouses, licences, a lawyer in Buenos Aires they both knew. They had a chance, and they did not take it. A chance for what, he was not sure. Desire was the least of it. But it was also, perhaps, a chance for desire.

He did not think of it during the day – there was always some other irritation to occupy his mind; a man's skin that was designed as a penance and not a protection; the changing vista, the clouds hanging in the branches of some forest, the feeling of legend from the landscape, and also of unfairness when you looked at such wide beauty from the narrow torment of your body; a chafed heel, an ulcerated shoulder, or the sense of your life gone astray. And then, around noon, there was the daily despair. It was a physical thing, like a drench of rain; you were dripping with it. It burdened every part and compartment of Stewart with a liquid grief, so that he wasn't so much riding as carrying his tears, brimming in some slopping leather bag, with gaps spouting in the seams.

And with the sadness came a decision. He would put his burden down. Every day, around noon, Stewart resolved to kill himself by the nearest means. He loved the force of the resolution; relished the relief. He craved death as much as water, more than food, and he fingered the handle of his knife at his side.

But he would have to pull away into the trees – and where was the right path among them, the most forgiving glade? The wound would have to be just so. The pistol in his saddlebag lacked shot. He might reach into his saddlebag, or fondle the leather plaiting on the handle of the knife. He might remember to put the leather in his mouth, because the doctor in him knew that this moment would pass, if he would only eat.

And yet, his throat was so dry. He might suck a little on the knife. Or he might nick the inside of his cheek to feel something sharp and taste the blood. Then it would come to him in a rush and he would stuff whatever handful he had been given into his mouth. After a moment, he would feel the prayer of it sweep through him and he was always glad, then, that he had stayed alive. There was always something to make him glad – the sharpness of grass, or a rock exquisitely veined with red, or pollen touching the child's skin and leaving its stain.

Story time. He looked at the green sward, the medieval

crags, the black brooding carriage, and he held his little girl by the hand. His Lily. His Rose.

By mid-afternoon words had left him again. He was not sure what remained in the pan of his skull, but the last thing to go was the mechanism whereby a man counted things. He could feel himself tick with each passing tree trunk, fifty, fifty-one, fifty-two – as though counting was the last tenacity. And then the numbers, too, were gone, and his thoughts were made of nameless rocks and trees, the nameless eyes of the child at his side, and the wide, nameless sky.

Dusk.

The evening, like the morning, was full of business, as he tended to López. After which, there might be food, or even music. As he turned to sleep, his mind would snag on some domestic thing the girl had arranged for him, a hot stone against the mountain cold, or the girl's own body bundled beside him: he would feel his own smallness under the stars, and there, on the side of the cold hill, he would long for something that was the exact temperature of Venancia Báez. His fingers twitched as he fell asleep, fumbling for the gaps in her imaginary clothes, and the feel of her skin was intimate as oblivion to him, and as large, and kind.

He thought about the last night he spent with her in San Fernando, at the mouth of the Tebicuarí. He could see her eyes in the dark. She was very clever, his wife. She had not come to the camp in secret – nor did she come openly. She came like a woman covered in dust, limping on bark shoes, and so she walked in past the sentries and then walked out again, back to the captured city of Asunción.

She slipped into his hut after sunset, and looked at him. Later he saw her body. Or some of it.

It was not just Venancia's body that Stewart had slept with in the early days of their marriage, but it was her body that was beside him now, as they lay and faced each other and talked – close, so as not to be overheard. The swell of her hip and the angle of her shoulder, her breasts falling out towards him in a line; it certainly was her body, or a swollen version of the same. But it seemed to him too lush, and hypocritical, now. Venancia's flesh, once so intoxicating, just irritated him: it made all the bites on his skin sit up. The whole pudding of it – his own starved, mortal shanks shivering beside her with something that might have been desire but felt more like tears.

'How do you live?' he had whispered, and she just smiled. Venancia grew things in the forest, or under the floorboards; she grew things in the dark. And even as he talked to her about a bank in Scotland, a broker in Buenos Aires, he was deciding not to touch her. She had given herself to some military fool, he decided, some Brazilian, saying, 'I have children to feed.' And how could he blame her? They were his children, after all.

Venancia's body. It filled the hut where they lay with accusation. It was not her fault. Stewart looked into her eyes (their brown plea) and knew that she might give her favours where she liked, but her life belonged to him. And all her cleverness, only to him. She had taken this journey, not to talk about money, but for love of him. Even so, the words that came to him were something like 'I do not', and then 'I do not', over and over again. A scrap of a phrase that begged many endings, one of them being – there was no doubt about it – 'I do not want you any more, Venancia Báez.'

High in the Amambai mountains, Stewart fingered the cold hair of the girl who slept beside him. It was brown. There was a white man back there somewhere, in her line. Some Jesuit.

'Poor William,' he wanted to say. 'Poor William Stewart.' Such scruples as he used to have. Now all he wanted was to hear the rasp and sigh of the girl's breath. All he wanted was to fling his life, one more time, into the body of Venancia (as was) Báez.

Later, he woke the girl to look at a low star which had gathered about it a light of great delicacy in the bone-coloured dawn. He was not sure she understood, but she sat easily on his legs and, after he had pointed and she had looked up, they stayed like that for a while, waiting for the day to begin.

She was younger, now. The farther they went in the northern hills the smaller and more helpless she seemed to him. So perhaps it was true. They were going to a more innocent place, after all.

In the morning, Eliza would climb on to the back of a cart and play the captive piano, still tied where it stood. She played 'La Palomita' while López, as often as not, shot someone. He did it personally – there were so few men left to do it for him; but also, it must be admitted, he needed to do it himself these days, like a morning expectoration or a fart.

When the time came to shoot his brother, however, the massively incompetent Benigno López, he spared the man no honour. He called upon the services of Bernardino Caballero, the highest-ranking officer he had left. Also he had everyone stand as though on parade. He signalled Stewart forward to check the condemned man's health and the comfort of his bonds. He pulled their weeping mother towards the stake, and shook her shoulder and cast her down, as if to say, 'See! See, what you have done to this woman your mother.' And Eliza, for the occasion, played 'La Palomita' standing up. She wore red.

Benigno was stripped down to his underdrawers, and the mound of his belly was immensely comical and afraid. It quivered and heaved, and was so inviting that López could not help but cut him loose one last time, to send him careening around in a circle, snorting like a pig. Everyone roared. They kicked or spat, while Benigno squealed. He seemed to enjoy it, in a bitter sort of way. He squealed fantastically well, and then he squealed even better. Then López gave a brief nod to Caballero, who had the man-pig pulled back to the stake and shot.

Eliza finished the last verse of the last round of 'La Palomita' and was helped down from the cart by Pancho, her son. She had not missed a single note.

After Benigno, López forbade the use of bullets, because they had not enough, and men were lanced where they stood. Particularly the men who had conspired with Benigno, but also, and sadly, the boy Paulino Alén, who came to the camp at San Fernando with a hole in his throat after the fall of Humaitá. He had tried to kill himself, and failed, so López made a gift of it and finished the job for him. Stewart might have balked at this particular death or at another, but there was always the general truth of the war, and the honour of their cause. Benigno had conspired – there was no doubt about that. He had plotted to slip a knife between his brother's ribs, to hand over the country to the enemy, to hoard supplies, to deny marching men meat, to divert from the front line all kinds of fat bacon and shoulders of lamb, lard and cutlets and blood sausage and tripes. It gave Stewart satisfaction to see the man die, because there was justice in it. It gave him pleasure to see Mother López caterwaul, the attitude she struck like The Virgin at the bottom of some savage cross. Also to see the tear seep out of the Little Colonel's green eye, before he turned to help his mother down from her cart.

Somewhere on the road Stewart had become a creature of López. They all had. They could feel him in their blood. The terrible rapine that might seize a man, the frenzy of hacking and slashing – that was López – the terrible urge to shit that might swell inside him when he had killed, so that soldiers dropped their kecks in the view of enemy fire there on the battlefield. It was not fear that made them so incontinent, but a madness of the body that filled them to bursting and demanded egress – of any kind: also carnal; the men being endlessly urgent and ignoble in that way.

Stewart, not being in the thick of it for the most part, kept his pants in order back and front. He confined himself to indifference – a narrow, whining sort of madness that might let a man die because he did not like the look of his ugly face. A civilised, smirking sort of thing, which stepped through the heap of enemy wounded and slit this, or that, throat. These were all pleasures. And he knew that once they slipped out of him, he could never call them back.

As the personal doctor of Il Mariscal López, Stewart lived close to the abrupt gesture; a wave of the hand that could kill a man. He tried not to fawn. He opened his medical bag with decisiveness and closed it with a satisfying click. Then he became too careful about his bag. Then he became too casual about his bag. He left the bag behind, as he squatted in a manly, companionable way and daily checked the presidential feet, the calluses and the many small joints. He rubbed López down like a horse, feeling the tendons where they joined the bone. He enquired after his digestion and went behind a tree to check his stools, which were always a matter for congratulation. He lifted his member and rubbed it with a chalk mixture, to give a more cosmetic consistency to the gonorrhoeal drip. He treated the body of López with cheerful hands. Not to do so endangered not only his personal health, but also the health of every man there, not to mention the well-being of the entire region of the Río del Plata.

And sometimes, when he sat with López talking about the need for heroes or the mechanising tendency in modern life (his foot idly tapping his doctor's bag), Stewart thought him the sanest man in the world.

In Tacuatí, the straggling army bunched up to a halt, and they stayed for a week. There was an *estancia* there: a horseshoe of sheds around an open courtyard where López sat at a table, and wrote. Then he sat back and looked at his notes. He talked to a queue of men and seemed to hand down judgment. Then he waved them away. He arranged the papers in front of him. He placed them in particular patterns. From time to time, he burned one.

There was no other madness.

Eliza encouraged the feeling of respite. She managed to give the place the atmosphere of a small spa. There was a little spring in the courtyard, and she drew wooden beakers of water from it, which she handed to the men herself; saying how restorative it was and extolling the pure heights from which it came. There was food, too, from the barns. And though they lived in uncertainty, there were things a man had not had, or heard, in some time, such as the sound of rain on his roof, for example, that lulled Stewart into an afternoon ecstasy of remembrance.

He was housed, for the duration, next to Eliza's quarters – a sympathetic billet: ever since they stopped, Stewart was fighting a sharp fever that followed its own clock; he could never tell what time he would be weak or clear-headed, and what time he would be stretched. It was a small, pungent room with no window and one rotting door. Where the dividing wall reached for the roof, there was a blessed, blunt triangle of open space; a dark gap through which the sounds of Eliza's 'drawing room' came to him as he lay on the floor. What a Babel! He would wake or drift to the sounds of her sons, speaking French to their Mama, or Spanish to each other, or Guaraní to the men. Once, Stewart thought he heard German or something like it – Swedish perhaps – something guttural and rational and quite gorgeous that was telling him to lie down and keep his clothes on. And once, a whole sentence in English, 'The book is on the windowsill', that was the most beautiful thing he had heard in a long time.

The girl lit a cleansing fire in his doorway and it flamed in the daylight, weakly orange, while the yard beyond buckled in the heat. Stewart saw things in the flawed air that he decided to tell no one about: not the girl, not Venancia, not his aunt, not his mother, not Eliza on the other side of the wall. He would tell no woman about these things that he saw. And he longed to rest his eyes on Eliza's boys, who stayed constant, all of them, and easy, through the haze.

Stewart could tell that they were fine young men, and very proud. Eliza had a certain way of sitting or being that could halt them at the mere sight of her – because of course they worshipped her, as boys do, and she adored them in return. Their father scattered them when he came into the room, but he too was indulgent and patient and kind. There was nothing degraded about this household. There was nothing that Stewart could sense of darkness, even when all was dark around him and his own death seemed as close to him as the family on the other side of the wall. Then closer. His own death scrabbled in the high triangular gap – he could smell the coming rot, he could see the long, black fingernails sneak in over the stone.

'Will you take a cup of coffee, my dear?'

It was hard to tell how sick or well he was when sentences like this fluttered down to him. Coffee? He must be dying. He looked at the girl as she dipped a rag into some water and wiped his chest. The rag, the water, the girl: these things were real. The coffee could not be real. He must be careful about coffee. He must stay alive.

Then he smelled it.

And Stewart decided that it was all real, in a way. Because the gods can make for themselves all kinds of felicity. The ease with which they run around, and chat and shout. The freedom they have. The lovely, ordinary nature of it all.

'Take your shoes off, my dear, and put your feet on this,' said Eliza, the cannibal. Eliza the evil one. Eliza who rushed, pregnant, into Humaitá to fling herself at Il Mariscal's feet and say, 'Why does your brother Benigno hate me? Why does he insult and humiliate me like this? Why?'

But Stewart was delirious, and death crouched between the thatch and the wall. Death was a nest of insects; a thick, seething, black triangle, all shiny and heaving and trickling down the wall to crawl over him. And he itched and whined in the straw while from next door came the sound of a stool being set down.

'Is that better?'

No. He was delirious and Eliza was just like any other wife. She must nag a little, and provoke; she must never be quite satisfied. Because this was the way of wives, it was their destiny: women must always be thwarted, and so men must always fail.

They had conjugal relations, Stewart thought, no more than twice the week of his fever, and this in a farther room. He heard much more than this, of course, but the actual events he distinguished from the less real by the whimpering, puppy-like sound that López made. At least Stewart thought it was López. If it was not, then it was a peculiar mewling for Eliza to make. But you never knew.

And so the week stretched into one long, golden afternoon, where they were, for the most part, as happy as anyone might be, the Devil and his whore. And Stewart was happy with them, on the other side of the wall, as they arranged their lives by rules both tender and aesthetic; as Eliza brought out one shawl or another to drape on the chair, or changed the lamp for a candle, because he preferred it so.

And Stewart allowed them a life like any other couple: a shared past shot through, as it may have been, by moments of great frankness; embarrassed, sometimes, by emotions it seemed their joined bodies were too frail to bear – López after the death of his father, say, or Eliza some ordinary Sunday afternoon, when it seemed to her she might drown in her own life and clung to him as a woman wrecked.

And so the fever waned.

Pancho called him. He grabbed the door frame with both hands and leaned into the small room saying,

'I think there is something wrong with Mama.'

Stewart peered into the boy's looming silhouette.

'One moment,' he said. And so, at last, he went next door.

He was right. It was lovely. She had covered the rough furniture with drapes of sage-green and grey. There was a pier-glass on the wall, a preternatural clock; there was the scent of lilac, and also a fusty magical smell that seemed to say 'Home'. In the middle of all this cluttered ease, Eliza sat with a distracted, strained attitude. She did not turn; but she answered the doctor's greeting, when he gave it, with,

'Yes, a very good evening.'

And still, she did not look at him. She spoke from the side of her face, so as not to disturb some forming thought that seemed to be gathering on the far wall. She squinted a little, as though trying to understand the shape of some stain; the lack of whitewash perhaps; an accident of light and shadow, or a horror of moss spreading in a corner by the door.

Stewart thought his delirium had spread, but there was no fever. He lifted her wrist and felt her pulse. Then he palpated, briefly, the flesh under her chin, by her ears, and along the base of her skull where it met her spine. Eliza's face, her grey brain, balanced there for a moment in his hands.

After which benediction, he sat down.

The creak of the rush seat seemed to catch her attention, at last. She looked at him; her head slightly cocked, like a bird's. It was a long look, and it was deeply estranged, both from him and from the world he was sitting in.

Stewart sought and found the phrase 'hysterical paralysis'. This is what happened to women in Edinburgh, he seemed to remember, from time to time.

Then she put her head straight and snapped to.

'Doctor Stewart,' she said, 'I felt the need of some arrowroot tea.'

'Of course,' he said.

'Pancho obliged. You know I hate him running errands for his poor Mama, but there is no better boy.'

'Mama,' said Pancho.

'Or I should say "young man". Come here to me, my darling.' And Pancho strode gallantly forward, and dropped on one knee. He looked at his mother as she looked at him. She put her hand on his shoulder and, when he felt her touch, he fell forward to lie in her lap.

Her eyes then were an evening blue. They were the colour of the light, when it goes.

'She has put me in charge of sleep,' said Pancho. Stewart nodded. He had come to talk to the boy. Or he had come to sit by the courtyard fire, where they might happen upon the subject of his mother, who did not, after all, drink her arrowroot tea, but fussed serenely around López when he arrived and called a soldier in to sing.

Then much bother about the piano, which must be unloaded at once and brought to her quarters. The evening made unbearable by music; a song called 'Barbara Allen'; notes that coated a man, and fingered every crevice. When the silence was finally clean, Stewart walked out to spit and look at the stars, and talk to the heir apparent.

The boy must be sixteen or so. His skin in the firelight

was an uneven and glowing brown and he looked altogether romantic as he squatted there; though also a little glum, as he stared into the tangle of flame. He was thinking, no doubt, of The War.

He had the clearest gaze. Stewart took comfort from his green eyes, which were a window of light in the middle of his face. He took comfort from the fact that, in this whole travelling circus, there was one freak who might be called 'the beautiful boy'. The boy who simply looks. And he was not the only one who felt it. Belief in Pancho was a general pleasure. The men looked at his eyes as you might look at the sky, for the solace of colour, and they indulged the boy and his jewel-like stare.

Behind him, his half-brother, the bastard son of Juana Pesoa, kept fierce guard, as always, in the shadows.

They were talking man-to-man.

'I am also in charge of the piano. I have my own brigade. We lift it in the evening, if it needs to be lifted. We keep the damp away. I have a man sleep under it, just in case. Not tonight though, as it is with my mother, indoors.'

Stewart did not ask who might want to attack the piano, but still the boy said, 'Just in case. And besides music is a noble business, is it not? This is what I tell the men, that music is just as mighty a business as killing is, and just as useful, in its way. I set them to care for "the beast", as they call it. Or, "his Mama's beast", sometimes, if they want me to hit them.'

And then, as though reciting and forgetting a list, he started again.

'Night-time security. What she calls "Sleep". I see to the bedding, personally. I make up the bed myself. It is a tender duty, you know.'

'Indeed.'

There was something the boy wanted to say.

'But sometimes in the morning, Doctor, the bed is just

as I left it, the sheets not even turned down. Other times it is so screwed and wrinkled I feel like scolding her. I say, 'Mama, what is the point? When I have four men outside your door, keeping their eyes open so that you can shut yours. You should become our night watchman, you would walk in our dreams.'

'She does not sleep,' said Stewart, carefully.

'She sleeps in the carriage for ten minutes at a time, I think. But at night she does not sleep.'

'She looks quite well.'

Pancho seemed to think about this for a while.

'She always looks clean, that is the thing of it. Whether or not she has slept, or in what tent or room. She always looks clean.'

'Perhaps it is because she is beautiful,' said Stewart, and the boy looked relieved. It was indeed a burden he carried – the unmentionable beauty of his dear Mama.

'Do you think so? It is hard for a son to tell. But yes I think she is beautiful, even though she is old, now. I think a boy might say that without compromise, about his mother.'

Stewart stood up. He was hugely tired.

'You must get her to take some air, when we move again,' he said. 'The coach is so enclosed.' And the boy prodded the fire a little miserably, and agreed.

It would all keep going, thought Stewart. After I am dead, and after López is dead. The son would keep going, while Woman – lovely Woman – kept turning the handle on the world's dreadful machine.

We really would be better off without them, he thought; as a breed. Apart from all the fuss. And it saddened him that a woman's needs should be so monstrously met, if not by her lovers then by her sons. That Eve should kiss not just Adam but also Cain. That it all keeps trundling on. It leaves her, and then it comes back to her again.

As he fell asleep, he heard her talking to the boy, through the wall.

'Pancho,' she said. 'Where did we get this thing?'

'I think we got it in the cathedral in Asunción.'

'Well it is a very ugly thing.'

And Stewart spent his dreams wondering what the thing might be.

The next evening, Stewart sought out the boy again. He could not help it. He wanted to talk to the future. He wanted to see those eyes.

'For all her nonsense, you know, mine is an important position. If we lose her we are absolutely lost.'

'Yes,' said Stewart.

Although it was the boy he believed in now, and not the mother. The boy's mother was a whore. It was never a word that made sense to Stewart, but it made sense to him now. It was the prickle on his skin of hatred or disgust – the unbearable tenderness where his skin met the night sky. The sensation of falling. Stewart thought that he might fly apart with it. It was a rage and a yearning, and the only word he could put on it was 'whore'. Everything was dirty and dark, now, and his waking dreams stank of Eliza, until he had to seek out her son and rest his eyes on him.

Pancho, as though he sensed his need, tried to put the older man at ease – but of course it was hard for a boy who had been reared as he had been reared to find the right tone. He settled on a story.

'I bet my boys they would not take the witch Cordal,' he said. 'It was in Humaitá, when she was still caged. Did you see her? If you threw her a bone she would twist it in front of her face like she had never seen a bone before, and my lads were all frightened – she would fling it back at them and they would scatter and shout – or she would gnaw at it, all leering, and once she put it into her private self, whatever you call it, her cunt, though not far. So I knew she was daring us, and I threw a belt buckle I had into the cage for the first man to take the witch Cordal.

'You should have heard my father laugh. He said he would write it in his "Maxims" that a dare is a mirror, because once I said it, of course, I was obliged to enter the cage myself, and attempt the deed. But I did it. Just about – the place being so confined, and the witch, as you may imagine, none too pleased.'

'I can imagine,' said Stewart.

'She bucked so much and spat. I swear it – I saw burn marks on the floor.'

'Really?' said Stewart, who was beginning to hear nothing now.

'She hexed my father, once, you know, but it did not work.'

Thompson's horse died. Stewart sucked its handsome tendons. He chewed them for days at a time. And, once he had eaten the inside of them, he wore the horse's shins pulled up his own legs, with the fetlocks stitched together, for leather socks or hairy boots.

One day, he looked down from the mountains back to the gently folding Cordillera, and noticed that the girl was gone. She had been getting smaller and smaller. It had been hard, for a while, to realise the lack of her. Stewart looked around him, over and again, wondering what was missing – was it his knife? The three bullets he had found to load into his pistol, if the powder ever came his way? When he saw that it was the girl, Stewart's mind went back along the trail looking, not for her, but for the man he had been when he had the girl by his side. Days back. Perhaps a week. When he found him – this past version of Doctor Stewart – he pulled him into himself for a fierce, short embrace.

Yes, the man told him, she was gone. She had been slipping into the bushes more and more often. Her looseness was turning to cholera, even though the air was now so clear. Yes, even when the cholera was leaving them, it was taking her with it. And at night her body had leaked in his easy embrace. And, sometime that morning, she had fallen down and Stewart had not picked her up. And why should he pick her up? There was no time. The Brazilians were hours away. There was no turpentine, nor any emetic to treat her with, and what little he had was kept for the exclusive use of Señor López.

At which, Stewart let his old self go again, and turned back to the black carriage that was creeping like a beetle up the flank of the hill.

By the banks of the Aquidabánmi, the ox that pulled the piano cart died, as did many of the men. They were on the brink of the high meadow lands, where the forest began to thin, a place blessed by hummingbirds and friendly breezes, also circled by the Karakara vulture, who must have known something about the stream there, because three hours after drinking the water they were seized, both animal and human, by griping pains. They could barely pitch camp, and that night you could hear López raving in the darkness, though maybe it was some other man – a strong man – bellowing at death. But despite the roaring, death had taken, as they saw when the morning came, the weakest oxen, and many infants, and considerable numbers of women and men.

López ordered the piano abandoned there, and he had to give the order twice. His own son looked at him, and then jumped to. And when they had it down off the cart, two of his boy brigade folded the huge cloth with that folding dance you see women make, shepherds coming to kiss shepherdesses, over and back, over and across, and over again.

Eliza was in her carriage for this. She did not pretend to watch, but the horses started away just as soon as the piano was left on the grass. Stewart, who stayed to tend the survivors, was left looking at the thing, standing proud in a field full of bodies, silent or groaning. The temptation was too much for him. He lifted the lid and played her out. As the line of fleeing Paraguayans trickled over the far hills, Stewart let his ruined hands wander over the notes. He found he was playing 'La Palomita', as though there was no other tune the piano knew, so he drummed the same note for a while, to admonish it. And when he looked away for long enough – at the beautiful birds, for example, or the beautiful hills – he found an old tune wandering out of his hands. Something Scottish, he thought, although he could not remember the name.

When he caught up with them that night, López was impatient at the delay. His stools were yellow he said. They smelled of smoke. Stewart prescribed charcoal. He said, with a laugh, that at least there was plenty of that about – then realised, as he looked at López, that he had just very nearly died.

But he had not died. He had been given something to eat, and he had lain down. He watched the stars while his back sought and swooned into the hard Paraguayan earth, and he listened, as they all did, to the fight in the presidential tent.

They fought in French. There was an occasional shadow-play of bodies on the canvas, but the figures loomed or receded hopelessly; or ate themselves, as they flicked from one to the other wall. It was hard to tell what was going on. Eliza was keening for her piano, of course. But she would not say it: she wouldn't mention it by name. Instead there was a litany of things she had to put up with: incessant travel and bad food and no help and badly washed clothes. Her throat was so full that she choked on the words, she had to squeeze them out of her, until her voice broke in a thin shriek, a wail.

'And when will we be married, you son of a bitch? When will you *marry* me?'

By the sound of it, she was up close to him. Stewart imagined that he held her by the wrists. She was trying to hit him, or bite him. Those handsome teeth. Of course, López could take out a pistol and shoot her. He could push her out of the tent and have her lanced before she stumbled to the ground. He could put her in with the prisoners and have her daily flogged. And then – and this was the greatest comfort to them in these last, terrible days – he could do none of these things, because he loved Eliza Lynch.

Silence. The president's doctor held his breath. Il Mariscal might be hit. He might be nursing a hurt lip, or crotch. The silence went on so long, he might be dead. Or she might be dead. Or nothing might be happening at all; they might be each reading their separate books. Then the sound of tears – Eliza crying in a rush, and slapping him (or could he be slapping her? He was a brute, but not that much of a brute), or were they slaps, after all? They had a rhythm – and the rhythm thickened and gathered into a dull hammering, and then, with a high, puppyish whimper, it was done.

'Yay!' said the bright face of the boy who was sitting on the other side of Stewart's fire.

'Yay!' said Stewart back to him, because children made the worst spies. And he waved the little stick he was chewing, briefly in the air.

When a man is inside a woman, he rules the world.

The River

Part 4

Flowers

January 1855, Río Paraná

AT LAST, A town of some size. I see it in a smoky distance, all flat and loose on the landscape, like something spilled out that no one has bothered to wipe up. The houses are jumbled and tiny, so far away; then clearer – a flag, a washing line. The red tiles I have seen along the river, which were always a sign, in their fat corrugations, of a rich man's *estancia*, now gathering so thick as we approach I wonder how they got so many. Red tiles. Hundreds of red tiles. Thousands of them!

This is how long I have been on the river.

I stand in the prow, face forward, belly forward. The boat thumps behind and under me, through my fat, hot feet. It is a lullaby sung in my bones. Still, the sleeping baby wakes to the sight of his city on the horizon; the blind baby delights in what I see. My blood paints him a picture of the future that approaches, and he beats out his answer on my tender hide drum.

And he does not stop. As my eye lingers and proceeds – on the rooftops, and the boats and the docks now coming into view – as I clasp my hands and wring them, almost, with relief and expectation, the child twists and bangs and hammers on. Is it a message or is it a dance? It is a wrestling with himself, an urgency to be free. I feel his impatience – but what can I do?

Look, look!

The baby not seeing but demanding, What is it? What is it?

Home. Where you came from.

Though this child has already come from everywhere: Paris, Rome, Madrid, Bordeaux. The only home he has had is me. And if you are to tell from the thumps and the kicks, the strength and meanness of his intent, he has difficulty in staying even there. My travelling boy. My man who would be on his way.

'They hit you hard, your children,' says my mother's wan voice in my head. 'They hit you hard and they start early.' It makes me weary to think she may be right. But I also know now, as she once knew, the pleasures of such submission – to the uncaring fists and the uncaring smile of your own heart's child. I will let you out of my womb, but not out of my arms. I will let you out of my arms, but not out of my head.

And also, 'Go, if you want to – this is a burden to me too.'

So I stand in the prow, very statuesque and still, while my belly boils. Along the bank small children start to shout and run as we glide past the first shanties: a melon patch, a scum fringing the water for the foraging pig, a girl who stands watching, her thin skirt bundled away from the water that runs, so flat, between her legs. It runs thus sheer – or so I have come to tell her – all the way to the sea. And she lifts her face to watch us slide past, and her look says that she always knew she would see this someday, a sight this fine, and when she catches sight of me, up there in the prow, she knows who I am, too.

But the smell of so much human habitation turns my stomach while the baby twists the other way. It is time to go in. Such spin and counter-gyration, as Mr Whytehead would perhaps put it, have me laid flat on my bed, sickened again by the lift and sigh of the river, and longing, just longing, for the ground beneath my feet once more.

I lie in the hot darkness of the cabin and imagine the ship making her way smoothly along the bank. I imagine it so hard I cannot tell if we are moving or still; but then, after the longest time, I hear the men shout and the slipping roar of the anchoring chains. The ship strains forward, and stops. We have arrived. I roll myself upright to look through the porthole, and see, on the quayside, a scrabbling crowd. They are altogether like the crowd I saw from the first boat I was ever on, the Plymouth packet from Queenstown. And so my life runs in circles, and not in a line, after all.

All my restlessness collapses into a silent wail, as I lie on the bed and think of all the things I have gone through, just to get back to the place I started from – all the journeys I have made, the seas I have crossed, and the love I have lost or discarded along the way. My family, both dull and vicious; I almost miss them – and I wonder where my father is, now.

I was ten at the time, and thought they were out to kill him. The crop had failed for a second time, and the bailiffs we were daily expecting turned out always to be the poor at the door, ever more indigent and ghastly-eyed. There was one woman who reached out a purple knuckle to graze my cheek saying, in a soft kind of way, that she would eat me, I was so lovely and so fat. As the countryside weakened – with the first, or perhaps the second corpse in the ditch – my father gained sudden strength to pack us up and out of there, off to the ship in the middle of the night, pursued, as I thought, by these skeletons. They were there on the quayside, lurid in the torchlight, beseeching the sides of the ship as they might some squat deity, the God of Escape. It is possible some of them drowned – I was terrified that they might, and there is something sickening, I still find, in the sound of a splash. But I only remember scraps. A face perhaps. Also, the first man's member I ever saw, nearly as thick as the two legs on either side of it. The man – was he sitting or lying? – he was, at any rate, dying; lazily so, with his hand idling in his flaccid lap.

It seems I am weeping. The tears slip out of my eyes, quite fast and silent, as though they have nothing to do with me.

We have arrived.

The worst Atlantic crossing you could ever have, or so they said in Buenos Aires: days and weeks of storm, the broken wheel, the men all sick. Most of this beyond my ken; my stupid body wracked by its own storm, rolling and heaving until I was afraid I might puke up the child itself.

And now, whatever is on that dock, whatever path starts there, a yard or two from the side of the boat, that is my life's own path.

And O! everything falls in one me in a clatter. I lie on my bed and it is only four feet away, my future, it is only a jump away. I could swim it. A fly from my future could come and bite me now, still lying in the past. And then I think that perhaps I will not make it. I will not be able to do it. I will never put my foot on the piece of wood that will lead to the ground where my path begins.

I do not cry, as a rule. I am not the crying kind. I keep my finger and thumb pressed down on the lids to save my face from ruin, but I cannot stop. It feels like all the bad times are back, hanging on to me – why do I think of them as women? – a grove of women weeping and clutching at my skirts, saying, You must not go on.

I am such a fool. The weeks after Misha left me in Paris, I thought once, were the worst weeks I would ever spend. Ditto the time after I was married off to that man Quatrefages. Ditto the inn at Artenay. I could give an inventory of the worst, which have turned out since quite well enough. What is Misha? He is like a doll to me now, with his little blue jacket and his braggadocio. I am indifferent to the memory of his mouth, or his throat. The only things that remain to hurt me are his lies. Look at this doll (I wave him about in my head) – how he lied to me. Ow. Ow. Ow.

And still I cannot rise off the bed.

Sweet Christ, we have arrived. And I think that here – four feet away from the side of this boat – I will be safe. I will be safe from M. Raspail, and Mr Bennett, and all the rest of them. I will be free of their jealousy. For they were all, I think, jealous of me, as a man might be jealous of a painting that he may pay for, but will never properly have. As men are jealous of all beautiful things.

I will have a carriage that is all in black. It will be my funeral coach. It will be the blackest thing you ever saw and my flesh inside it, the whitest. And if López abandons me here, I will ride about in it quite naked and unseen, and my name will be If-You-Dare.

Open the door.

This is what I think about, as the tears wreck my face, and the baby kicks and wrestles to be free. I think that my name is Mortality.

Poor pregnant Dora, who thinks she can kill a man just by the way she looks at him. There she is on the bed – her skin a rash, her feet so big she must cut the heels off her shoes. Her belly is quite sacred, you know. And as it grows, poor Dora withers away. What can save her? Nothing but love, of course. And a little bit of money.

I am so far from myself I do not hear Francine come into the room. She lifts me by the shoulders and I weep and say I cannot, she must not make me. I also say (at least I think I say) that, if I die, she must know that I forgive her all that she has done to me. Ashamed already of my blabbing – we are both ashamed. Francine says nothing, but lays me back down while I weep some more. She wipes my hands with something cool and also my face.

'What must I do?' I am saying. 'You see what he is.' And more such until Francine says,

'You must love him. There is no other way.'

My obvious Francine. She is right. And a glow spreads in my blood with the rightness of it. It happens all at once. I have found a place in my soul where I can stand – the place where I love López. It is quite elevated and lonely, but also easy; also warm. I am staring at the ceiling. I have found it. My tears have stopped.

Then, with a crack, my tins of powder and paint are slapped on to the dressing table. A fall of lilac as she lifts my dress and lets it drift across my feet.

'Let us show them a little bit of France,' she says.

I sigh, and my sadness turns delicious. I have arrived. I am in love. The stage is set. This dress was the newest colour in Paris two months ago, and it is the newest colour on this vast continent: it is the future, and it is wrapped around me.

Still, I am frightened. I cannot manage myself properly in public any more. I know this. Look how I cry and tremble when I am alone. It is the baby – the size of him, now making me so stupid and swooning. And although I can keep my head in company it is only for a short while. Everything must be brief, now. Dressing. Walking. Everything must be brief.

I am muttering this as a kind of refrain as she gets me into my clothes. Drawers, petticoat, embroidered petticoat, stiff jupon petticoat, Balbriggan stockings, corset. My belly fights back against her lacing. We are in the middle of the push and shove of it, when my entire bump goes hard. And with it the clenching, a feeling on the skin as you might get on your scalp when your hair is pulled too tight. It crawls from either side of me, and meets out front. I push the maid away, and sit, and think, counting slowly, and passing my hand over the skin.

Is it starting?

Francine looks at my questioning touch, and says,

'You will feel it when it comes, for sure.' The hardness melts back to the usual mound, and we get the laces tied – quick, quick – while my belly is unawares.

Chemise, undersleeves, dress. My wonderful lilac hat.

And so I sit and compose my features. And so it is time.

I must love him, because through such narrow gaps in our lives we all must squeeze and crawl. I must love, not his greatness, but the sadness in his brown eyes. I must love, not the ring, but the dear hand. This is the only way forward, the only way through.

But when he comes into the cabin, resplendent in blue, I have no time to tell him that I love him, now. I kiss his sweet mouth and say that I have five minutes, maybe seven, in which to be radiant and whole. After which I am an animal again. I have five minutes by the clock, I say, as we mount to the gangway and the breeze takes my veil, after which I will have fainted clear on to the floor.

And my noble Love presses my arm so tightly to his side, it seems I rise with the pressure – tight, tighter – until, on tiptoe, I float down and through the adulating crowd, their faces all smiling and pushing. I fling up a hand to save my face from something thrown. A flower. Scarlet, like a great gob of blood, come sailing through the air at me. And I know I must concentrate on one face at a time, smile at one child at a time. An old man. A woman. A man. A girl. Their hands are thrust towards me, but not open, not in supplication. They dab little circles in the air – bravo, bravo. One bully-boy is clearing the rest back to lay a branch of palm under our feet, and they laugh and cry out; not López! López! but Barrios! Barrios! which must be the name of the boy with the palm, and I feel – how could I not? – that I am being welcomed in, as though by a family: Look, they say. Here is Barrios, our fool.

Still, a clock is ticking in my blood. Five minutes, five minutes. And the feel of the glad earth beneath my feet makes my belly all hard and hurting. I have held off for this, it seems. Closer, closer, he presses my hand as we walk to the place where the carriages stand. Here we are at a disadvantage, being on foot, but we play it like a couple strolling in the Bois: he shows off his French manners and doffs his French hat and keeps moving as I dip and smile, thinking I have never seen such a crew for hair, a family with one eyebrow between them, even the women need to shave. Also counting in my head from one to sixty, because by fifty-nine, I decide, I will have pressed the side of my face into the welcoming dirt. But by forty-something we are there. Miltón hops into a carriage so he can pull me into it. López hands me from below, and with the slightest help I am sitting pretty and giggling like a girl.

A flower lands on the floor by my feet. Another. It is raining flowers. The horses are solid and easy as we push through the throng. Miltón stands on the dasher as though on the prow of the *Tacuarí*. The sun shines through his ragged pants, turning them to gauze, and again he is mysterious to me; his thin bones and his soft, old face. He waves, and the crowd shouts. Which is the sound, too, of the blood in my ears, as the clock of my body begins to chime.

*

I had a laughing labour. At least for a while. They say it takes women funny, and every woman a different way, but the rush of my breaking waters made me laugh and the tightness of my belly was so like the pain of laughter that I felt I might as well join in. It took me over, too, very like laughter does. It had me hanging on to the end of the bed, insensible with that mirth that is close to pain. Oh Lordy. Oh Lordy. Don't say another thing. And then, Here it comes. Something funnier than the last. Something so funny I must die. It is possible I was a little insane.

I was in a strange room: it was white. It was already, I think, a day since we had arrived. There was a worried-looking matron leaning towards me, clucking and kind. On the windows were dull red curtains, a hundred years old, so rotten that when I grabbed on to one it opened under my hands. It struck me as odd, the way the cloth did not so much tear as give; hundreds of threads and cross-threads, each disengaged. And as the cloth tore, or sometime later, I felt the same thing in me, a rending or a loosening, I cannot say which.

Francine entered with the doctor's bag and I realised I was clinging, not just to old curtains, but to whatever remained of my mind, and what I had kept it for was just this moment – the one when the doctor walks in the door with his wicked pad of chloroform. And I know how frightened I have been, all this while, not of the pain, which is every woman's lot, but of dying, and, more than that, of the baby born dead; my Love standing there, looking at me, with some poor scrap of flesh in his hands.

The bag comes in but the doctor does not follow it. Francine goes back to the door, and there is an altercation. Miltón is there, also Stewart, I am sure of it. Drunk, I think, the man is drunk. The world has gone mute. I think I am screaming. Francine scrabbles in the bag. Miltón stands in front of me with his finger to his lips and he is so intent that I should be quiet that I stop and listen, suddenly, to the room. And yes, I say, I can hear them. They have a high clear sound, very clean. They gather in the shape of the room, Miltón's daemons. They are in the crook of a corner, or in the slant of a shadow falling from the shutter on to the floor. The three lines that make up a corner are the three notes of their song, or perhaps it is just one note – very beautiful. It is an A: I could play it on the piano. And although it is just one note, it feels like a whole symphony to me, as though it must be approached and left with many other notes. And still it comes out true – an A – simple and pure. I felt this in a flash, the shape of the room, the shape of the daemons there, the need for silence as, inside me, the baby set sail.

So much I remember: the baby riding high and large under the bone until I thought that I might split, not in pain but, as a fruit might, in pleasure at the ripeness of itself. The head came. He turned into the world like a screw twisting out of me, and his nose looked quite large. I thought this while the rest of him was still inside me, and the timing of it seemed so odd or unworthy that I laughed, and the laugh pushed his shoulders out and the rest slopped clear. And he drew breath.

A boy. I knew it. I will call him Juan Francisco, for his father. And I will sweeten it to 'Pancho', for me.

His own cry seemed to astonish him – or so I thought. But I am already too fond. And then, sometime later, my Love was there. He took the boy by the neck, twining his fingers around the tiny bones of his ankles, and raised him high over his head, offering him, it seemed, to the ceiling, or the window, or the street below. And, as he did so, he shouted. He roared. This all to Miltón's great irritation, who bustled over and scolded like a woman. López handing over the baby then; almost slinging it at the matron who had attended me, whose name I now know to be Juana Pesoa.

And then later he is in the crook of my arm. They say you must love a child – but not too much! They say you must do this, or that. But a word like 'love' means nothing to us. It is not even a feeling I have for him, or he for me. It is a silence, or very like a silence. It is the inside shape of me – and it is the outside shape of him. It is nothing that you could stick a word between.

And now I fret at the way his father lifted my boy, as though daring fate: the ghosts or gods of this place. Though I know that we make our own lives. Who knows it better than I, having made my life at last – with this journey, this man. A woman's crowning achievement, Miss Miller used to call it. Well look at me now. I have a child that will never know hunger, and more than that, Miss Miller, I have had a child who will always be rich. And even as I look at his ugly, tiny face, I wonder at it: how careful – through all my mistakes – how very careful I have been.

The only peculiar thing about all of this being that when I look for the house, some weeks later, in order to find the woman and thank her (perhaps the one friend I will have in this place), I keep missing it. I ask for, and am directed to, the house of Juana Pesoa, but I drive my little phaeton around one corner and the next. This happens so often I have a boy lead the horse by the bridle to the door, but the house we stop at has just one storey, when the house I gave birth in had two. Or so I remember. When the curtain ripped in my hand I was standing at a window looking down into the street. There were people going about their business, down there, unawares. But this house has blank walls, a fancy wooden grille over the one window, which faces, across a lane-way, another wall.

When I knock at the door, it is indeed opened by the servant of Juana Pesoa. To still my agitation the mistress of the house shows me the room where Pancho was born. There is a window on to the courtyard and, hanging in the dusty light, the curtain still torn.

'I thought I was high up,' I say. 'I thought I was on the first floor.' And she looks at me.

Clean Linen

March 1870, Cerro Corá

IT WAS NECESSARY was to bury him before he began to rot. He was very fat, still. His eyes were neither shut nor open: there was a bland rind of white under the lids, which seemed, in their gentle curves, like two little smiles. Eliza walked the length of his body, from head to toe. Death made him smaller: she was brought short by reaching the end of him. She stopped, then turned and walked back up to his head. She toured the length of him in this way, once, twice more; and when a young Brazilian captain came over she pushed him away from her and did not break her stride.

She halted at the midsection, and looked at him. López lay as he had been dragged out of the river; his toes pointing gracefully down and his arms by his side. The water had mixed with the blood of his wound, leaving tidemarks on his shirt; the last piece of clean linen in Paraguay. It made it look as if he had died, not of a bullet but of some small, domestic indignity. It looked as though he had died of a stain.

Eliza nudged a pale arm away from his side; then she drew her foot back and kicked him in the ribs. The last air rattled out of him with a flabby sound and, as though frightened by it, she kicked him again, quickly, in the neck. Then she walked back to his feet. On the next turnabout she kicked him in the head and his skull was so heavy and hard she seemed to hurt her foot. The head spun away, then lolled back, while she lifted her toe behind her and dabbed it in the air. His eyes rolled fully open on the return; you could see them stare, as though to protest the kick to the blades of grass that grew unseen, close to his dead eyeball.

By this time, the men were gathered at the edge of the trees, to look. No one moved. The Brazilian general, Camarrá, had a contingent ready to set around her, because the Paraguayan women had started to wail the death of López. It was a foiled, pathetic cry, as though they might as soon tear the body apart as bury it. And, if they could not kill him, because he was already dead, then they might settle for killing her.

Eliza listened. She bent from the waist and took something out of the corpse's boot. It was a knife, but instead of lifting it and lowering it into her own heart, she crouched and slammed it into the ground, just there, where his eyes were fixed on the blades of grass. She talked to him in English as she dug, so that no one would approach. You could hear the metal eating the earth and the hard-sounding phrases as she spoke. Sometimes, too, little whispers in French, which was the language they used when they were alone. She paused now and then, and sat back, because the knife was small and her hands were small, and the hole she had in her mind's eye would not be emptied of earth until it was night.

She cried for a while in the middle of the afternoon and scrabbled faster, scooping the dry red earth with her bare hands up and away to form a shallow bowl, which might, when you looked at it, be enough to keep the wild animals off. Then she stood, and organised herself. She brushed her skirt and pulled each sleeve down to the wrist. She tucked a stray lock behind her ear, then felt around the back of her head and freed the mass of her hair. The stuff fell down behind her, and she shook it out and swung it to one side, before gathering it to be wound into some mysterious knot. It was so deftly done; her hands moving, once, twice. Then one hand held the pile, while the other reached for the pin that had appeared somehow between her teeth, as though she had coughed it up.

She glanced at the crowd. She walked around the body of Francisco López so that it lay between her and the grave she had made for it. Then she bent down again and started to push, then roll him in.

And so it was nearly done.

Stewart looked around the camp they had set the night before, now smashed and overrun. They were in a wide valley, a high bowl in the mountains – the Cerro Corá. A man with a pack mule had told them the name of the place, and then he walked on. They had let him go – as though this was not a war, with the imperatives of war, but simply a road they were on, where a man might travel the opposite way.

López was losing his touch – he who understood more than anyone what a war demands: that you must shoot your own brother, you must shoot your brothers-in-law. You must make your mother swear that you are the only legitimate child of your father Carlos Antonio, the previous Dictator López. You must whip one story out of a man's back and then whip a different story out of his front. You must always change the details or, if the details remain, you must change the conclusions. You must make the facts of the matter shift and wriggle, so that when the time comes, there is nothing real for the enemy to kill.

But the man went by, alive, and his valuable mule was

let go with him, and he walked until he found the Brazilian army, and he led it back to where they were, like pulling a toy on a string. And so it was that the man who betrayed López, in the end, was the one to whom he had been most indifferently kind.

They debouched into the valley from two sides, hidden by the folds in the mountains; and, without stopping or regrouping, without a strategy of any kind, they ran towards the Paraguayan camp. Perhaps it was apparent that they did not need a strategy, and this last discourtesy made Stewart look about him at the fleeing, scrabbling crowd, who picked up what they could by way of food or children and ran towards the stream of Aquidabánmi. Perhaps 'crowd' was too big a word for them now. They were a travelling show, an eviction, a village wandering from some clearance. They were people who had no lives left to lose.

Despite which, the Brazilians were upon them like a band of grinning robbers, whistling to each other and whirling weapons over their heads; blades and lances – it was too close for shooting, and too scattered for much close work. A man, galloping low and hard, scooped off a man's head with his sabre, and was cheered as though for some trick, as the surprised neck shot its exclamation of blood in the air.

A stumbling man turned to shoot Stewart, and he had the face of a middle-aged boy. There was some disease that did that to you, Stewart thought, as the pubescent old man lifted his rifle to his shoulder – now, what was it called? The shouted gutturals of his Portuguese sounded, at this close range, like something twisted, perhaps evil; like Spanish gone askew. Stewart thought how foreign it sounded. Then he remembered that he was British, so all languages were foreign, really. Finally he realised that if he was British then there was no reason to kill him, because this wasn't, strictly speaking, his war.

With sudden conviction he lifted up, for the wizened child's attention, an empty bottle of turpentine in one hand and a Smellie obstetrical forceps in the other; both snatched from his open bag. The child looked at them and stumbled onwards, his legs still going crosswise in their fatal dressage. The rifle lingered on Stewart's face, the angle became more acute, and then it slipped away – at which precise moment, the boy pulled the trigger and, still shouting, swung the muzzle around, and ran on.

Stewart looked at the forceps. It was shaped like giant scissors. Each leg was a loop of metal ribbon which was shaped to fit the soft contours of a baby's head. Perhaps the loops were intended to fit around the baby's ears. Stewart was not entirely sure. He had brought the forceps with him from Britain in order to deliver Pancho, the first son of Eliza Lynch. It was the last thing he had about him of 'William Stewart, physician-accoucheur', and he was amazed that it had survived all this time: it had not been whittled down for cutting or stabbing, nor had it been chopped up for shot. Stewart used it, mostly, for cooking – it was handy when you wanted to extract something, or turn it over in the campfire. But there was something, evidently, in this set of blackened tongs that meant that he was either a doctor, or too mad to kill, because the Brazilians rode past him now, as he gazed at the forceps that had delivered him his own life. And, by the time it had happened, by the time it was known – whatever knowledge that rushes through a battlefield so fast that fighting men look at each other, and falter, and stop. By the time it was over – which was very soon. Stewart found himself standing in a meadow, alive.

The work that had been done was the shooting of Francisco Solano López. There were few enough rounds fired, and Stewart thought he might have heard the particular shot echoing around the bowl of the hills, long after it had hit the man's escaping back.

One soldier claimed he had seen it, as they stood, and then sat, in the shadow of the trees to watch Eliza Lynch. He said it happened in the middle of the stream. The horse had fought to get out from under him as Il Mariscal jerked bolt upright – almost surprised – and then pitched forward on to the animal's neck. The man said the horse was having none of it, and upped López into the stream, where he thrashed a little before the bubbles came. So it was the horse that killed him as much as any Brazilian, he said. Another few feet and he might have made it, he might be gone clear, or he might be captured and sitting here with them now. The thought amazed them all so much they fell silent, and looked to where the man lay to check that he was still dead.

A few crossed themselves.

Another man said that the horse knew it was time. The thing they hate, the thing they fear most, he said, is to crush a man. And worse than that to have a dead man on their backs. He said, too, that López loved that horse. All horses, he said, after a while. He said that López loved every horse he ever rode. And that the horses repaid that love. Or usually they did.

Stewart wanted to walk away from this, but he could not, corralled as they were under Brazilian eyes.

'Doctor,' he said again to the sentry. '*Inglese. Inglese.*' But the man was nervous of him – the sandy red hair, he supposed; the fact that his face had peeled and crusted so badly in the last, long months in the sun. He did look rather like a disease, and a foreign one at that. And so he grinned, in a winning sort of way, and went back to the men.

They sat and were obliged to watch Eliza, as though in expiation of all their crimes, as she rolled the body, first one end and then the other, towards the hole. The legs of Francisco Solano López went in first and then, very slowly, the rest of him followed, turning as it went, so that his face surfaced one last time before disappearing into the ground.

Then she stood – as though, Stewart thought, to show them all the state of her dress. 'Look what you have done to my mousseline,' her hands might have said. She swept them downwards in a tragic dumbshow that might also have meant, 'May God have pity on women. The things that fall out of us that we can never pick up.'

She walked over to where Pancho lay and knelt beside him. And still no one dared to help her as she pushed one arm under her son's knees and the other under the small of his back. She tried to gather him up like this, as you might lift a sick child, but she could not. His stiffening body came up at the legs in a kind of comical kick, which forced the torso back down. Eliza dropped one leg and then the other, and then tried again. She started this time with a hand under the small of his back, then she reached for the knees, but the span of her arms was not enough to compass the length of her dead son, and she ended up circling his torso with both arms and, half-dragging, half carrying him, on her knees to the grave.

It was almost dark. Stewart had leisure to watch all this: the boy's arms falling out wide as his kneeling, dragging mother pulled him towards the gap she had made in the grass. His head was flung sideways, to show his mother the skin of his ear and throat. And his eyes were bent towards the men.

The Little Colonel looked across the grass at them. His face was livid with the sunset. It looked like a saint's face – he was so young, and his green eyes were glazed with the red of the flaming sky. Eliza let him drop at the lip of the grave, then lifted and pushed his head and shoulders into the hole. She lifted and pushed some more. But it became apparent that she, herself, was in the way and so she stood up to move around the other side. She must have trod on her own dress then, because halfway up she was jolted to a halt, and something tore. Eliza looked at the line where her skirt was joined to the bodice, and a sound came out of her crouched body that Stewart would remember for the rest of his life.

'Why did you not help her,' Venancia said many years later. And Stewart looked at his wife with fond amazement.

'I would have been shot,' he said.

But thinking, not of Eliza, nor of the dead bodies, nor even of how one action of his might have begged another, but of the river playing with the mist, and the evening gathering of birds in the Cerro Corá.

In fact someone did approach her, early on. At first he was not stopped by the guards – perhaps because his face was so raw-looking and bare. He stopped before he reached her and signalled in a strangely covert way. He stood with a leaning look to him, craning towards her, and his hand fluttered in the middle of his chest, as though to say 'Pssst!' When she lifted her head and looked at him, he straightened up and smiled. Then the guard hustled him away. It was the eldest son of Francisco López, Stewart saw, the one he had by his first mistress, Juana Pesoa.

That evening the captured men – Creole Spanish for the most part, along with those Guaraní of discernible rank – talked about destiny. Stewart was amazed at their temperament; but, 'Philosophy is the luxury of the defeated,' said his wife's cousin, Frederico Báez. They told stories of the day's battle as though it had happened many years ago. Stories of their own escape, mostly – rehearsing them for their own amazement, the sequence of events that lead to the fact that they were still alive. The war was over. It was like blood returning to a deadened limb and some of the men cried; there was such anguish in the air that they kissed each other on the cheek and on the mouth and fell asleep, some of them, in each other's arms.

As for Stewart, he said that there were many different ways of tracing a life, but sometimes you think you would have ended up here no matter what. You would be the person you are, in the place where you are, watching a particular woman bury her son. And the stories you will tell your children; of journeys and chance encounters, of stray bullets and rolls of the dice – they may be true, but they are not necessary, after all.

'Then why are you still holding those scissors,' said Frederico Báez, and Stewart saw he had not let the blackened forceps out of his hand since noon.

There were many more stories told on the long walk home. One was a story of Eliza climbing a mound of corpses – like a rag-picker or a woman bereaved – and looking for a single face. It seemed that everyone knew this story, and each man had a different face in mind. One said that it was the face of a lover, a Brazilian who would step into the breach when López was dead. Another said it was the face of a woman that she was looking for, and when she found it she scored her ring across the cheek and eye, like she was trying to get blood out of the corpse. One of Il Mariscal's women, most likely; of which there were so many. But that is the problem with revenge – you cannot kill the dead. The grief of it, he said, when your enemy is gone and you can not hurt them, any more.

A Little Dog

1873, Edinburgh

VENANCIA WAS AS happy as Stewart to leave, after the last little baby died. Besides, it was hard to spend money in Paraguay, and it seemed they had a lot of money, now. The problem with Paraguay was that everything had to be imagined and ordered and shipped. And of course it grew more gorgeous as it crossed the ocean – a chair, a shawl, a glazed china rose: whatever gee-gaw it was, it became the most remarkable gee-gaw in the world, until you opened the box. There was something about the air of Asunción that made things shrivel.

This was, finally, the talent Eliza had, Venancia said. A talent for shipping. And before they left, she took from La Recoleta a small, handsome, wrought-iron dog, with a narrow-bladed back. It was some time before Stewart realised what it was – a boot-scraper from outside Eliza's front door. Only one? The other was already taken, Venancia said; she had to pay a boy to hack this one out of the mortar where it was set.

Venancia was nothing if not tough; Stewart knew this, though the cold air of Scotland seemed to make her timorous and excessively kind.

'Oh yes,' she would say to some local biddy, over tea. 'Oh, I do so agree.'

And Stewart would move to the window, to admire the view.

Sometimes he discovered her hidden away in a room, sucking maté out of that disgusting gourd. She had a terrible greed for asparagus, and she reared her own chickens in a coop near the house. Other than that, they seemed, both of them, unmarked by the war and the lean years they had endured.

Venancia's looks were much worn, of course, but that was the children. She might be any age, he sometimes thought, from thirty to dead. Stewart had always liked old women, though he never expected to find himself in bed with one, or even, as occasionally happened, in a kind of accidental congress, which always left him feeling faintly hilarious.

In the early evening, when she was most busy, he might find himself following Venancia, for no reason, from room to room until she shooed him away with both hands flapping, and this always amused him, as though, together, they had done something quite witty.

This was the woman he had longed for, from San Fernando to the Cerro Corá. She stood in front of him – a woman who had the same name as the woman in his head. This, he finally thought, was love. And, indeed, when she moved close to him there was sometimes a fluidity; a looseness that was like the looseness of a man's tongue in a woman's mouth, or the shifting play of remembrance, or the sense of flesh giving way.

Stewart came up to Edinburgh one autumn day to tend to his legal affairs and meet with his pregnant daughter and walk her down the Royal Mile. She looked quite Scottish – so, though she had missed her mother's good looks, at least she had Stewart's breeding, and he was desperately proud of the contents of her belly, which had something, and nothing, to do with him. It was like throwing your voice, he thought. Or catching a fish by letting go the line.

So their progress was quite stately and domestic and gorgeous, as Stewart doffed his hat to this acquaintance or another, while his daughter panted gently by his side. Such respectable reproduction on the Royal Mile – it was very like a vista: the future opening ahead of him, even as he felt his own life close.

As they passed St Giles, however, the street suffered a subtle alteration and Stewart looked around to see who was watching them. It was a servant in livery – as negligible a presence as it was proper for a servant to be. Perhaps that was the thing: he was too absent. It was as though he surrounded himself with stillness, and in that stillness Stewart suddenly remembered trees. Not plane trees, or elm or even oak. But trees that ticked in a man's eye as he passed; trees that were each, if you stopped to look at them, a madness of variation and character. 'If you die here,' they seemed to whisper, 'I will eat your bones. But very slowly.'

It was the darkie, Miltón. A little cleaner than when he saw him last, but still the same Indian who, from San Fernando to the bank of the Aquidabánmi, ate clean grain while Stewart ate mouldy; who leaned forward one night and whispered in Stewart's ear, 'Water, Chambertin, Latour, champagne,' like he was putting his tongue in there, and not words.

Stewart felt a little violated by his eyes on his daughter. Or perhaps blessed. Because the man smiled at them – and it was such an open, friendly thing, that was the mystery of it. It was the smile the girl gave him as she held on to his stirrup, high in the Amambai mountains. Deliberate and yet free: it was a gift. It was always so much more than he deserved, Stewart thought – wherever these people got it from.

Then he looked around, in a panic, for Eliza Lynch.

She had passed in front of him. She had crossed the

pavement not two feet away and was walking up to a door on the Royal Mile. How could he have missed it? There was something quivering about her, as though the street was her stage, the very stones rapt. A hood of fox fur played with the idea of falling back from her gold hair as she waited at the door. He could not see her face, then she turned slightly, and brushed her cheek with the back of a gloved hand. The glove was russet-brown, and the sleeve of her dress red – an autumnal theme: she was the season itself, all aflame with a rich decay and gloriously sad. She was also an old tart. Perhaps it would pass in Paris, but that gold hair was quite scandalously bright under an Edinburgh sky.

It would not do to greet her; even so, it thrilled him to see her so close. Eliza Lynch: changed – old perhaps – but the woman herself, in whatever flesh. The door closed behind her and Miltón turned to the carriage from which she had just lit; a fine little cabriolet, with a little dog on the seat. The dog – or could Stewart be imagining it? – was dyed the same colour as its mistress's hair.

Stewart's heart was pounding as though he had escaped some terrific danger, a bullet, or a mud-slide – but the street looked just the same. As he walked on, a heat gathered between his shoulder-blades that might have been Miltón's stare. Or, more like, the urge to turn back and stroll past, at just the right time. He was almost resolved. Oh, to face her again, eye-to-eye. The pleasure of it. He would pay good money to have the advantage of surprise: to let her know, by a coldness, a slight smile, an inclination of the head, that no, he did not forgive her. He did not forgive her anything. Not the war, not the money. He did not forgive her his entire life.

'Are you all right, Papa?'

The last time he had seen her, she was in chains.

She must have spoken to the Brazilian general, Camarrá. Eliza was thirty-five when López was killed, too old to play the innocent, too recently bereaved to play the whore. Stewart could imagine the high, hurt tone she adopted with him, but she would have to offer something other than her body. Money, certainly – there was no doubt that money would, in such a situation, change hands. But a lot of people had money. She would have to offer something else – that indefinable thing she had. Her fame. The shift a woman makes when she says 'I am beautiful' that a man is helpless to, whether or not it is strictly true.

Or he might just have liked her, as men tended to do.

Or, 'Save me,' she could have said – and indeed the López women would have killed her with their bare teeth, given half an hour.

Whether Camarrá was a decent man or a politic one, Stewart saw her, at any rate, climb into a gunboat at Concepción. Never mind the chains, she was followed by her trunks – every last one of them – also by her younger boys, her retinue, and the widow Díaz.

She was getting away.

So Stewart and the other prisoners trudged down the river path, while from his horse General Camarrá saluted, with greatest pleasure, the most reviled woman from here to Buenos Aires, and the boat found the current and floated towards Asunción.

*

Stewart did not wonder what she was doing, so many years later, in his own home town: she was paying a visit to her lawyers, just as he was doing. They were due in court in three days' time, because this is how it ends, he thought, not in death but in litigation; a matter of fifty thousand pounds lodged in the Royal Bank of Scotland under his name, a promissory note that Eliza claimed to hold. This was a woman who had taken the gold combs from out of the prostitutes' hair, a woman who had bled the country dry. She had written to him personally. Quite a diatribe – she made free use of the word 'disloyalty'.

'Disloyalty.' Stewart closed his eyes. He laughed. And yet, he did feel disloyal. For no reason at all, he felt disloyal, too.

Eliza Lynch claimed that the money was duty on the export of yerba maté, lodged abroad for the use of the Dictator's children. Let her say what she liked. López never married her. And if the money *was* hers, why then it belonged to one Xavier Quatrefages, her lawful husband. 'A very minor beast,' as she called him one night by the graveyard at La Recoleta. 'But a beast, all the same.'

He had always remembered the name.

'Papa?'

'Yes, my dear, perfectly fine.' Though he was not fine. He wanted a drink. He wanted to get his daughter away from Eliza Lynch. He wanted to go home, and scrape his boots, and see his wife.

Acknowledgments

I must acknowledge the work of Josefina Plá (*The British in Paraguay in the 19th Century*, Richmond, 1976) and of Helene Clastres (*The Land-Without-Evil: Tupí-Guaraní Prophetism*, University of Illinois Press, 1995). As for the rest: Eliza Lynch seems to provoke in her English-speaking biographers all kinds of sneering excess. Some facts seem to remain constant and it is around these facts that this (scarcely less fictional) account has been built. This is a novel, however. It is Not True.

Thanks are due to The Arts Council/An Comhairle Ealíonn; to the ever-wonderful staff at the Tyrone Guthrie Centre at Annaghmakerrig; and to the library of Trinity College Dublin.

Special thanks to Mario Rosner of Buenos Aires for a likely picture of the *Tacuarí*, to the friends who read the manuscript, and to Shane Enright for additional library work.